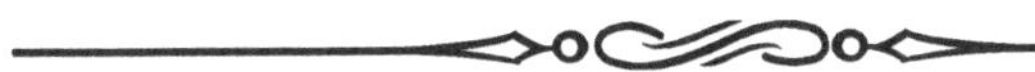

Witches Loving Werewolves

ELA BAMBUST

~ A Sapphic Love Collection ~

First Edition

This document was professionally typeset by Cassidy Marble cassidy@marble.sh

Table of Contents

Any Witch Way   **1**

No New Beginnings   2

World So Undecided   7

The Stillness of Remembering   12

Another One of Your Plays   17

Discord and Rhyme   22

No Choice But To Follow That Call   26

Welcome To The Human Race   31

I See Pictures In My Head   36

Don't Put Your Blame On Me   41

Life Before Was Tragic   45

The Sky's Open Wide   50

Come And Put The Blame On Me   55

Find My Own Completeness   60

Clad In Black, Don't Look Back   65

Kiss Your Fist And Touch The Sky   70

Epilogue   74

Mutually Assured Seduction — 79

The Duel — 80
Meeting Girls — 85
Geography and a Cup of Coffee — 90
Butterfly Hisses — 96
First and Fourth Dates — 101
Battle Of The Herbos — 106
Aftermathematics — 113
There and Back Again — 118
Meet The Parents — 123
Scared And A Little Hopeful — 129
Unexpected Visits — 134
Double Dates — 139
Even More Confidential — 144
New Beginnings — 149

Part-Time Monster — 154

Time Out — 155
Backstroke of the West — 159
Red In The Face — 165
Be The Change — 171
Taken In Vain — 175
Over Dinner — 180
Improvise. Adapt. Overcome. — 185
Friendly Fire — 190
Out Of Left Field — 196
Union And Reunion — 201

About the Author — 208

Book I

Any Witch Way

1

No New Beginnings

The sun set on an uneventful day. It wasn't fully done setting yet either, slowly sinking in the sea like someone carefully lowering themselves into a bath that was slightly too warm. The orange glow lit up the piers and bayside buildings facing it, bouncing off the almost-but-not-quite melted snow on the beach. Wind whipped little festive flags strung between lanterns and a small dog yipped and yapped at a dancing newspaper.

I drank it in as best I could, letting the image of the setting winter sun, the sounds and smells of the ocean, fill my thoughts, overtaking any semblance of self, until I *was* the scene. And then I took a little break to take a bite out of my hotdog, because the meat vehicle needed sustenance. Sitting down at the edge of a little wooden pier, my feet dangling just a little above the water, I chewed, doing my best again not to let my mind wander too far. Nothing good lay out there, in the deep nothingness of idle thought. Just bad memories and regrets of missed opportunities, two and a half decades of chances not taken. I broke off a piece of the sausage — I'd die before I called it a wiener, thank you — and offered it to my companion.

"Brrp", he said, and bit down on it and a part of my finger. I scratched him behind the ears while he seemed lost in an attempt to lick the inside of his own nose.

"Atta boy", I said in between bites, loosening the harness a little bit. I got looks, once in a while, but didn't let that bother me much. People would just have to accept that they lived in the vicinity of a weirdo who walked his cat. Or that there was a cat who lived near them called Pancakes, which was printed on the side of the leashed harness he wore.

I finished my 'meal', for lack of a better term, and almost tossed the wrapper into the water out of sheer lack of consideration, but just barely stopped myself, before stuffing it into my pocket. It was getting cold. We had only a few minutes of daylight left. "You ready to go, Pan?" I asked the cat, who looked at me as if to remind me of the fact that all the anthropomorphisation in the world wasn't going to get him to actually understand what I told him.

That said, he seemed to be very comfy where he was, so I decided to stay here a while longer. Sure, it was cold and wet and my jeans were starting to cling to my ass in that unfortunately familiar way they did when I sat down on something wet, but, well, what was I going to do? Argue with a cat? I'd look like a crazy person.

I lowered myself onto my back to look up at the evening sky, painted in blues and pinks with some clouds in between them, and Pancakes took that as the perfect opportunity to step onto my chest and curl up. Well, it looked like I was going to stay here for a while longer. One hand on his dumb little head and the other under my own, I sighed. Pan started to purr a little bit.

I didn't have the worst life. Retail was... well, it was retail, there was no getting around that, and tourists had a tendency to live life like making me hate mine was their personal goal. But I had a small apartment, a small cat, and a small amount of spending money that usually went to splurging on something like an album or a book once a month. I didn't need all that many new clothes. Jeans, sweaters and shirts were good for me, thanks. Sometimes I even remembered to exercise for a few weeks.

But there wasn't much more to it than that. It felt like running out the clock, sometimes. Like I was missing something. A purpose. Well, that was in part fixed by Pan, who was gently shoving his cold nose into the underside of my jaw. Taking care of a little creature had made the monotony a little easier, at least. I enjoyed food, when I could afford to make myself *good* food. Music was nice. But that was it. I felt like I was living someone else's life, and not even the fun parts. The parts that were cut out of the montage for being too dull.

But for Pan's sake, at least, I puttered on, making ends meet, living life from sunset hotdog to sunset hotdog. Well, there was more to it than hot dogs. But the sunsets were nice. Even in winter, a bit of sunlight on my face was nice.

Pancakes shifted and slid off my chest and onto his dumb little face with an indignant "*Mrrp!*" and I took that personally. We both got up, I regretted sitting down on a wet pier as my clothes clung to me like a cold shower curtain, and I took Pan's leash.

"Let's go home, buddy." Hands in my pockets, hoping those would warm a little bit, I went down the boardwalk. Pancake's little bell jingled as he walked in front of me. He knew the way home. A few girls walked past, delighted at Pan, who held his head up with the kind of pride only cats can have. He knew damn well he was being looked at, and might even have been aware of the fact that he was cute *and* adorable. I lowered my face into my collar. The last thing I wanted was for the girls to go from looking at the cat to looking at me.

The disappointment was usually too much for people to hide. Not that I was ugly. But bland was an understatement. A beard that grew in too fast and then immediately thinned out. It was impossible to keep down, but also impossible to grow out without being see-through; it looked permanently unkempt. I'd long given up on looking presentable. And smiling just made it worse. Someone had tried complimenting me once by telling me I looked like "PG-13 Charles Manson", whatever that was supposed to mean, and I hadn't been able to smile into a mirror or a camera since.

The girls just glanced at me and their gaze slid off me like water off of a duck. Good. That was probably for the best. Pan and I kept walking, until we got to our street. I lived in a little apartment just off the seaside boulevard, facing exactly the wrong way to catch either morning *or* evening light. Somehow, the apartment also managed to not have a view of the sea, or much of anything for that matter, save the concrete wall on the opposite side of the street. But it was cheap, and it was home. Cozy? No. But it was a roof and walls. It's where I kept my energy drinks.

The elevator was broken, because of course it was, but I didn't mind. It was mandatory exercise, which I could use. Whenever the winter months rolled around I had a tendency to store fat very quickly and very easily. I'd sort of melted a little bit, in a way I didn't really like, so having to do seven flights of stairs was a good way to work a little bit of that off. Besides, it gave Pancakes a way to get rid of some energy.

He was quite young. I'd only picked him up the year before. He'd been a rescue. Someone had found a litter by the road and had put them in a cardboard box. What was I going to do, *not* pick up a kitten for a dollar? I've never been the best person, but I'm not a *monster*. It was a *kitten.* He was *orange.*

I hadn't been in the best place, but having a little tyke like that to take care of had really helped me focus on something outside myself for a while, and I was happier for it. He'd been very affectionate from the get-go, but also a little food criminal who did little food crimes and stole my food if I looked away for even a second. Which was how he got the name. It had taken me almost an hour to get the syrup out of his hair and off of his dumb little idiot face.

I opened the door and he immediately began to spin in little circles, waiting for me to take his harness off. As soon as I did, he sprinted into the apartment and I heard him crash into something, and immediately after that the sound of something breaking. I bit my tongue and followed him in to assess the damage.

The room was quite sparse. A small sofa in front of a small television. Little coffee table covered in cups and magazines from that time I'd tried to get into biology and finance for a bit. I should've really thrown them out a while ago, but there was a part of me that reminded me that I probably needed *something*. A stack of magazines as thick as my leg about every subject I could think of made me feel like I was at least trying.

My literature degree mocked me from the far wall, letting me know it was never going to drag me out of retail. It was the first thing I'd ever put up in here, and only found out afterwards I wasn't allowed to put holes in the wall. Oops. That was my deposit gone.

And speaking of things that were gone, there was a bowl that had been on the table. I had bought that bowl with the express guarantee that it was unbreakable. Obviously, whoever had guaranteed me that had never come into contact with an excitable cat. The cat in question had disappeared, probably hiding from its own hubris and noise.

I started picking up the shards with a resigned sigh, and managed to *immediately* cut myself. How in the hell an unbreakable wooden bowl managed to have an edge sharper than most knives, I didn't know. I sucked my thumb as I brought the rest of the pieces to the tiny kitchen and dropped them unceremoniously in the sink. That was a future-me problem. Today-me was going to relax a bit. Maybe watch television. Cuddle with Pancakes. Have a snack. Go to bed.

I walked back into the living room. Something in the back of my head was trying to bring something to my attention, but I was too lost in thought, trying to plan out the rest of my week while tallying up what finances I had to see if I could afford to buy a new fruitless fruit bowl any time soon. I sat down on the couch, and my brain was screaming at me to look at the room.

There was a hole in it.

A whopping big hole, just in the middle of the air. In my living room. At this time of year, no less. "Um", I said. Then some of the magazines fell upwards into it, and the part of my brain — still screaming — reminded me that this was *not* normal. I jumped backwards. Or I tried to, anyway. Instead, I started to fall over as the gravity in the room seemed to shift. Towards, quite obviously, the hole.

Most importantly, I saw Pancakes, panicking, holding onto the side of the couch as he started to fall at the hole of nothing. I regretted taking the harness off of him, now. If he'd had the leash, I could've at least held onto him while I made myself to the front door. I started to crawl across the floor, feeling the tug of gravity start to change, when I realized two things.

The first was that I was absolutely going to make it. Gravity was changing, sure, but not fast enough for it to grab me. The door was close by. In an apartment this small, *everything* was close by. I would be out into the hall in seconds.

The second was that Pan was absolutely not going to make it. And Pan was... well, he was my Pancakes. He was my boy. Not that looking in the mirror was easy at the best of times, but if I left now, I'd never be able to face myself again. I turned around. Pan was barely holding on with his front paws, the rest of his body pointing straight up at the hole. I got up into a crouching position, leaning away a little to keep from falling forward. The cat was losing the fight against the force that was drawing him in.

Well, if he was gonna go, at least he wasn't gonna be alone. I leapt forward just as he lost his grip, and wrapped my arms around him. He squealed in protest as I grabbed him, and we fell into the nothing.

2

World So Undecided

I didn't know what I expected. In my defense, the last time I'd seen Doctor Who was like, seven years ago, and even then I'd always zoned out during the intro. But generally, when falling into a hole in the world, I felt that some kind of infinite black void or whirling vortex of colors was appropriate. Instead, the world became hues of... tasteful off-white. Still whirled a lot, though.

"Well, that's... um..." was all I managed, before the panicking ball of fur and, more pressingly, teeth and nails in my arms started to try and wriggle itself out of my grip. "Pa— Panc— *Stop it*", I mumbled between my teeth, as I tried to hold onto him, but eventually relented, and immediately Pancakes relished in the freedom of freefall. He hung in mid-air in front of me as the two of us tumbled through the eggshell void.

"Mwrp?" he said as he tried to orient himself in a vague direction that could be considered down, and only managed to make himself spin slightly.

"Yeah", I said, feeling slightly victorious about being able to say 'I told you so' to an animal that had to be taught to poop in a box. "Are you calm now?" Pancakes managed to turn to look at me, and then tried to swim towards me in mid-air. Not quite calm yet, but at least he seemed to be panicking less.

"Mwee", Pancakes exclaimed as I reached out and grabbed him under the armpits, which was a strange sensation without gravity weighing him down. I held him to my chest as I pondered our current situation. So, there appeared to be just... nothing in every direction, but at least it was fairly easy on the eyes.

There was also a slight rustling noise, like wind blowing through the leaves of trees. "You know", I said to nobody but Pan in particular, "this is quite nice." As I was falling through the void and was therefore lacking in any wood furniture or surfaces to knock on, irony hit me in the face like a cartoon frying pan.

There was a '*VWERP*', followed by a '*GLORF*', and capped off by a '*BWAAAM*'. Everything went black. Then white again. Then something like a purplish orange, and then with the sound of a cruise liner being crushed like a soda can, the whole world came back. Well. A world. In a rush of sound and fury and a lot of air being blown in every direction, I appeared some five feet above the ground, knees up.

I wished I'd had the time to say something witty or funny like an 'ah, crap', but gravity actually hit harder than animated characters would've had you believe. I immediately ate a facefull of... snow? It took me a moment to register that it *was* snow, because it was in my eyes, nose and ears, but after I got up with a gasp and a whimper I confirmed that it was, indeed, snow. At least a foot or so. And I was naked in it. But that wasn't my first and immediate concern. Not really. I looked around. "Pan?"

When I had popped out of whatever I'd popped into, there had been a noise unlike anything I'd ever heard, like ten-thousand people opening their candy at the movie theater, all at once. What followed now was more of a disappointing '*pwarp*', the last breath of a desperate trumpeter.

What appeared to be a large, fluffy dog appeared in the air, and fell onto the snow. When it raised its head, I immediately lurched back. I was smart — and educated — enough to know that this wasn't a dog. Dogs are smaller, and don't look like the wolves in nature documentaries. Wolves do. I started backing away slowly, but the creature's eyes immediately trained themselves on me, and I froze.

"Meow", the wolf said. I frowned. Wolves howled, didn't they? I read once that dogs bark because they're descended from wolf pups who were the smallest and cutest and easiest to domesticate. But I'd never heard of them meowing. Apparently, neither had the wolf, because it looked cross-eyed at its own muzzle. "Mrrp?"

Looking down at my own nakedness again, something was starting to click. It hadn't originally registered, my senses being too busy to register "cold" to really record any other useful data, but now it was becoming clear to me that this is not what I looked like.

I hadn't been out of — Okay, that wasn't true, I *had* been out of shape, but I hadn't been that badly out of shape. But I'd definitely put on some extra weight during my extended stays inside and my general lack of a life outside of work (and Pan).

This body, however, was *lean*. Lean like that of an athlete. It was also taller than I had ever been, and with a more slender frame. My family had always prided themselves as being "country people, through and through", despite my mother having been an interior decorator and my father being a third generation 'finances guy'. But we were definitely *built* to have a little extra. This body didn't have extra. It didn't have any place to *put* extra.

The long and short of it was that this wasn't my body, another reason not to look *further* down. That would feel inappropriate. It wasn't my business. But if this wasn't *my* body... I looked at the wolf again. "Pan?" I asked.

"Myew", the wolf said, and got up. It tried to lick its own back and fell over onto a fresh bank of snow. Immediately after that, there was another noise, like a bunch of grapes being squeezed through a straw, and a stack of magazines crashed through the air, on the ground between us. Now more in charge of its senses, the wolf barreled away in the other direction with a kind of lisping hiss.

"Yeah", I said to myself, "that's him." Pancakes was trying — and being remarkably successful — at climbing a tree. He'd crashed into it at first when his legs had turned out to be bad at the kind of vertical jumping cats were supposed to be good at, and then also bad at clinging to trees in a similar way. I walked up to it just as he scrambled up onto the first branch. "C'mon buddy", I said. "It's okay." I looked around and rubbed my arms. It really was very cold. I wouldn't mind having a large, warm fluffy animal to be at least close to. Behind me, more magazines tumbled out of the air with various sputtering noises.

"Wreow!" Pan argued down at me. "Breow", he added. I rolled my eyes. It was going to be one of these. At least he was undeniably him. He still had the same look on his face, despite it being so different. And he seemed to recognise me too, which was something. I doubt he'd argue so vigorously with someone he didn't know.

"Listen, I know it was loud and scary. So are you." Pan eyed me suspiciously, and I was once again reminded of the fact that my lot in life seemed to be arguing with this cat-turned-puppy.

"Mweh", Pancakes said as he tried to get his feet under him on a branch that was already shockingly thin for a wolf that size to sit on.

I rubbed my face. "How about", I said, "if you come down, I promise not to eat you and wear you like a coat when the hypothermia hits, and you promise not to eat me for sustenance?"

"Brf", Pan said, and fell off the branch with a yelp. I jumped forward to catch him and realized that wolves weighed something around the 'fully grown adult'-mark, and weren't snatched out of the air like cats were.

"Get off", I grumbled into the fur. Pan did so, and for the second time, I picked myself up out of the snow. Pancakes looked at me expectantly. There was a primal part of my brain that was telling me he should be wagging, but it seemed he wasn't *that* much wolf just yet. As I let my joints pop themselves into place again, I looked around, taking stock. There had to be *something*, right?"

I looked over at the stack of magazines, haphazardly piled and strewn about the snow. They were, quite obviously, the same ones from my living room. I hopped over, trying to keep moving so I wouldn't freeze my toes off. Vaguely remembering what they were about, I found one about landscapes and traveling. That one might help me figure out where I was, although what science-fiction I'd read made me feel like my chances of figuring that out were minimal at best.

Leafing through it and jumping from foot to foot, I was completely unprepared to be hit in the face with a boot. Thankfully, there was nobody in it, or the impact might've seriously hurt, but as it was, I lost my balance anyway and crashed into the snow a third time. Because Pan was the only witness, I was free to pretend like I hadn't just whooped in icy surprise, and just got back up as the hole in the air spat out thick, black, wool clothes. I practically dove onto them. It took me longer than I would've ever dared to admit to try and fit my upper body into a shirt before realizing it was pants.

Finally wearing surprisingly non-itching clothes, I hopped up and down a few times to get my blood flowing, but I couldn't get my teeth to stop chattering. Despite the clothes and the cloak, it was still, quite obviously, freezing. Next to me, Pancakes was sniffing through the magazines, and I took that as a reminder to get back to figuring out what to do next.

I looked at the trees again. Most of them were... Pine trees? Maybe? Whatever, Christmas trees. Pointy. Although there were a few that weren't, like the one Pan had tried to climb, without leaves. Other than that, the sky was a perfect milky white, with no visible sun. My only real option was to try and find... something. Anything, really?

"What do you think, Pancakes?" I asked, grabbing handfuls of the magazines and stuffing them in my clothes like I thought I'd seen in a movie once. Pancakes looked up at me and meowed, so there was that. I looked around. There was ever so slight a slope to the little field I was on. I figured, if I walked downhill, I'd eventually end up at a river or a valley and that would, hopefully, lead to some kind of civilization. I looked at Pan, and knelt down, grabbing his little face in my hands. Well, it wasn't so little now, but he was always going to be my little idiot, no matter how big he got. "We're gonna get out of here, alright?"

"Frrpt", Pan said, and I kissed him on the forehead. Deciding that I had best get going, I got up and started to walk, and dutifully, Pan trotted alongside me. It was good that he wasn't his tiny cat self. He would've had a rough time getting through the snow. Now it barely came halfway up his legs. Not that either of us had it *easy*. The snow was quite thick and hard to navigate, even while trying to go downhill.

After walking for a while, I realized that the terrain had flattened out. No more downhill. Well, nothing for it but to press on. Trying to go in a straight line, I looked behind me every once in a while to make sure. My stomach was starting to rumble uncomfortably, and I realized that I hadn't actually eaten before we'd arrived here.

The second unfortunate realization was that the sky was turning slightly bluish orange; the sun was setting. There was a slight hill, but I figured, if I got to the top of that, maybe I could see something more. It took some huffing and puffing, but even halfway up, I saw something ahead. An interrupted patch in the snow. I hurried a little more and realized, to my horror... that it was a stack of magazines. Well, part of one. I'd gone in a big circle.

"Ah, crap."

3

The Stillness of Remembering

A part of me wanted to do a big dramatic yell, falling down on my knees in the snow next to the pile of magazines. The more sensible part told me the last thing I wanted was more snow on my legs. It was growing properly dark now, and I had no idea where I was, where I was supposed to go and, most importantly, what to do.

Annoyed, I kicked the magazines. Listen, when alone with only a cat who seems to be a dog for a while, one is allowed a little bit of a petulant tantrum. Even in the dark, I noticed something under the magazines. I threw a couple more of them aside and uncovered what appeared to be, by touch, a leather bag. An old timey-one, too. I set it upright and opened it and began to root inside. There seemed to be multiple little glass and wood... things in there. A book or two. And something else. Something made of metal. Curious, more than anything, I pulled it out.

"Ah", I said, like I knew what it was. It was a little C-shaped piece of metal, with a little cord to what seemed to be a rock. It *felt* familiar, at the very least, even if I couldn't quite place it yet. There had to be something... Thinking back to the magazines I'd leafed through, an itch at the back of my brain was trying to figure it out. "Hold on..."

There was a specific guide about old-fashioned wildlife, currently residing under my left armpit, that talked about ancient firestarting methods, with something that felt very similar to this. Pancakes poked me with his nose while I retrieved the uncomfortably-warm magazine from under my coat. "Blerp", Pan said.

"I know, buddy", I said, absent-mindedly scratching him behind the ears. "I'm hungry too." The light was fading fast, and I was having a lot of trouble making out the words as I flipped quickly through the pages. If only I had a light. Pan nudged me again, bumping me with his forehead, which had been cute when he used to do it as a cat. As a hundred-fifty pound wolf, he knocked me on my ass. "Alright", I mumbled, and got up, stuffing the magazines and the device into the bag. Pancakes helped by batting at my hands every time I picked up one of the various books. With all the literature inside, the bag weighed quite a bit, but the body I'd landed in had little trouble carrying it. Heaving it onto my shoulder, I tapped Pan on the shoulder. "Come on", I said. "We should keep moving, we can't stay here."

We both looked up. I'd hoped for the moon to be visible, or at least give me enough light to read something, but it was barely visible through the cloud, like a flashlight through a glass of milk.

Walking again, I tried not to give in to despair. This time, I went uphill, hoping that, if I kept going uphill, I'd at least find a place from where I'd be able to view my surroundings. Not that the terrain was working with me. What I'd originally guessed — and hoped — had been the side of a mountain of some kind had turned out to be one bump among many, although there were degrees of bumpiness. I definitely got the sense that I was always going *up*, at least.

I remembered reading that the moon moves across the sky quite quickly, and I didn't want to run the risk of going in a circle again by trying to follow it. Pancakes was meowing at me more consistently now, but I didn't have any food to give him, and he seemed to realize it the longer we went on. Occasionally I ran my hands through his fur, for both our sakes. Not only did it clearly seem to comfort him, but it also kept my hands warm for a bit. And, well, sometimes squeezing a large animal can be good for the soul.

The problem, of course, was that it was getting colder, I was getting consistently hungrier, and maybe worst of all, my mind was starting to wander. Much like my slowly growing desire to consider eating Pancakes, my mind was also slowly starting to cannibalize itself. Worries started to cloud my mind, and ganging up with my chronic depression and seasonal depression.

"Don't panic", I whispered to myself. "This'll work out. It'll work out." I'd repeated a mantra like that to myself before. Several times, in fact. Like the first time I'd been evicted for missing a rent payment a few years ago. I'd survived by falling asleep in train stations and hanging out in cafes or diners for a night, but eventually, I landed a job and things worked out. They always did.

It *had* to work out. I had been sucked into a hole and spat out into another world in a body that wasn't mine, and the thought of everything ending like that, without even knowing where I was, was existentially terrifying. I looked up. If I could see the stars, would they be the same ones as the ones I came from? Had I been thrown into the past? Or was this a different planet? Was home somewhere up there?

Pancakes still walked dutifully next to me, although he seemed to be suffering a little bit too. The poor guy was hungry, and I didn't have anything to offer him. I was still some ways removed from offering myself to him as food, although I had no illusions. Pancakes would absolutely eat me if he could. He just didn't seem to realize he *wasn't* a tiny cat.

Which was weird too. I looked at my hands. They were long and slender. Even the nails seemed to have been trimmed, where I'd had a tendency to just bite them off when they got too long. Whose hands were these? Was someone else in my place back in my apartment? What kind of person was it?

I glanced down again, even though I was covered in thick clothes. Whoever he was, he was muscular, and took care of himself, in a way I'd never had. And he had fairly nice clothes, even if they were very... medieval. I tried to figure out what that might say about him. It wasn't hard to detach myself from the body I was in. It was something I'd had a lot of experience with, after all. My own body had always just been a fuel-inefficient meat-mecha.

What would he think about me, when he was in it? My meager apartment, my disappointing physique and appearance, even the croaky voice.

"Hmm", I said, as if to test the man's voice again. I hadn't really given it much thought before. Even that was melodic. Slightly higher than my own voice had been. "You know", I said, "this isn't so bad." Still a lot of rumble and bass to it, reminding me of my old fart-in-a-trash-can voice, but it was easier to tune out.

"Mwef?" Pancakes said. I rubbed him on the head, and he pushed against my hand.

"It's nothing. A— are you okay?" I asked, not really expecting an answer. Cold was starting to creep into my bones, and it was getting progressively more difficult to think. Rubbing my hands together, I set off again, losing all semblance of time.

It was starting to snow.

"Fuck", I mumbled to myself, and put my hand on Pancakes' shoulders. The last thing I wanted was to get separated from him. But my mind went darker places now. Lost in snowfall, at night? Everyone knows that's... well, usually fatal. I didn't need a survival guide to tell me that. But other than the trees around me, there was no real cover anywhere. The best thing I could do was keep moving. Even though I no longer had any sense if I was going up or down. I was just moving, almost on instinct.

I felt like it was getting darker, and colder, although that could've just been my imagination. Maybe the freezing weather had seeped through my clothes and into my bones. Maybe my mind was just getting foggy. Or maybe there was so much snow in my eyes and eyelashes I couldn't see anything else anymore.

Pancakes' whimpering, complaining meow was the only indication I got that something was wrong. I hadn't even realized I'd fallen over. Strength had just sort of drained itself from my limbs without my knowledge. I felt his warm breath on my face, and the next thing I knew was a heavy weight falling on top of me.

"Ughhh", I mumbled through frozen lips. "Pan... you little bastard." He licked my face as he tried to curl up against me. I wrapped an arm around him and buried my face in his fur. It was cold, matted with snow, but it was warmer than anything else around. "Thank you."

Then it all went black, and the maelstrom of insanity I'd expected when I'd fallen through the cracks in the world finally showed itself. Like being eaten alive by a kaleidoscope, trees in every direction in every color, singing lullabies to the moon.

Dreams had never been my forte, but I was pretty sure this was one. It wasn't *quite* a nightmare, but there was definitely a sense of powerlessness. Weightlessness. But there was also a sense of freedom. I had no body, and could fly around as I wished. I was a ghost on the wind, and I flew around on a purple snowflake for a while until I landed on a small cat's nose.

"Pan?" I said. Then Pan turned into a wolf, and then several wolves, and so did I, and I was carried by the scruff of my neck to what seemed to be a nest. "Hmm", I said. "Woof." Then all the wolves around me turned into towering figures and suddenly I was my old self again, curled up and vulnerable and exposed.

Okay, so it *was* a nightmare. I felt vulnerable and visible and everyone around me, faces impossible to see or discern, were judging me, hating me for what I was and what I looked like. I was being *mocked*, and how couldn't I be, I was *revolting*.

But I wasn't, though! I was tall and presumably handsome now. I tried to stand up on legs that weren't mine, and fell over, and went from dog to cat to nothing again, a little ghost to fly around. Okay, so *not* a nightmare again, then.

I changed the world around me, made it a little more palatable. Warmer. I added some blankets, and a stove. If I was going to freeze to death dreaming in a snow-bank in the middle of nowhere on a deserted planet, I was at least going to be *warm* while doing it.

Gosh, it really was getting warm. I tried to push Pancakes off of me, but he gave way surprisingly easily. My arms sank right through him, like he was *empty*. I panicked and bolted upright.

"PANCAKES!" I shouted at the thick blanket in my arms. In front of the fire, Pancakes shot upright and immediately hissed at me. I blinked at him. He blinked and then glared at me, before curling up again and closing his eyes. I looked down at the blanket again. It was a thick, fluffy comforter. I looked around. I couldn't still be dreaming, right?

Dreams didn't have this level of... fidelity, usually. And they didn't tend to smell faintly of sheep. "Hello?" I heard, and I nearly screamed in startled confusion. Someone had walked into the room. It was a woman, with short, black hair. She was wearing something straight off of a ren faire, although with a bit more... effort put into it. It was period appropriate. "Did you say Pancakes?" she asked. She had an accent I couldn't quite place, elongating vowels in places I hadn't heard before. I nodded, and tried to speak.

"Ghg", I said. Swallowing and trying again, I slowly found my voice. I — I "did", I said, then pointed at Pan. "It's his name."

"Ah", she said, "we were wondering about that. You've been mumbling it in your sleep. We figured you were just very, very hungry, but we couldn't exactly feed you while you were asleep. I'm glad to see you're up." She put her hands on her hips and smiled a bit, looking at me. She had fiercely brown eyes, close to being orange in the light of the fire. Behind her, another woman walked in.

"Octavia, knock that off. Don't talk to 'im like *that*."

"How am I supposed to talk to him then, Ma?" The first woman, Octavia, turned around with a frown. "Clearly he's not well and he deserves to know what's wrong, doesn't he?"

"Well, yes", Octavia's mother said, "but you know what kind of man he is!"

"Excuse me", I said, pulling the covers away, realizing I was naked and immediately covering myself up again, "what kind of person am I?"

"Well, yer the witch from the other side of the mountain, aren't you?" 'Ma' said, almost accusatory. "You ent been around these parts for a time, but we seen you skulking around. Must've hit your haed bad if you didn't even use your tinderbox, with all that kindling you were carrying around." Behind her, Octavia left the room and came back with a tin cup of something steaming.

"Uh... yes", I said, pretending like I knew what she was talking about. "Hit my head quite badly. Could you remind me... where am I?"

"Oh, heavens", the woman said with the voice of the tired and annoyed, and waved her hands in the air as she left the room. "Save me from men and witches alike."

Octavia stayed behind and gave me the cup. It smelled like heaven. "You're in Condaire", she said. "This is soup. You're the Witch Of The Mountain. And, apparently, you have a wolf named Pancakes."

"Apparently I do", I said, took a sip, and burned my tongue quite badly.

4

Another One of Your Plays

Thankfully, I recovered quickly. I had all my fingers and toes, and aside from some painful skin, I didn't seem to be suffering any major after-effects of my little snow-bath. I must've been found close to the village and not long after I'd passed out. I spent a lot of my time leafing through the magazines that were actually pertinent. Sadly, most of them were completely useless to me. I got the feeling people here cared even less about the Dow Jones than I did. But there were a few that, now I had the light to read them in, seemed to be at least a little relevant.

I also found out that what I had failed to identify in the dark was a tinderbox. Which would've made fire. I swear I didn't imagine Pancakes laughing at me as I slapped myself in the face with the booklet that explained its use to me. But after only a couple of days, I was strong and fed enough to be up and about. Dressing myself in the wool clothes — I tried not to think about Octavia or her mother undressing me — I tried to figure out what I was supposed to do in thanks. I didn't exactly have any money to pay the family that had taken me in, for the food, the care, or for taking Pancakes on his daily walk. The Witch's bag was full of bottles and pouches, all neatly organized and labeled (if illegibly so), and not a single one had anything I could identify as currency.

Several of them I'd considered giving to them, but I didn't think they'd be particularly interested in a small box of mustard seeds or whatever cantaloupe mold was supposed to be. I was still studying the contents of the bag when Octavia came in and saw me sitting on the edge of the bed.

"Glad to see you're up", she said with a very genuine but somehow strained smile. I did my best to return it, but quickly stopped when I realized how awkward I properly looked. Come to think of it, I didn't actually know *what* I looked like. I still had no real grasp on what my face looked like, but I could already feel facial hair growing in. It made an insufferable grating sound when I ran my thumb across it. Octavia wrung her hands together, and she moved her mouth a few times like she wanted to say something. The overall effect was of someone trying to keep a frog from escaping their mouth.

"Something's wrong", I said, cutting that particular knot for her. "Have I been here too long? I promise I'll be gone soon if you can tell me which way to go…"

"That — That isn't it, sir", she said. I raised an eyebrow. It was weird to have a fully grown and clearly quite capable woman call me 'Sir'. I'd always been a 'Hey You There' or the occasional 'Mister', but never a *'Sir'*.

"What's up?" I asked as I stood up. She wrung her hands more.

"Well, it's father, y'see. He's got a cut on his leg and it 'ent healing properly. Since you're a witch and all, I was wondering…" She bit her lip, and I realized that she was the one who felt like she wouldn't be able to pay me. This was probably a terrible time to tell her I *wasn't* the witch mentioned. The least I could do was try to help, right?

"You, uh, want me to have a look, yeah?" Octavia immediately grew beet red, then blushed. I frowned slightly. The 'demure damsel' wasn't my favorite trope, but she seemed to hold me in some esteem now that I was dressed in my wool blacks again. "Lead the way", I said, grabbing the bag and reaching into it, mentally running through everything I'd picked up the last day. It *sounded* like an infection, and other than "um, boil water I guess" I wasn't sure what else I'd be able to contribute. And if it was broken, the best I could probably do was maybe make a splint and try not to throw up.

Octavia's face lit up and she spun on her heels, leading me out of the room. As she went ahead, I leafed quickly through the various wildlife survival magazines, although most of them had helpful advice like "call someone", "bring your own first aid kit" and "get to your car." She led me out of the room, which had been small and cozy, into a larger living room. It was all fairly well furnished, but I didn't really know what I'd expected. Medieval farm equipment? Maybe a hole in the wall instead of a window?

As we walked in, Pancakes got up off the floor and stretched lazily. He'd been sitting up in front of the fire there, presumably after having been let out for a bit, his legs tucked under him. He still needed to do his business, and I wasn't going to hold the bedpan for him. He walked up to me and I scratched the top of his head. He gave me a soft "brrp", and I was once again astounded by how large wolves were.

Another door, into what appeared to be a private bedroom, and a sleeping man. The window had been covered, presumably to allow the large man on the bed to sleep. And large he was. I had to take a second look. I used to think *I* was large, but this man could probably have tossed me one-handed without too much effort. He was a *tree* of a man.

"Da", Octavia said, "you awake?" With a groan, the figure on the bed sat up, and Octavia opened the curtains.

"I'm awake, Vi", he said, "though I'd much rather not be." He pushed himself backwards to lean against the headboard. Now that the morning light shone on him, it was easier to see his features. He had the kind of full beard mustaches wished they could grow up to be. "This your man?"

I'd expected Octavia to blush demurely again at the implications in that statement, but instead she shot her father the kind of glare usually only seen used by customer service employees. "No, Da, and you'll be good to leave that be. But the Witch is here to have a look at your leg." He started to grumble, but Octavia hurried over to him and poked his chest with a finger. "You've been in bed for *three days*, Da. If that doesn't get any better, we'll have to have old man Willie take your leg off." Crossing his arms and sniffing loudly, the man sat back but said nothing. "Good man", Octavia said. She looked at me. "Go ahead, sir. He'll not complain." She glared at her father again. "He better not."

"Yes ma' am", I said, hurrying over. I didn't want to risk Octavia's wrath. I uncovered the indicated leg. It was bandaged quite well, although they were clearly already a bit bled through. "How long's it been since that was put on?" I asked.

"Ma put it on when she put me to bed", the man grumbled. "You tellin' me she did bad work, Witch man?" I shook my head vigorously. I had never applied a bandage in my life.

"Not at all", I said, "just that it needs refreshing."

"How do I help?" Octavia asked, standing next to me. The demure air was still gone, thankfully, eager more than anything.

"Uh... can you go boil some water?" I asked with the straightest face I could manage. "And get some fresh bandages." I started to undo the bandages a little awkwardly, and it was quite clear that this was not healing well. It *reeked*. I gritted my teeth and mentally went over everything I knew. Okay, so this was clearly infected. High school biology meant that this was... uh... bacterial, probably. "How'd you get the cut?"

"Pasture", the man said. "Grazed a piece of kit David — the, uh, farmhand — had left lying around." His tone told me David had probably gotten more than an earful, and it wouldn't be his last. "No rust or anything, just well-used."

Okay, so... bacterial infection. What did you need for bacterial infections? Well, clean bandages and sterile water, right? That's what the boiling was for. And um... antibiotics? I obviously didn't have any antibiotics.

However, there was something. I went to my bag and rummaged through it. Not the survival guides, those were largely useless and assumed I had access to a pharmacy. But there had been a little 'what to do in the post-apocalypse?' There had been something there. "Penicillin!" I said out loud. The man in bed frowned at me.

"No, it ain't that high up my leg", he said. Suddenly he looked worried. "I don't think?" Barely resisting a chuckle, I shook my head.

"No sir", I said. "Pencillin's medication." The look of relief on his face was almost comical, and I didn't have the heart to tell him I had no idea what I was doing. The article mostly outlined what I needed to make it myself, the mold that had been used, and how injecting yourself with homemade penicillin had a high chance of giving you an infection so bad you might as well start chopping limbs right off the bat. "Hold on", I said to myself. The mold grew okay-ish on bread and vegetables, but especially on...

I dove back into the bag, retrieving various different bottles and flasks, until I found one I'd seen just a little bit before. Maybe this Witch had discovered what had taken my own country until the nineteenth century to figure out. Finding the right ceramic bottle, I held it up triumphantly. "Cantaloupe Mold Extract".

For a moment, I felt really, really good about myself, until I realized I had no idea what to do now. Going back to the booklet, I wondered if the witch had gone through the trouble of the entire distillation process, or if this was just... powdered mold. The distinction, according to the survival manual, would likely mean the difference between killing the man or saving his leg. I swallowed and undid the cork. There was a fine powder inside, and a very faint smell of alcohol. It stung my eyes and I pulled away slightly. Okay, that was a good sign.

"You alright there, boy?" the man asked, and it was all I could do to flash him a reassuring smile.

"Yes sir", I said. "Just making sure I've got my, uh, amounts right. You don't have a scale here, do you?" He shook his head. "Okay", I mumbled. "All right." Octavia walked back in with the fresh bindings and a steaming bowl of water. She put it down next to the bed, but I took her arm and nudged to the room next door. She frowned but followed me. "Look", I said, trying to figure out how I was going to say this, "I'm still... a bit unwell from what happened in the snow. I can help, I think, but my memory is, um, not working like it should. I'm going to need your help with some things."

She gave me a weird look — and who could blame her — but she nodded, if a little hesitantly. "Will Da be okay?" she asked.

"I think so", I said, holding up the box of mold extract. "We're going to have to inject him, which I've n— I can't for the life of me remember how to do. But if we do that..." I thought back to the magazine, "three times a day, he should come out fine."

Octavia's mouth moved as she repeated what I'd said to herself, and then she nodded. "Well, unless your memory comes to you while we work", she said, "we'll just have to do this together, aye?" She gave me a beaming smile that contained more confidence than I'd experienced in my life, cumulatively, and then went back into the room. I shook my head in disbelief and went in after her.

Cleaning and dressing the wound was a disgusting task, but it wasn't hard to get it right. Octavia dispatched of the old bindings, promising to burn them later, while I washed the leg mostly unsteadily. Finally, with her help, I figured out how to dissolve what I had to estimate was about two hundred milligrams. There was a very small measuring cup inside the bag, but the Witch's handwriting was such a thin little scrawl I had to guess.

Finally, I managed to not only find but operate the needle.

"C'mon, Da", Octavia said as her father squirmed and grimaced, "you've wrestled a bull, no little needle's going to scare the likes of *you*." More grumbling, more trying to keep a man twice my volume down, but eventually we got the needle into his arm.

I was washing my hands in a washbasin outside, kind of enjoying the cold of it. Made the whole thing feel a little more clean, and after that, I didn't know if my hands were ever going to feel clean again. Octavia joined me.

"You did good", I said, feeling like I had to say something. She gave me a smirk.

"So did you", she winked. "You looked like you were going to faint there, several times." I bit my tongue. I'd hoped I'd put up a better front than that. "But Da's asleep now, and I hope we can all rest easier for it."

"Yeah", I said and took a deep breath. We stood together in silence for a moment, until she gave me one of those looks, the ones I'd seen girls give me before. Not the *really* bad ones, but one of those that made me feel like she could look right through me.

"What's next for the Witch, sir?" she asked. And then, as if she could read my mind, "Any trouble remembering where you live?" I clenched my jaw and looked at her. I gave a short nod. "I'll walk you there t'morrow, sir Witch", she said. "I reckon it'll be good to be out of the house."

"Yes, ma'am."

She started to turn to go inside, and then paused. "What's your name, sir?" I blinked. Was this a trick question? Did she know the Witch's name? Was she trying to figure out if I wasn't who she thought I was? Or was she genuinely interested? I couldn't just give her my old name, regardless.

"Just… just Witch is fine", I said, and realized that I'd possibly never hear my old name again. There were worse things, all considered.

5

Discord and Rhyme

"Just head down this road, and you'll approach your home from the south", Octavia said, raising her eyebrows as she looked at me. I pretended to adjust the shoulder strap on my bag, and then leaned down 'to check on Pancakes.'

"Thank you", I said as I ruffled the hair on Pan's head and gave him the scritches on the back of his head that made him stick his tongue out. "For your directions, I mean. And, uh, for the help."

"Don't mention it, Sir Witch", Octavia said with a smirk. "You may have saved Da's leg. You're allowed an eccentricity or two for that, yes? I've heard about you, Witch. You're an odd duck." I couldn't help but smile back. She had no idea.

"When was the last time I've been to this village?" I asked, like it was something I was having trouble remembering. She looked at me quizzically, like I'd asked her when the sky was going to turn green.

"You've never set foot in town, Sir Witch", she said, "though you've been in the vicinity, and I know Old Man Willie's come up to your shack for the cabin you had fixed two winters back." She squinted at me. "Are you sure you're well enough to go up the mountain on your own?"

I held up a hand. "I'm sure", I said. Part of it was that I didn't want to appear lost on the way there, or that I had no idea what the building was like. I looked down the road. In the light of day, it was easy to see it, slightly elevated even under a blanket of snow. But it was the kind of thing I would've missed at night. "Just down the road."

Octavia nodded. "Yes. And if you don't find it, you know your way back." She grinned as she turned and walked away to the village, snow crunching underfoot.

"Um, have a nice day!" I tried before she was out of earshot. She didn't even look behind her as she waved over her shoulder. "It was nice to meet you", I mumbled to myself, before turning around and heading up the mountain. I'd been offered a hearty meal by Octavia's mother, as thanks for helping her husband. I made her promise to reapply the bandage twice a day, a number I'd sort of plucked out of thin air, but it felt like it would at least be better than "once every few days".

The day had gone by quite quickly, and it was already a ways into the afternoon, although Octavia had assured me that there was enough light left for me to walk all the way there and back, although I hoped in my heart of hearts it wouldn't come to that. Much as I didn't actually hate the idea of coming back to town and seeing her again, I didn't want to go through the embarrassment and potential unmasking that would come with having to admit to not being able to find my own *house*.

"Alright", I said, "let's go, Pan."

"Mwep", Pancakes said resolutely, and we walked up the road. It wasn't a particularly eventful or even uncomfortable climb. The road curved around the summit, and I finally got a view of the surrounding landscape. The forest I was in, which was mostly pine with a smattering of not-pine, stretched almost as far as the eye could see, although there was a large lake somewhere in the distance. From this far away I had no idea *how* far it actually was, although I guessed it was probably pretty big. In the far distance, I saw what I *thought* might be a small town or village, but it was hard to be sure. So, if I had it right, I was currently taking the road going north. There was another going south from the village, and a mountain range to the west. As I rounded the top of the mountain, I finally saw, up ahead, a rooftop sticking up through the trees. Another hour, and the Witch's cabin came into view.

Well, it was technically a cabin. It was as if someone had been given seven cabin building kits and been told not to stop until they had one big one. As if someone had started and had refused to stop. It was several cabins, smashed into each other at various angles until what came out on the other end was less of a building and more of the architectural equivalent of a map of Norwegian fjords.

"Bweh?" Pancakes asked, cocking his head. I gave him a pat on the head.

"Yeah, me neither buddy", I said, and walked up to the building. What was interesting is that there was a path up to the house that was devoid of snow. Getting closer, I noticed that there seemed to be a trail of... something. Salt, maybe?

On approach, the house was downright intimidating, if not because of the absurdity of its architecture then because of its sheer size. And right in front of it, right next to the front door, appeared to be a smaller version of the house, with a much larger front door. Pancakes stuck his face inside and gave a little "Mwee" of approval.

"So you're in the Witch's wolf's body, huh?" There was a little engraving above the door, covered in snow. "Let's see what this... hmm." I looked at Pancakes. "Says here your... well, your *body's* name is Princess."

"Mrew!" Pancakes objected. I shrugged. Well, that was... something. I considered briefly the possibility of what would've happened if the Witch had been a woman. For some reason, the thought of it was more than a little anxiety inducing. It had to be that. I didn't have a history of panic attacks, but the way my heart was pounding... that had to be it.

"Let's go inside", I said, forcing the thought out of my head, although I still heard my blood rushing in my ears. I pushed the front door open. Inside was a large open room. Kitchen, living room and dining room all seemed to be one large space, although at the center of the space was a spiral staircase going up. "That'll be the bedroom", I said to myself, hoping to distract myself. I was still out of sorts for some reason. I took a deep breath. It was starting to get dark outside.

Throwing the bag on the table, I took stock of my environment. There were several doors into the room, so I started to check. There was a pantry, stocked with dried and salted food. Several smaller storage rooms full of vials and bottles. There was a door leading to a well and an outhouse out back, and even what appeared to be an oven of some kind. I'd only ever seen something like that in a pizzeria, but I assumed it was for making bread.

The kitchen, too, had a box with a variety of dried food and some cheese in it. I grabbed a small piece and nibbled on it. Above a large bag by the door was a note covered in the Witch's scribbles. I focused on the taste of the cheese to keep myself grounded as I tried to decipher it. "Oh!" I said, "This is feeding instructions for Princess!" I pointed at Pan like he'd be able to understand me. He sniffed my finger, then gave it an experimental bite.

I pried the bag open. Inside seemed to be a mixture of dried meat and some kind of treated bread. "Fead twiſe a daye", the note said. "In cayſe of illneſſe or Prinſeſſ being otherwiſe unwell, mikſe three partſ goatſ milk with one part meat chopped into ſmall peiceſ." Other than the archaic spelling and almost illegible handwriting, it was not hard to figure out what this was for.

"Well, that's good to know", I said and scooped up some of the food in a small wooden bowl that had been left in the bag, and put it on the ground. Gratefully, Pan immediately started to chow down on it. "Good boy", I said. I almost called him Princess, which would have been weird. The weird thing about him having turned into what appeared to be a girl wolf must have still been bouncing around in my head. Why *was* this messing with me so much? I could feel my heart thumping in my ears louder and louder, and decided to step outside so I could catch my breath.

The moon was already in the darkening sky. Looks like it had been... uh... waxing, I believe the term was? Whatever. It was full now. I looked at it and steadied my breathing, trying to get my heart to stop trying to force itself through my sternum, but it wasn't working. What *if* the Witch had been a woman? What would've happened to me, then? I couldn't have just turned into one, that kind of thing was something for weird anime and fetish stories.

Even thinking about it made my teeth itch and my scalp burn. I scratched at my head hoping it would at least make the discomfort go away a little bit, but it was barely helping. Everything about this was insane, and I hadn't even had a chance to really think about any of it, to let it sink in. I'd been too busy recovering from my arrival and trek through the snow. But I was really, very likely, stuck here. Somewhere I'd never been, in someone else's body. It was an agonizing thought. The only solace was that I had Pan with me, and he was currently large enough to eat his old self in a single bite.

I felt my breathing quicken, and there was nothing I could do to stop it. I grabbed my head and tried to sit down on the porch, but fell forward on my hands and knees. My entire body felt like it was on fire. My breathing became labored and rasping, so loud it almost sounded like ripping cloth. I dug my hands into the snow in front of me, but I could barely see them. My eyes were filled with tears.

It was too much. It was all too much. I was terrified and alone and confused. I didn't know what I was supposed to do or where I was supposed to go. There was nothing I *could* do to fix my situation, and nobody I could talk to. No online friend groups I might talk to, no therapists or help centers. It was just *me*, in the middle of nowhere, and it was *terrifying*.

I cried in deep, heaving sobs, at the moon, my unfamiliar voice weird and unfamiliar in my throat as the howl bounced off the trees and back to me. I tried to get control of myself but I couldn't even make myself stand up straight. It was like my entire body was forcing me to stay curled up like I was.

Then, behind me, I heard the door being nudged open. I turned and saw Pancakes push his way outside. He froze, and looked at me. "Meow?" he said.

"Woof", I responded, then blinked. Um. That was... not what I'd meant to say. I tried again. "Woof." I looked down at my nose, fearing the worst. It was a lot larger than it had been, and a lot fuzzier. With a little black dot at the tip. I looked down. Two large paws stood in the snow. I lifted one, and then the other. "Oh no", I tried to say. Instead, all that came out was a profound "woof."

"Mrow", Pan said, and I could've sworn he smirked.

"Woof", I frowned at him, and nudged at him to go back inside. Somehow, he understood what I'd said and what I'd meant. Well, that was something at least. And my panic attack seemed to have subsided. That was something. I took a step, realized I was having to juggle having two extra legs, and fell face first into the snow. "Bf."

6

No Choice But To Follow That Call

I ran. When turned into a wolf by the light of a full moon, that seemed to be the right thing to do. At first I felt very silly. Extremely silly, even. Several situations popped into my head that made me self-conscious enough to stumble over the two extra feet I had suddenly found myself burdened with. I considered, for example, the possibility that I hadn't actually turned into any kind of wolf, and that I was just kind of running on all fours through the forest naked. The worst thing to happen, in that case, was for that particular delusion to wear off. Reality is what we make it, and all that.

That was the biggest one, really. The idea of being watched while I did something as silly as running full tilt through a forest. What made me realize that that was probably not the case was the fact that I wasn't really getting out of breath. My breathing increased, sure, and my heart thundered in my chest like a staccato drumbeat, but it plateaued fairly quickly, and I could just... keep going for much longer than I would've been able to if I'd just been human.

And it really was liberating, too. At first that feeling of being watched refused to go away, until I realized that I *was* being watched. By me. The little person in the back of my head that scrutinized my every move, the one that told me that I was wrong or gross and not to try new things and for the love of god don't you dare smile at people you know what we look like when we *smile* — *that* voice. It was watching me. So I gave it the very simple retort that I was a dog, thank you very much, and all dogs are perfect, no matter what size.

It didn't really have an answer to that and while I could still feel its prickly gaze, it just didn't seem to have any real criticism anymore. For the first time in what felt like forever, there was no real need for me to watch how I was going or how much space I was taking up, not running from anything but also sure as hell not staying in place either.

So I ran. I ran my little doggie heart out, my breath trailing behind me in the air whenever I dared look behind me long enough. Not that I could really afford to do that much. At the speed I was going, there was a good chance I'd smack into a tree. So I kept my eyes ahead, and just went. Not really anywhere in particular, although I made sure to loop back around until the house came into view. It was like my senses were not just on edge, but like finding my way back was... natural. Instinct, I supposed.

I paused from time to time, taking the time to let the world sink in now that it wasn't actively trying to kill me as much. If it was, I was absolutely dealing with it way better this time. The night sky was different than it usually looked. Before, the description of a 'wine-dark sea' had been so silly to me, but the sky was dark blues and blacks accented by stars in a way that made the simile feel perfect. And the landscape, in stark contrast, was just blacks and whites, snow covering dark trees. It was beautiful.

"Wref", I said to myself, and realized that properly saying words without proper lips or the kind of flexibility the human tongue has would be difficult. That's fine. I'd met dogs, they could communicate a great deal with their exceedingly expressive eyebrows. I was just going to have to train some facial expressions. That is... if I talked to anyone.

I stopped. I'd just finished a quick run-back to the house, and came to a realization. If someone from the village saw me, there was a chance they would be less than friendly to me. Other than Pancakes, who had been found by my side, displaying all the ferocity and hunter's instinct of a lethargic hedgehog, they probably wouldn't be very fond of wild predators near their village. I couldn't afford to be seen like this.

Well, at least that meant not having to learn facial expressions. I frowned and looked up. The moon was high in the sky. How long had I been running? Would I turn back when the sun came up? I swallowed for a second. I sure hoped so. While this was all liberating and "returning to my roots" and stuff, if I was stuck like this I was going to be in trouble *real* soon. I had grown very attached to my thumbs over the past few years, and I wasn't keen on learning how to clean myself using only my... blegh.

I trotted back to the house, the whole "free spirit" fantasy thoroughly ruined by the idea of learning how to write by using my nose, and also growing quite hungry. I wondered briefly if I should wait until morning to eat, or if I should try my hand — paw? — at the home-made kibble prepared by the Witch.

That was a strange way to think of the house and body's previous inhabitant. Maybe I could look around the place, see if there were any books around, or a diary explaining everything in excruciating detail to make my integration into the place a little easier. Ideally one with his name on it, so I knew what to call myself.

I hadn't really given that any thought. I hadn't wanted to give my name back in the village, because the chance was that someone would've gone 'hey, why are you telling us your name is Mordreth when you told us last week it was Barry?' and I just didn't want to risk that. But I might be here for a while, and I had to say something in case I didn't find a trace of the original Witch's name. *Should* I use my old name? I didn't like the idea. It had always been a very pedestrian name. It was no Eugene, thankfully, but it was nothing as easygoing as a Jack or as interesting as a Marcus. No, my old name belonged in the world where I'd left it. Which brought me back to the original problem.

As I was thinking to myself, I saw something speed across the snowy field in front of me. I was trying to decide if I should do something, or if I needed more information first. My legs, however, needed no such thing, and had kicked into high gear in hot pursuit of what my animal-brain had already figured out was snack-sized, and possibly a hare. I could tell because I had once taken the time to study the difference between rabbits and hares. Rabbits looked like a ball of fluffy cuteness that nonetheless had the capacity to blow up at everyone at the office. By contrast, hares looked like strung-out authors rapidly approaching forty who had just dropped a plate of food coming out of the microwave at 3 AM.

This one had big "I missed my first deadline and I have five messages on my answering machine" energy, which was probably related to the fact that I was currently chasing it faster than I had ever chased anything in my life, and I didn't even know why, though I could hazard a guess.

Was I really going to just... do that? Take a life in order to sate my hunger? More importantly, could I also eat it raw? I'd considered going vegetarian at some points in my life, from an animal-cruelty *and* just a sustainability perspective. On the other hand, fake steak just wasn't the same, so I'd also faltered on occasion. But like... it was one rabbit. Or hare. Whatever. But also it was *raw*. And I'd be killing it.

While I pondered the ethical implications of killing and subsequently eating my kill for the first time in my life, we ran circles around the building. Every time the hare tried to run into the forest, I managed to get ahead of it, but I also couldn't quite make myself actually strike the killing blow, *well aware* that all this was doing was getting the hare more and more upset, and I should either let it go or do something, but *also*-also I was kind of having fun?

As I pondered these varying conflicting and confusing conundrums, a black shadow flickered across my vision, and the hare was gone. Well, not gone. It was eight feet to my right, and Pancakes was standing over it looking more triumphant than I had ever seen him look in his life. Oh no. He was going to eat it.

"Waf", I said, and realized it was going to be very hard for me to tell him to put it down and not eat it, without being able to say anything. But he was absolutely capable of being terrible at eating a hare and choking on a bone or something. But if I could take it from him, maybe I could put it somewhere and then when I had hands and fingers that could hold a knife, I could try and put myself to the less-than-ideal task of teaching myself how to prepare a dead animal. I took a step forward.

Dead hare in his mouth, Pancakes took a step back. He had A Look in his eyes. It was a look that all animal-owners throughout history have known, and all of them dread it. It was a single word, expressed in the entire body but most visible in the eyes.

"Play?" Pancakes' eyes said. I shook my head. Even though he didn't, Pan's eyes seemed to nod yes in response. I shook my head again and took a step forward. Pan hopped backwards. Oh no. Maybe if I was fast enough, I could snatch it out of his mouth before he—

He sprinted away in a burst of speed. As I broke into a run after him, I realized to my horror he was running to the house, which was the worst place for him to run. He was leaving a trail of blood behind him in the snow, but inside the Witch's cabin, the mess would likely be a *lot* worse.

"Woof!" I yelled, in vain. This was going to be hell, wasn't it? He burst through the door, and the speed of him running through the half-open door almost shut it behind him, and I had to paw at the wood for a second before I could even get it open. When I finally stepped inside, Pancakes was innocently sitting in the middle of the room, cleaning his paw with big laps of his tongue. *"Woof"*, I said with all the threat I could muster, and glared. He hopped up on all fours and took the hare in his mouth again. I grabbed the door handle in my teeth and pulled it closed behind me. There. Now at least he wasn't going anywhere.

I turned around, and immediately jumped for it, hoping to take the little bastard by surprise. Where had all this activity been when he'd been a kitten?! It couldn't be that he was hungry, could it? I'd fed him when we got here, and that had been at sundown, which couldn't have been more than... wait.

I looked out the window. The sky seemed less 'wine-dark' and more 'yellow snow'. When had *that* happened? I glared at Pancakes. "I'll let it slide", I growled at him, and realized I'd actually spoken. Good! That meant I was turning back into a human. Human meant hands. Hands meant I could grab Pancakes by the scruff of his neck and make him spit the hare out. It also meant that my clothes, which I had stepped out of when I'd turned into a wolf, were still in a pile outside, and I was going to be naked in just a few seconds.

My heart started to hammer in my chest, like it was trying to power a locomotive, and my eyes rolled up into my head. There was the strange sensation of falling while sitting still against the front door, and my breathing became labored. It didn't last as long as the first time, the sensation of my skin being on fire subsiding quickly. I could feel the wood floor on my bare legs. I took a deep breath, my heart still pounding, putting my hand on my breast. Breasts. Chest. Lady's chest. Breast.

My eyes shot open. I looked down. I looked back up. "Pancakes", said, in a very light voice that sounded husky and musical at the same time, "what the *fuck?*"

"Mreff", he said through the hare's hair. Yeah, I wasn't expecting him to give me any useful input. I was trying to get a hold of my situation. Okay. Okay. I had breasts.

And a high pitched voice. And incredibly soft skin. And slender hands. But that didn't mean anything, right? I mean, I couldn't just have been turned into a woman, right? Oh god. My heart hammered in my chest like a fifty-ton-woodpecker, and my lungs were working *hard* to keep up. I closed my eyes. This was all too much to keep up with. Another world. Another body. Another name. Another body, this time a wolf. *Another body, this time a woman?* What was I supposed to do?

I opened my eyes. Okay. I rubbed my hands on my legs and wiped off some of the wet snow and blood. From the hare. I hoped. First thing's first. I had to do something I had t—

My train of thought was interrupted by a knocking on the door. *WHOMST?*

"Excuse me, Sir Witch!?" Octavia yelled. "You left some of your books behind, and I thought you'd want them! *Oh lord there's an awful lot of blood here.* Is everything okay in there?!"

7

Welcome To The Human Race

"Um, he's not home!" I yelled. Gosh, my voice really was quite high. Well, not even that. I spoke the way I usually did, but the low rumble that usually made my chest vibrate was absent. I took a deep breath and realized I was quite cold, wrapping my arms around myself. Right. Naked. And quite sweaty now, too. I squeezed my eyes shut, trying not to think too much about how I looked right now. "And I'm not decent!"

There was a pause. "Are you all right?" Octavia asked, clearly still in front of the door. "Are you injured?" I could hear the concern in her voice, and I knew I had to say and do something to put her at ease. I stood up carefully and opened the door ever so slightly. It was nice to see Octavia again, at least.

"Yes! Um, yes, I am", I said carefully, and looked inside for a moment. Pancakes was making some truly disgusting noises as he ate the hare. Well, too late to stop him now. I was going to have to clean it up afterwards. "Pan— Pancakes caught a hare, and dragged it inside", I said, "and it got all over my clothes." Well, at least part of that was true. Octavia smiled carefully.

"Glad to hear that", she said. "That... that you're all right, I mean!" She was stammering now, and blushing slightly. That was unexpected. "I can wait until you've fetched yourself a spare set of clean clothing, if'n you like."

On the one hand, I wanted to ask her to leave, and leave the magazines by the door. On the other, I was naked, scared, hungry, confused, a *woman*, and fairly certain the Witch wouldn't have any clothing in *this* size. I had to say something. "Um." I couldn't think of anything else, so I looked at her, and she looked at what I presumed were two eyes looking back at her through only the smallest gap in a door. "Um", I repeated.

Blushing again, she turned away. "I apologize, I don't mean to stare." Her breath was a little cloud in the winter morning air. It was almost like she was out of breath. "I can wait here. It's no bother at all, miss."

Once, when I was younger, I'd been learning how to ride a bike. Without training wheels, I had to carefully try, over and over again, on the sidewalk. There had been few parts of me that hadn't been scuffed, back then. But I had kept trying, until one day, I'd fallen down again, but rolled onto the road. The car coming towards me was barely moving, its driver having kept an eye on me. Nonetheless, it had hit me, and sent me flying. I'd broken my arm, and had given me a fear of bicycles *and* cars that had taken me years to properly overcome.

That was *nothing* compared to the impact of being called 'miss' by a beautiful woman. Something about the way she'd said it had wrapped a hand around my brain and squeezed it like a stress ball. My heart caught in my throat, blocking the "Thank you!" that tried to edge its way past, and I slammed the door shut. Okay. I had to put something on. Maybe there would be *something* upstairs? I got up carefully. My knees were still shaking, and my body felt weirdly heavy, until I realized I'd essentially been on my feet and/or running a day and a night. I probably needed some sleep, too.

Clothes first. Focus. I carefully walked over to the spiral staircase in the middle of the room, and started to climb it. I found myself in the middle of an intersection of hallways. Why was this building laid out like a maze?! It didn't even look from the outside like there was *room* for a lot of hallways. Whatever. If *I* was the Witch, the bedroom, and presumably some kind of storage for clothing, would be close to the stairs. I would want to be able to get to the front door and back to bed quickly in case of visitors.

It took me *three doors* until I found a room with a big closet and a bigger bed. I threw it open and found... a lot of black clothes that were all going to be much too big for me. Whatever. There were belts. I was going to have to make do. I quickly threw on an overly large cotton shirt which rubbed uncomfortably against my skin, and then shoved my legs into some pants. Or I tried to. They were much too large, right up until they got to my hips, where they were suddenly too narrow.

"I'm going to scream", I whispered under my breath, and was once again surprised by my own voice. I suppressed the giggle that was bubbling up at hearing that voice. Now was not the time to give in to what was undoubtedly either hysteria or madness. Octavia was waiting.

I squeezed uncomfortably into the black trousers, and then kept them in place with a black leather belt. Those weren't going to fall down for sure. I'd have trouble getting them past my hips a second time as things stood anyway. Finally, I put on some socks. Surprisingly, they seemed to be made of silk, and it was surprisingly nice to take a second to put them on. Okay. Focus. I hurried back downstairs, making sure to tiptoe around any blood on the ground. Pancakes had fallen asleep in a little ball near the window. Good.

I opened the door again, fully dressed this time, if a bit haphazardly, and wiped some of the hair in front of my face. That, at least, seemed to be roughly the same. "Hi", I said. "Sorry for the wait."

"No trouble at all", Octavia said, and then squinted her eyes at me. She saw my look of confusion, and then shook her head. "I am so sorry, Miss", she said, poking me right in the brain, "didn't mean to stare. You just remind me of someone." She handed me the magazines. "It's just that I've never seen you 'round these parts before. D'you mind if I ask... are you related to..."

I nodded. That was the perfect explanation. "Yes, I am!" I said, maybe a little more enthusiastically. If I was the Witch's, say niece or sister, that meant I could just make up whatever and it wasn't likely to contradict any stories he'd already told. "I'm a cousin. From overseas." I had to give more. "There's been a... a fire! Everything I had, up in flames. Which is why I don't even have most of my own clothes." I gestured at my outfit.

Immediately, Octavia's expression went from polite suspicion to concern and shock. "Oh, goodness, love! Your cousin should've said something when he was in town yester-day, I could've given him some of my own clothes for you." She put her hands on her hips and rolled her eyes. "Men. D'you know if he'll be back any time soon?"

"No", I said truthfully, shaking my head. "I have *no* idea. Uh, why?"

"Well, if'n you want, we can go back to town, get you something that'll fit you a mite better, yeah? I think most of my dresses and skirts would do you fine, even if you're a bit more... endowed around the hips." I saw her look down at my waist, and I looked at her to compare. It was only when we made eye contact that we both realized we'd been biting our respective bottom lip. "Uh, if that's alright with you, 'f course."

"Y-yes. Of course. Yes, thank you. Yes." I blushed, and Octavia giggled. "Uh, when do you want to go? I'd offer you tea or something, but I honestly think I need to clean up first before I have any guests over." I opened the door a little bit more to show her the damage Pancakes had wrought. There was a mess of blood and fur close to the door.

"Ah", Octavia said. "Cold wet washcloth. Before it seeps in too much, I think, should do you right." I grimaced.

"Might be a bit late for that, I'm afraid. Baking soda ought to work, though."

"Soda?" She looked at me quizzically, and realized that baking soda probably wasn't around yet. I rubbed a finger against my chin and was delighted at the absence of a grating noise, of a stubble of any kind. I was so soft, I completely forgot what I was doing for a second. Octavia waited patiently before leaning forward a little. "Miss?"

"Oh, sorry!" I shook my head. "I'm sorry, I don't think I, uh, have what I need to make that here. But I might be able to figure something out." I hurried over to the washbasin in the kitchen and grabbed what I hoped was a dishrag and not some deeply treasured scarf, and threw it onto the stain. "I'll figure something out later with vinegar or something." My grandmother had told me about it once, and I hoped she hadn't been talking nonsense. "Sorry about that."

"You've nothing to excuse yourself for, love", Octavia said. "Well, if you like, we can head back to town now, and get you some clothes." I looked back at the room. I hadn't slept yet. I was barely standing, and really hungry.

"I've not eaten yet", I said. "Only arrived in the dead of night, I'm afraid, I'd love to, otherwise." I gave her an apologetic smile. Much as I liked the idea of a walk with Octavia, right now I liked the idea of sleeping more. My brain conjured up an image of soft, warm sheets, big pillows, as I'd seen them on the bed. Resting on one, letting my eyes drift closed, Octavia lying next to m—

"That's entirely fair", Octavia said. "I'll be by later with something for you to try out, then. You take your rest, Miss. Oh, I'm afraid I didn't catch your name."

I panicked. I had to say something. "I... uh... Mi— May— Maya", I stammered, and I could feel my cheeks heat up. It was the first thing I could think of, and something about it just felt right. As names went, this one was pretty good. Octavia seemed to have noticed my reaction, and had seemingly taken the wrong conclusion, because she was blushing too. "Um", I added, "what's yours?" I already knew, but, well, she didn't know that.

"Octavia", she said, and then she softly bit her lip and looked at me carefully and went. "You can call me Tavi, if'n you like."

"Oh, that's... that's really pretty. Octavia." I tried out her name with my new voice for a second and smiled at her. "Lovely meeting you, Tavi", I said, sticking out a hand out of force of habit. Her smile turned into a grin and she shook it happily.

"Nice to meet you as well, Mi-May-Maya. You don't strike me as much of a city girl", she said. "Are you a Witch as well, if'n I can ask?"

"Uh, sure. I mean yes. Yes, I am." If knowledge of stuff they didn't have in the middle ages was going to be my biggest skill, it probably made sense not to pretend like I was some upper-class socialite or something. "Though I don't know as much as my brother does."

"I thought he was your cousin."

"Uh, yes, that's what I meant", I said, then yawned dramatically. "Sleep deprivation must be getting to me. Thank you so much for bringing these to me, Tavi." I had an idea, to somewhat salvage the situation and not make things even weirder or worse, while also sparing her some of the awkwardness. "Tell you what, why don't I come by tomorrow, after I've had a chance to get some sleep. If I don't make it, I'll ask my cousin to come by. And then you just let me know what I owe you for your trouble and the clothes."

"I couldn't possibly", Octavia said. "If I'd known he was taking care of family, I wouldn't have delayed your cousin yesterday. But I hope to see you again, Maya. A beauty like yours is a rare sight 'round these parts." She blurted out that last sentence quickly, and she spun on her heels then hurried down the steps and down the path. Clearly it had taken her some effort to get them out. Obviously, it had been worth it, because I was still reeling.

"Octavia! Two of them, you mean?" I shouted after her. She turned around.

"What?"

"Two beauties", I said, feeling braver than I ever had in my life. "Around these parts. They already had yours." Octavia's face grew beet red.

"Best be careful, Maya!" she replied.

"Oh? Why?" I worried that maybe I'd overstepped her boundaries.

"They say there's wolves about", she said, winked, and ran down the road.

8

I See Pictures In My Head

"Are you *absolutely* sure this is, like, fine?" I asked, hoisting myself into the practical tunic. I'd noticed that a lot of the clothing worn by women in the village was a little more… progressive than I expected from the kind of medieval stylings I'd expected. The dress-part was split at the front, allowing for a lot more freedom of movement, the obvious trade-off being the difficulty of enforcing gender roles. And even then, it still easily went halfway down the thighs.

"Yes", Octavia said from the other side of the heavy door. I'd waited a day before visiting her. The night before I'd turned into a wolf again, but this time I'd been prepared. I'd put a fire on, laid a bunch of the large blankets in front of it, and had spent most of the night cuddled up with Pancakes. "As I said, I'm more'n happy to part with them if they go to a good cause such as yourself." I couldn't help but blush a little bit. She was being so *nice!* It was a little difficult to really appreciate it, though, as I tried closing the… front bit, and had no idea how. There were strings or laces or something.

"Um, Tavi?" I asked, and got a little 'hmm?' of confirmation in response. "How do I close the… uh…" I tried to think of what these things were called. Come on, I'd seen *Pride and Prejudice* a dozen times or so, I *had* to remember. "…Bodice?" I tried.

"I can help if'n you like", Octavia said. "Are you decent enough?" Reflexively I just responded in the affirmative, and she opened the door. As soon as she saw me, her face went beet-red and she turned away. "Miss Maya", she stammered, "I thought you said you were decent." I looked down. I hadn't put the trousers on yet, and realized that maybe she *hadn't* been expecting to see my bare legs. I quickly turned around and covered myself up.

"Sorry", I mumbled, "still not used to all this."

"You've nothing to apologize for, Maya", she said as she stepped closer. "Only caught me off-guard is all. I take it where you're from, they don't dress as we do." I nodded and turned around again. Only a few feet away from me, I thought she was staring directly into my cleavage, until I realized she was taking a look at the bodice. "How'd you not know how to lace a bodice?"

"Never wore one", I said honestly. "Is it just like tying..." I had almost said 'sneakers', but I got the distinct feeling she wouldn't quite know what I was talking about.

"Like lacing a boot", Octavia said. "Allow me." She took the two pieces and deftly wove them together, then wrapped them around my waist. Her fingers were doing careful work and I made sure to keep my arms and eyes pointed up, so I wouldn't constantly be looking down at her, or at my increasingly prominent bust.

And I had an okay time ignoring everything going on, right until she had to tighten the thing, and she gently pressed a hand against my abdomen to pull the strings tight. Something about the intimacy of the touch against my stomach, even through what felt like thirty layers of clothing, made my heart flutter.

"Are you all right?" she asked. "You're twitching." Her hand stayed firmly in place.

"I... yes", I stammered. "Just... not used to this."

"You didn't have anyone do your clothes for you?" she asked, and seemed genuinely surprised. "I'd think someone such as yourself would've had servants lace you up."

"I... *what? Servants?*" I was almost offended. I hadn't been able to afford food some days, the idea of having servants was so wild to me, I didn't know what else to say.

Octavia smiled up at me in confusion. "Really?" she asked. "I apologize if I've offended, Maya", she said as she finished the lacing. "I just figured you were noble in one fashion or another." She stood up in front of me. "The way you carry yourself, I mean. You've the air of someone with an education. Not like us country folk, leastwise."

"I... not really", I said, embarrassment creeping up and trying to change the subject. "I used to work in... uh..." Trying to figure out how best to translate 'barista' to medieval-speak, I stammered for a moment, before settling on something that made sense at least. "I was a sort of servant", I said. "Mostly, um, food. Preparing drinks and so on."

"Oh!" Octavia said. She seemed pleased. "So you're saying I needn't worry about upsetting any upper-class sensibilities."

"Eat the rich", I blurted out, and then slammed my jaws shut so hard it made my eyeballs shake. Octavia's head turned so slowly I was almost expecting a sound effect, like the sound of creaking metal. She stared at me for what felt like an eternity. Finally, she opened her mouth and let out a hearty laugh that immediately broke the tension.

"Stars, Maya!" she laughed, "Do all servants speak like that where you're from?"

"Oh, god no." I couldn't help but scoff. I'd always been unpleasantly surprised at how some of the people I'd worked with, who had spent decades slaving away for companies who would ditch them at the drop of a hat, who would never once question the validity of that system. "No, it's not a popular opinion where I'm from, either."

"Well, you'll find that people here don't much hold nobility in high regard", Octavia said, "but not out loud, y'hear?" She stepped around behind me to tighten the laces there too and I felt a little bit like a stress-ball being squeezed. "Too much?"

"Yi", I squeaked, and the pressure let up. "You have trouble with nobles here?"

"Not really", she said, "but technically there's a baron who owns this land. He leaves us — and your cousin — alone, on account of us not having enough to tax. Decent enough sort, I suppose. There", Octavia said, and put her hands on my waist. "You're all done."

I turned around to thank her, but her hands stayed in place, and suddenly we were face-to-face. She didn't pull her hands away. In fact, she didn't pull away at all. "Yeah", I said. I didn't know what else to add. I'd never been in a position like this. Was I supposed to say something? Did women act like this around each other? Sure, I knew they did in queer movies, but that was back home, and I never knew how much of that was real.

"Can I help you with anything else, Maya?" she asked, and her lips were curled in just the slightest bit of a smile. I became aware of my own being dry. When, with titanic effort, I drew my eyes up to hers, I realized that I'd licked my lips when looking at her mouth and oh god what would she think of me and why did she bite her *own* lip and smile like that and look at me with those slightly closed eyelids??

"I..." I said and spun around. "I should go!" It was the first and only thing I could think of. I didn't know what to do and the last thing I wanted was for her to think less of me. Especially if she found out I was the Witch she'd treated just a few days before. I was expecting her to be mad at me for being so rude, but to my surprise I heard her chuckle.

"Very well, Maya", Octavia said as she walked over to the table. She'd filled a large sack with clothes. "Don't forget these." She smirked as she handed it to me, and I took it with a guilty blush. "Please, do consider coming by again some time", she said. I nodded. I wanted to. If I was suddenly a woman now, then it would be nice to have someone around who could show me the proverbial ropes and I could use my alleged 'I'm not from here'-ness as an excuse.

"Okay", I said quickly as I walked to the front door. Octavia made me feel weirdly appreciated, but also strangely vulnerable. More than anything, right now I wanted to sit on a sofa and, with Pancakes on my lap, read a bit before the sun set. Moreover, I was wondering if I was going to become a wolf again. The moon wouldn't be all that full again tonight, so I was curious. "Thank you again, Tavi."

"Any time", she said as she held the door open for me. "I mean it. My door's open to you at any time."

"You mean your family's door?" Octavia shared a house with her parents, after all.

"No", she said with a sweet little smile. I took a few steps away from the house, but she halted me with a word. "Maya", she said." I turned around. "Just one question, if I may."

"Hmm?"

"Why'd you leave your home country?" she asked. "If I may be so bold as to ask, of course."

"Oh." I hadn't expected that one. I wasn't really sure what to say. I could allude to my earlier comment and claim to be some kind of cool revolutionary on the run, but I didn't think I had the energy — or the education — to follow that one through. "I suppose", I said after a few seconds, "I didn't quite fit in."

That answer seemed to satisfy her, and she waved me off with a little goodbye, which I happily returned. I was humming to myself as I made my way through town, the bag slung over my shoulder, when a shout stopped me in my tracks.

"Miss!" The man approaching me didn't look familiar, but he didn't seem threatening or threatened, so I just calmly waited for him to approach. He had something wrapped in what appeared to be brown paper in his hands. "You're the Sister Witch, aye?" he asked. A little perplexed at his strange phrasing, I nodded anyway.

"I'm his sister, yes", I said. "Is something wrong?"

"Not at all", the man said. "But Octavia came by the house this morning, said on account of your brother fixing her ol' Da's leg that I ought to pass you along a just reward." He handed me the parcel. "That's a prime cut, that is", he said. As I took it from him, he licked his lips a little, like he was a little sad to let go of it. It squished. "And I'll thank you not to burn that all the way through", he added. "My Bess was well cared for, so you best not spoil that meat, you hear?"

"Yes, sir", I added with a smile. I was about to turn around, but he was fiddling with the hem of his shirt in a way that made me feel like he had more to say.

"I was wondering, Miss", he said, "if'n you could ask your Brother about stopping by." I raised my eyebrows.

"Is something wrong?"

"Day before yesterday", he said, "I burned myself warming up after a day outside, you understand." I nodded. That made sense. "Only, I'd been seated on a cold bench for an hour or two, and so when I came inside I turned my backside to the fire—"

"I understand!" I quickly interrupted him, and then actually thought about what he'd said. I was sure there was something I could do. "How, uh, how bad are the burns?"

"Just superficial, Miss", he said, "but well, they're right up in there, you see, and—"

"Okay I think I have some aloe cream or something I'll come drop it off as soon as I can bye", I sputtered and turned around before this man could tell me everything about the condition of the skin between his cheeks. "Promise!" I added as I hurried home.

The way back was easier now that I'd walked down it a few times, and I was home before long. Pancakes was happy to see me, although I couldn't help but suspect that this was also related to the smell of fresh beef in the package. For a brief second, I considered figuring out how to cure or salt the meat or whatever it was that was done with meat, but I realized I hadn't eaten yet and that I was probably going to be wolf tonight. I put it in storage and put the sack of food in front of the door. I figured that'd keep Pancakes from getting to it at least.

Finally, I threw off my coat, threw some logs on the fire, grabbed a magazine, and went to sit down. Not strictly speaking a sofa, the Witch seemed to have nonetheless created a cozy corner using blankets and stuffed pillows, which the other house I'd seen so far lacked. I was happy to find that I wasn't the only one who preferred sitting on something soft.

Pan quickly joined me with a "mrrp!" and put his head on my lap. It had taken some pushing to get him to realize he was no longer the size of a dinnerplate, but he'd finally caught on. Sipping a cup of tea and scratching the dog-sized cat behind his ears, I realized how comfortable I was. Much more than I'd ever been. My legs curled up underneath me, I was smaller than I'd ever been, and being able to touch my face without the usual stubble was certainly nice. It was like there had been an itchy spot on my back my entire life, and now that it had been scratched, the lack of discomfort was tangible.

It didn't last, of course.

9

Don't Put Your Blame On Me

"Pancakes." I paced left to right. "Pancakes, look at me. It doesn't make sense." The overly large puppy kept licking his own paws. "I'm going to need you to listen", I continued. "Sure, some of it does. So it turns out that I go full wolf around the full moon. Perhaps a day before and after. Ish."

I'd read once that a full moon only *actually* lasts for a split second, but that, because of how bright the thing is, it just appears that way. That made sense to me. So me being a wolf coincided with about a day before and a day after the *actual* full moon I guessed, which had seen me turn back into a human halfway through the night. It had been a little awkward.

"So that part made sense, right? Werewolves! Heck, maybe *you're* some kind of werewolf and you got *me* infected somehow. Or maybe the Witch was already a werewolf and I just got here and took his place."

Pancakes yawned but dutifully sat in the middle of the main common room where I'd put him. I needed to talk to someone, and Pan was the only one close by I could rant to. He pawed behind his ear, and I gave him some scratches while I put more of my thoughts in order. Okay. So. Being a wolf was... not the worst, the urge to pee on things notwithstanding.

"So I did some digging", I said. Pan tried to eat my hand a little bit. "Turns out the Witch is a journaler. One of the rooms upstairs is a study. I don't even know how I didn't find it. Anyway." I started pacing again. "Except that he keeps some kind of weird cataloging system and it's not alphabetical or in order of writing, so I'm having trouble digging through. But I did find this." I held up a journal.

After turning back in the middle of the night, I'd been unable to sleep, so I'd spent until dawn digging through the journals. The Witch cataloged everything. The plants that grew in the valley, how they needed to be treated to get certain effects and how to cure common ailments. At first I'd just been looking for words like 'wolf' or 'werewolf' or a diagram or something, and putting everything back where I'd found it, but after a while I realized that some of these were probably going to be useful in the future.

So I'd started taking my own notes. I didn't know where he got them — I'd expect paper to be more than a little rare in a land like this — but the Witch had empty notebooks by the crateful. I'd taken one for myself, and instead of messing up this extremely meticulous person's filing system, I'd just started noting down the location of every notebook I came across that talked about remedies, and then another for plant treatment, and then finally notes for things that might come in handy, like maps to a nearby creek so I could refill water should I need to (I'd been boiling snow so far, which seemed to work but was a bit annoying).

"So I found this one, right? As far as I can tell, this is one of the *earliest* diaries." I waved it around for emphasis. "And it mentions the reason he came to this valley in particular. He talks about a 'Family', capitalized like that, and the research he's done into movements, *especially* around the full moon." I crouched down in front of Pancakes and took his face in both hands and squeezed it. "You know what that means, right? He knew about it. And look", I said, holding up the journal and showing it to my sweet stupid meow meow, who just licked my face, "he made diagrams about stellar movements so he could predict when the shift would happen, to the hour, and then there's a note here, *ſee journal 544 for recordingſ of movementſ of The Famelye*' which doesn't even make *sense* because there's no way there's five-hundred of these things. *Anyway.*" I took a deep breath. "So he was busy following this pack, and he wrote down everything." There were more journals. "There's the occasional additional mention of 'the Family', but always in like, coded language, it looks like."

I sat down next to Pan and wrapped an arm around him, then buried my face in his fluffy coat. Pancakes said "mrrp" and shoved his nose in my ear.

"But in all of these", I said, tossing the journals across the floor, "there's literally only *one* mention of what they look like in human form. Hold on." I crawled across the floor to find the right one, and leafed to the offending page. I'd read and reread it a dozen times to make sure I hadn't missed anything. "Says here: '*Appearanſe regular. Not worth diſcuſſing ande or conſidering further.*' That's it." I tossed it aside. "It does not mention any of them having their bodies changed. *Anywhere!*"

I put my hands behind my head and laid down. Pan put his head on my chest, and I scratched him behind the ears. He went "Brep" and drooled a little bit.

"Nor does it mention why someone would turn *back* into... what they looked like before the shift." I sighed. After I'd turned back, I hadn't really fit into the clothing Octavia had given me. Well, it did fit — the Witch didn't have the most imposing frame — but it didn't *fit*-fit. My hips didn't fill out the dress. My waist didn't support the bodice. My shoulders felt uncomfortably wide. I rubbed the stubble on my face. I was back here. And it bothered me, and it bothered me that I didn't know *why* it did.

Pan whined a little bit, and I liked to imagine it was because he felt bad for me. It was more likely because he was still upset that he hadn't gotten any of the steak from last night. I'd made the right choice putting it away, and it *had* made for a very good midnight wolf-snack.

"But!" I said "All is not lost. It looks like our Witch was a *real* Witch." I frowned. "Well, I suppose he already was because Witches were always just, like, clever people, but point stands. He was a *proper* magic Witch, looks like. He just didn't do a lot of it, because — and I quote — *ʃuch frivolityeʃ are to be avoided for they avoid real work and conʃequenceʃ*. Who looks at magic and goes 'that's for lazy people'?!" I shook my head. "Anyway, looks like he succumbed anyway, because in his *latest* journal", I tapped the one on the ground next to me, "he mentions experimenting with *'otherwiʃe frivolouʃ magicʃ*' to do... something. Then there's a lot of stuff about synchronicity — sorry, *'ʃynchroniʃitye'* — and about creating a consistency of presence. The point is that I think that's what he did that caused me to be here."

Thoughts raced through my head while nothing at all raced through Pan's head. He snored a little bit, and I lowered my voice so as not to wake him up.

"But you know what that *means*, right? That means magic is real, and who knows what else it can do? For one, it might help me figure out what the whole werewolf thing is about." I scratched my neck, annoyed by the hairs growing back this fast. That meant I was likely going to have some kind of shaving tools. Blegh. "I also need to remember that there's a clan of them around here somewhere, that he's been studying. I might need to go through the rest of his journals and see if I can find any other mention of them."

It was worth seeing if I could replicate the whole process, to see what it was about. If that turned me into a woman again, it was worth figuring out why that happened too, and why that didn't bother me, and why turning back *had*.

Finally, I had to go into town and give... the butcher? Anyway, I had to give the butcher his butt-cream, because I had managed to get my hands on some aloe vera, and turning that into a paste hadn't been too hard.

"So now I guess I'm going to learn how to do magic while trying to make myself useful", I said. "And I kind of want to see Octavia again, but a part of me feels strange talking to her while I'm like... y'know, this." I gestured vaguely at myself. "It felt more comfortable to talk to her when I was... uh... the same height." I blushed a little bit, remembering what it had been like to be face to face with her. "And I'm worried that maybe my behavior will be different now that we've met when she didn't recognise me, and *also* I don't like the idea of not being fully honest with her.

"Frrp", Pancakes snored. I was going to have to buy some more food when I was in town, too. I wasn't quite feeling up to putting out traps the way the Witch had, and I also wasn't in the mood to eat rice for a few weeks, especially considering how little rice I had.

"Okay", I said. "In order: go to town. Maybe see Octavia. If I feel up to it. See about her dad's leg, replace bandage. Butcher Butt Cream. Get food. Come back. Research wolf magic. Try not to get eaten by the pack of wolves that apparently lives around here."

I was trying to think. I was forgetting something. I was trying not to think of something. Pan lazily opened his eyes and looked at me. Now that he was a wolf, his eyes were more blue than they'd been, and he was looking at me intently.

"Don't give me that look", I said. "I like Octavia, I do. And I don't *want* to avoid her. I just don't want her to find I'm not... who I looked like. Or that I'm a *werewolf*, for that matter. I know what medieval folk were like." I thought back. I'd read stories when I was a kid, of the origin of the werewolf myth in Europe and how it had been used, much like accusations of witchcraft, as a way to lash out at, oppress, or otherwise demonize people with various disabilities. And almost always it had not ended well for the accused.

"Mwem", Pancakes said. "Mew. Mrowl."

"Yeah", I groaned. "Me too. But I just... She makes me feel nice and she doesn't... well, the way she looked at me when she gave me those clothes was really nice..."

"Mwee", Pan said.

"You shut your mouth", I said, like what he said had any meaning and I wasn't just projecting thoughts onto him because thinking thoughts to myself was too oppressive and scary and carried with it pitfalls I might not find any way to climb out of. "I know. I *know*. I just... want her to look at me like *that*. Like we're equals. Like we're the s— Like I'm not—" I glared at Pan. "This is your fault."

"Wrowl?"

"You know what you did", I said as I rubbed the spot between his eyes. "Okay. Maybe I can force the change a little earlier, so I can visit again as..." I smiled at the thought. "As Maya. That'd be nice." I perked up a little. "And it would mean that I get t— that she won't get suspicious if Maya doesn't show up for a while. And that she won't get mad at me for not visiting sooner." I nodded. "Yeah, it'd be good to avoid suspicion. Now that she's seen Maya, Maya has to be around more."

That made sense, right? Like, if people came up here looking for her and she was nowhere to be seen, it would be weird, and if she never visited people might suspect that I was some kind of shape-shifter, and then they might figure out I was werewolf, and then all hell would break loose.

"Yeah", I mumbled. "That makes sense."

I almost convinced myself, too. But something niggled at the back of my head, like Octavia wasn't the only one I was lying to. Oh well. It was Pan's fault anyway.

10

Life Before Was Tragic

So I could do magic now? A part of me felt like I should've been taking it slow, but once I found out that that was just, like, a thing I could do? Not even Pancakes falling asleep on my lap could stop me. Not that it was easy, of course. The Witch had been very uninterested in getting magic to work, preferring to focus on natural and practical remedies where possible. However, a lot of things that hadn't made sense to me, symbols in the byline of his journals, words I couldn't place, started to form a picture in my head of how things might work.

The first and obvious order of business, of course, was to try and figure out what was up with the lycanthropy thing. While I didn't really *mind* being turned into a wolf — it was liberating, quite fun, and sleeping while curled up with Pancakes was quite nice — there was the real danger of some random villager seeing me and hunting me down. The same went for Pancakes. Maybe I could turn both of us back.

But that meant starting with the basics. The first hint I'd found was in an older journal, a project the Witch seemed to have started up but had then abandoned, a sort of manual. Maybe he'd once considered taking on an apprentice, or becoming a teacher. Regardless, the fundamentals of magic were outlined, very roughly, the way someone trying to explain advanced mathematical concepts might outline the basics for a returning student.

It wasn't easy to make sense of at first. The symbols were arcane, the language was worse, and the Witch had clearly assumed that the reader would have either some kind of supplementary material at hand, or some understanding of things already.

The first test was outside, of course. I wasn't going to risk blowing up the Witch's house. If I understood everything correctly, magic was essentially a kind of... mathematics? It had very clearly defined rules, and was a lot less esoteric than I'd anticipated. At first I tried to make sense of the vocalizations, the hand movements in quickly drawn diagrams, the poses and symbols that were supposed to be drawn on the floor.

That's when Pancakes, trying to lick the back of his own head and falling off the couch gave me an idea. Well, not that specifically, but it shook something loose in me. A memory.

"Stand in the corner, and if you spin 720 degrees and fire rockets straight down, the game thinks you're moving up in every direction at once and will clip you through the world floor." I remembered it specifically because it was something I'd been watching when baby Pancakes fell off the couch for the first time.

I scratched him behind the ears while I drew the last of the symbols in the snow. It was probably not going to work, but that was okay. Once I realized what the Witch was *actually* doing, it was easy to see how I was supposed to do it. Sticking the landing wasn't even the point yet.

Pancakes sat down obediently when I handed him a small dried sausage, and I stepped into the magic circle. If I had it correctly, all this was supposed to do was create some light. Holding my hands like *this*, saying the weird noises like *that*, and light that was supposed to hit my hands would, in theory, sort of... stop, about an inch from my hand, and ball up there.

Now, everything I'd learned in physics back in high school had taught me that light didn't work that way. Light followed some really complex but ultimately very clearly defined rules. You couldn't scrunch it up like a newspaper. The universe didn't work that way.

Of course, the universe didn't stand a chance in the face of speedrunners. I exhaled and hummed the last syllable of the impossible word, and I saw the glow in front of my hands. I jolted in surprise, and the light stayed in place for a moment before dissipating. Okay, that was fine. That was *fine*. Magic worked. I could do magic. All I had to do was break reality a little bit, and it seemed to snap back just fine.

Of course, I'd also seen the kids' movies about hubris, I'd read Icarus' story of girl-bossing too close to the sun, so I wasn't going to overdo it. Once I realized what magic actually entailed, a part of me really understood why the Witch didn't seem to want to bother with it. It seemed the kind of thing that might invite *"attentſion from thoſe inviſi-ble to the nayked aye"*, in his words, and I wasn't risking that. So I stuck to small things Technically, if reality could be broken, time probably could as well, but I wasn't messing with that.

But I could do magic now, and it was kind of hard not to get overly excited about that concept, to the point where, for a while, I forgot about the whole 'turning into a wolf' thing. What had stuck with me was the fact that the lycanthropy had come with a very strange side effect.

Of course, the Witch had been spectacularly vague when it came to the kind of magic that could change someone's form. He hadn't, it seemed, been interested. So it came down to me to try and figure out what I could based off of his cryptic notes, and the kind of weird logic that seemed to keep the universe together, especially if I wanted to try and replicate the effects. For now, Pancakes didn't seem especially bothered, but I got the feeling I would be more productive if I had some experience under my belt, even if that meant being turned into a woman again. That thought didn't bother me at all. I had the clothes to change into if I managed to do it, after all.

There was also the other reason, of course. Tavi came by a few more times, asking after Maya. She was always disappointed when I told her she'd been traveling — "to gather supplies" was my go-to excuse — but perked up when I told her she'd probably be back at the end of the month. I didn't know, of course, but the two changes had gone hand in hand, after all. And a part of me, a very silly part of me, had felt a really strong flutter in my chest when her face had lit up at the news that Maya would love to visit her again.

She asked after Maya a lot, when she came by, asking how 'she' had been doing, and if Maya had mentioned her at all. I didn't want to seem creepy, but her enthusiasm was both infectious and a little flattering, so I told her Maya had inquired after her too, which was clearly a satisfactory answer.

So I kept plugging away at magic in my free time, though there was less and less of that as time went by. While the Witch had been extremely remote and had filled his day with study of plants and just surviving on his own, I came by the village quite often. Every time, someone came up to me with some ailment or another. A sick cow here, an injured child there. Being mostly on their own, these people knew how to survive, of course, but with what I picked up from the Witch's journals and my own magazines, I could at least increase their standards of living a little bit.

It was, all things considered, a fairly comfortable way of living. The most annoying thing was shaving every morning. The Witch, it seemed, had facial hair that came in fast and hard, so I had to learn how to use a straight razor, and quickly. I had more than a few nicks and cuts in the beginning, and I learned early on that, no matter how annoying, boiling water every morning was paramount. I made the mistake of shaving with cold water exactly one time, and shaving dry half of that. My skin was sore for three days. That *would* be another advantage of turning back into a woman, I thought idly more than once.

And I did, slowly but surely, make strides in that field. I could do magic now, after all, and magic was just... tricks. It wasn't looking reality in the face and daring it to change, it was more like... pointing over its shoulder, going "What's that?!" and then running in the opposite direction and getting done what you wanted before it caught up with you.

So two questions remained: How would changing shape work? Was there some kind of inherent 'shape' that things were supposed to have, and could I swap those out? Was that what happened with the whole werewolf thing? After all, if it was 'just' magic, then I'd be turned back from a wolf into a person as soon as reality realized I had a tail too many, so there was clearly some kind of permanency component to it.

The moon probably played a part, so I tried to look into what the Witch had written down about the moon. Too much, apparently. He'd been exhaustive in his studies of the moon and its effects on... animal behavior. The Witch would've made an excellent field biologist, but he made for a terrible teacher of magic. But the moon probably played a part. I mentally put a pin in that. So, body changing, or at least the wolf-and-woman parts, were connected to the moon somehow. Moonlight was just reflected sunlight, so I had to guess it was less the light and more the possibility of something 'breaking' when it was both night and being hit by a large concentration of sunlight mixed with... something else.

Maybe I'd been infected with something, some kind of disease — I *really* hoped it wasn't rabies — that reacted with moonlight in some strange way. I'd have to wait to do experiments with that until the next full moon.

The other burning question was what had caused myself and the Witch to trade places. To SWitch, if you will. Had he done so deliberately? Had he tried to pull me through for some reason but had caused myself and Pancakes to end up in his body and that of, I presumed, his own pet wolf? Was there a version of him in my world, walking around in my body, with a wolf in Pan's body? I had to assume as much, and the thought of Feral Pancakes was both funny and terrifying.

But why? His latest journals, which I had read front to back several times, kept mentioning "*fynchronifitye*". Synchronicity, the idea of things that *seemed* to be connected but had no real cause-and-effect link, was somehow a part of this.

"I wish he actually said what he meant sometimes", I mumbled mostly to Pan as he kicked his legs in his sleep. I gently stroked the fur between his eyes as I dug through the journals again. Maybe he needed help with something? Or he needed to keep something synchronous? Was that a word? Did he need something from my world?

The infuriating thing about his journals was that they were stuffed to the brim, top to bottom, with What and How, but not a whole lot of Why. The Witch was an enigma, and I wasn't likely to figure out what he wanted out of his journals. He was too analytical for me. So I focused on magic for my own reasons, and I made sure to write down a whole lot of why in the ones I started.

Why was I learning how to make butt-creams and joint-balms and penicillin? Because I wanted to be helpful to the people of the nearby village. Especially since they always paid me in things I could use. And... well, I made a small note of the fact that I didn't hate the fact that it let me see Octavia every once in a while as well, as she was always eager to hear more from and about 'Maya'.

Why was I learning magic? Well, because it was *there*, obviously. I wanted to know how the world worked in a way that had never made sense to me before. But also because I wanted to understand what had been happening to me, and how to recreate the scenario, so that I could turn it back if I had to. Especially as the days ticked forward to the next full moon.

Oh, and I made sure to write down everything about Pancakes. Anyone coming after me deserved to know about Pancakes.

11

The Sky's Open Wide

I practically counted down the days until the full moon. I made sure to stay active as well, of course. The Witch had kept his distance from the village for what I presumed to be reasons of either social anxiety or regular old not-liking-people, but I didn't have any such compunctions. But even though it pained me, in the last few days I did stay near the cabin. I didn't want to risk messing up the timing, for one.

The other reason was that I had additional research to do. With the help of Pancakes, who supplied me with hugs, cuddles and the occasional distraction by crashing full-tilt into the sofa, I had been plugging away at the actual magic the Witch had performed so close to the full moon a month ago. With some luck, if I could figure out what he'd done, I could maybe get an idea of what he'd been *trying* to do. The odds were low that he had actually intended to drag a complete stranger into this world.

But I was pretty sure the moon was connected, somehow. Had whatever had gone wrong also turned me into a wolf? And a woman? On top of getting a better chance to figure out what had happened, that was the other reason I was excited. Getting to be a wolf again would be educational, sure, but I also kind of missed the way Pancakes would get all excited at me being the same size as him, and being able to express a similar sentiment through wagging *had* been nice.

And it would, purely for research purposes, be interesting to turn into a woman again, and had *nothing* to do with the way Octavia would get all excited at the sight of me. Not at all. So I counted down the days and wrote down several different 'spells', which read a little bit like a glorified cheats manual straight out of an early 2000s gaming magazine, and prepared for the day itself.

The biggest obstacle I'd run into with this magic and trying to expand on it was the lack of feedback. I had no idea how magic had even been discovered, because the strange combinations of words, poses and motions, sometimes accompanied by certain colors, items and even articles of clothing, that caused reality to break for a moment seemed completely arbitrary.

What I needed was breakpoints. I'd learned a bit of programming in high school, and I had remembered the concept of stopping whatever was happening so you could look at your code in action without trying to read everything at once like it was the matrix scrolling past. Sadly, that's *all* I'd remembered, and I had no idea how to apply that to this particular instance.

So, instead, I had set up several magic circles just outside the house that would make certain symbols light up — something that was easy enough to do — whenever certain magical effects happened — which was a lot harder to do — and then maybe try to find a way to burn them into some wooden planks — which was likely to burn my house and/or the forest down.

I was all set. A part of me had expected that I'd be anxious. After all, for the next few days I'd be changed into a different body from the one I was in most days. It didn't turn out that way, though. Maybe it was because even in this new body I had a kind of low-level anxiety about having to inhabit a body in the first place — a fate nobody should have to go through if they didn't want to. Whatever the reason, the thought of being wolf and woman for a few days genuinely didn't bother me.

The night itself I made sure to put some extra logs on the fire. I wanted to spend the first night, at least, going for a run through the forest. Stretch those puppy legs. And when I got back, the last thing I wanted was to come back to a freezing cold cabin.

I made sure to give Pan some extra food too. He'd been a really good boy these last few days, even though we hadn't been by the village for a bit, and I knew he kind of liked the long treks through the snow. That, and I didn't want to have to fight him for my own food when I no longer had thumbs.

One thing I'd half-noticed last time, and I was curious to really try to pay attention to this time, was that I didn't seem to be all that tired. I had spent most of the night awake as a wolf, and then most of the day awake as a woman, and excited to see the world as either, I had spent only a very minimal amount of my time during that full moon actually asleep.

Was I getting energy back from switching from one to the other? Was one form "asleep" while the other was awake? Did that mean my body wasn't really changing but being swapped out? So much to try and figure out, and no way to really control any of it.

Pancakes looked at me, said "Yip" and tried to lick the back of his hind legs and fell over. He was the greatest cat in the world who also happened to be a wolf and in that moment and any moment before it I had never loved anything more. He kicked himself in the head and then bit his foot.

"Pan", I said to him, "you're so stupid and I love you." He looked at me and panted happily. I rubbed the top of his head. "C'mon, it's about to be sunset, let's head outside and get ready." I tossed one last log on the fire and stood up, grabbing my coat from the hanger, and held the door open for Pancakes to head outside. I kind of wanted him there, for moral support. I had the feeling it would be nice to have a friendly 'face' around when I was changing and this time maybe not going through some kind of panic attack.

The sun was still clinging to the horizon like a kitten on a "Hang in there!" poster, and the sky was painted in every color imaginable, provided your imagination was limited to orange and purple. It snowed slightly. I walked to the circles, Pan close next to me, and did a check of my handiwork. The biggest circle was supposed to throw up a magic sigil if *any* magic was happening. Then there were a few different ones. One I hoped would burn a sigil into a plank if there was a wolf. I even managed to make that sigil look vaguely like a wolf.

Finally, a few different sigils. One that would burn if moonlight was indeed important, one for *any* kind of transformation magic, and then a few different ones for different kinds of magics. Teleportation, object swapping, even illusions and light distortion.

Standing in the first circle, I did the light-creation magic moves again. That one was easy, and it made Pancakes go "Mwee!" Immediately, the sigil lit up too. Good. It still worked.

It was rapidly getting darker as the sun set. Something I'd noticed last time was that, even with the moon visible in the sky, the change didn't happen until it was proper night, proper dark. I still had a minute or two, so I blew air into my hands to keep them warm, which only helped a little. I beckoned Pan over and shoved my hands in his fur. Much better.

The sigil lit up. Right, Pan was a wolf. "Okay nerd", I said, pointing, "sit." I couldn't have him in the circle while I changed. I needed to observe everything. Okay. I cleared out a bit of snow and looked up at the moon. Any second now. I took off my coat and folded it. I wasn't taking off my shirt and pants until I was in full wolf-form. No way was I going to be sitting butt-ass naked in the snow.

I looked over the various circles again just in time for everything to explode around me in a violent cascade of light. Every single one of the circles and sigils was sparking like crazy. Wait, no. I squinted through the assault on my senses. Through all the lights and colors, I saw there were a few that weren't lighting up! I saw the sigils burning into the wood and scorching patterns deep into it. I'd actually be able to make use of some of this... well, when I had thumbs. For now...

Not so much. I shrugged the shirt off my head, and fell into the snow. The lack of cold on my paws, on my fur, was genuinely delightful. I shook, a motion that came natural, to get any snow off of me, and then trotted over to Pancakes. The 'wolf' sigil turned off when I stepped out of the circle.

"Woof", I said to Pancakes. He cocked his head, then seemed to recognise me, opened his mouth, and very gently and carefully clamped his muzzle over mine.

"Wghh", he replied, and he was right. I blew some air into his dumb face and he backed off with an offended look on his face. Now, time to get this dumb baby inside, and then go running. I nudged Pan to the door and pushed it closed behind him. Maybe catch something? The thought of actually killing my own food with my own teeth and then eating it raw hadn't sounded particularly appealing before, but it was a lot more palatable now that I was like this. Oh well, I was just going to have to play it by ear, teeth and tail.

With an explosion of speed and energy I'd never felt before I'd landed face-first in the snow here a month ago, the gently drifting snowflakes turned into a hyperspace-tunnel in front of me. I'd forgotten how freeing it was to run through the trees, dodging on auto-pilot.

After a few minutes I had to slow down, and I was happy to just jog in a large circle around the cabin, just burning through some energy. Even though the sun was down, my eyes had no trouble adjusting to the darkness, and the snow seemed to illuminate everything.

My breath formed little clouds again and I stuck my nose in it and swirled it around, but stopped when I heard a high-pitched yapping noise. I looked around carefully until I realized that must've been my own laugh. Shaking my head, I turned around and came face to face with... another wolf. I almost reprimanded Pancakes, until I realized a few things in quick succession. This wolf:

1. Was not Pan.
2. Was wearing a shoulder bag of some sorts.
3. Was a girl wolf.
4. Was laughing at me.

"Mrr?" I said and cocked my head. She laughed again, then kicked up some snow at me. I shook my head as the powdered snow landed on my face, and then kicked some back. She deftly jumped aside and crouched low, her tail wagging excitedly.

Well, if that's how she wanted to play it... I jumped up and forward at her, but she dodged again. I growled playfully and gave chase. She ran. I followed. Then she turned around, ready to kick up snow again, and I turned around. Now she was chasing me, and it was only after a few seconds that I realized that I was having *fun*. I was actually having more fun than I had in quite some time.

We chased each other in circles around my cabin, until I was genuinely too out of breath and I needed to relax. She led me to a stream and a small pond, where I made the dubious decision to drink from groundwater, but only after she did. Then, we looked at each other, because that felt like the right thing to do. She was a pretty wolf. I was trying to figure out for myself how I knew she was a girl. It was something about not just the way she sat, but the way she held herself, the shape of her muzzle.

But then... I looked down at the pond. Yeah, it figured I was a girl too. Something about that made my tail wag. Strange. I looked back up at her, and she was wagging too. Maybe it was to do with finding someone like ourselves.

I began making my way back, until I realized that that might not have been the best idea. For one, it was probably almost dawn. Last time, the transformation had taken longer than I'd anticipated, and my perception of time seemed to be a bit different. So, for the sake of safety, it was probably best not to lead anyone up to my cabin, no matter how much fun they were to play around with.

Especially now that we were calming down, it was dawning on me that she was probably someone from the pack of werewolves the Witch had talked about. Well, I wasn't sure who she thought I was, but I didn't want that pack to find out, especially not where I lived.

I turned around and started to walk away in the wrong direction, parallel to where I was going. Behind me, the lady wolf took a few steps too, so I steeled my heart, and growled as I turned around. The wolf seemed genuinely surprised and froze in her tracks.

Before she could do anything to make me regret being so mean, I broke into a sprint, and only after making sure after an hour or so she hadn't followed me, did I double back to the house. I felt genuinely awful. She'd seemed nice, and I was glad that my first encounter with the pack had gone well, but I couldn't reveal myself yet. Especially if I was going to turn into a very naked woman soon.

The sun started to come up just as I reached the front door, and as my limbs elongated I hurried inside and scurried up to the hearth. The fire was still smoldering but I tossed some new logs on there, then warmed my hands.

Maybe because I'd technically been naked for most of the night, even as a wolf, but being nude in this room didn't bother me. Before, I'd never been comfortable without clothes, but something about being like this as a woman... I looked down, and felt my cheeks redden a bit as I looked back up. It felt a little voyeuristic, but then again, who wouldn't like to look down and see some—

My thoughts were interrupted by a knock on the door. I ran over to the couch, shoved a protesting Pan off of the clothes I'd prepared, and got dressed as quickly as I could, before dashing to the door and opening it just a crack.

"Maya!"

"Tavi!"

12

Come And Put The Blame On Me

"I'm delighted to see you've decided to grace us with your presence again", Octavia said with a disarming honesty as I let her inside. She looked around curiously. Pancakes raised his head from where he'd fallen asleep in front of the fire, sleepy indignation in his eyes. "Your brother not home?"

"No, he had to head out for a few days. Uh, cousin."

"Sure", Tavi said. "Anyway, he mentioned you might be returning this-a-way, so I've been wondering if you'd like to head into town. With me."

"Oh!" I'd been planning to do some observations and see if I could learn anything about my wolfish predicament. I hadn't even had a chance to get a look at the sigils that must've been burned into the wood, and what more I might learn from it.

On the other hand, getting out of the house for a bit and among other people did sound nice. Especially if I got to do it as Maya. I was more comfortable around others for some reason, like it was easier to be genuine when I didn't have to be scared about creeping people out.

"Uh, sure!" I said. "Anything in particular?" I went to grab my coat, when my stomach growled, and I had to give Tavi a sheepish smile. I hadn't gotten around to actually eating yet. She put her hands on her hips and raised an eyebrow.

"Am I going to have to make you eat, girl?" she asked, and then fished in her bag. "Here, folks have been meaning to hand these to you." She retrieved a loaf of bread wrapped in cloth, several jars of preserved fruits, and what looked like weird misshapen purple carrots. "Well, to your cousin, but to you both, I suppose. He keeps waltzing into town, helping people, and then scurrying off before folks can say thanks."

She put them all on the counter. "I... thank you", I mumbled. It hadn't really occurred to me to really... get paid. People had occasionally stuffed something in my hands as a thanks for what I'd done for them, but I was already grateful for the fact that people seemed to be putting up with me being around in general. This was... "It's too much", I mumbled.

"Nonsense", Tavi said. "That's not even a large part of it, neither. You and your cousin provide a service to our little town, now, and we're aching to express our gratitude." She took a step closer. "So that's them sorted. As for me..." I swallowed nervously as she took off her coat and folded it over the back of a chair, then stood in front of me. What was she planning?

Nervousness turned into weird excited anxiety when she put her hands on both my shoulders. "Wh—" I said, like a poet. She looked at me with that little mischievous smirk and those eyes, and for a moment I felt like she was about to close the distance a whole lot more. Then she steered me to... the same chair.

"Sit", she said. "We're not doing anything or leaving at all until you've had something to eat." She turned around and opened a few drawers until she found a knife she was happy with. "I'll make you something quick and easy for the road, we can get you some soup or stew when we've reached town."

I hadn't expected that. And a part of me really, *really* didn't like what was happening. Sitting down while an (admittedly very beautiful) woman cooked a meal for me was strangely abhorrent to me. It reeked of the kind of relationships I'd seen my older relatives have, which framed me in the position of a kind of paterfamilias. No matter how much I looked like a woman, that role was not one I was familiar with. "No", I said, and stood up.

She spun around, realized she had the knife still out and now pointed at me, and then put it down. "No?" She frowned in confusion. "You don't trust me to make a decent meal, Maya?" I bit my lip and tried to find a way to express how I felt without hurting her feelings, which seemed dangerously close to happening now.

"That's... that's not it", I said. "I just... don't like... people doing things for me." That was true at least, even if it was coming out extremely stilted. "I want to help. I *can* help. I'm not... I'm not so helpless that I can't take care of myself, if that's what you're thinking."

"Not at all, Maya", she said, leaning against the counter. "I'm just wanting to repay kindness with kindness is all." I took a step closer and put a hand on her arm. For a second I was worried she'd pull away, but other than what appeared to be the slightest jolt, all she did in response was look away. Her cheeks reddened, but I didn't know if that was out of embarrassment or frustration.

"I'm sorry", I said. "This is just... not a kind of..." I was trying to find the words. "I have a really hard time accepting acts of service like this. I really *do* appreciate it." I perked up a little. "Why don't we both make something for the road? Have you eaten yet?"

She shook her head. "Something small, last night, but nothing substantial this morning yet. I figured I'd eat when I got back." I nodded, then grabbed the loaf of bread.

"Then how about we both make something, and we see what we feel like on the road?" I offered. "That way, the both of us are being productive and I don't feel like..." I hesitated. 'Like I'm taking advantage of you', was what I wanted to say, but that felt deeply unpleasant to even say out loud.

"Like you need others to take care of you?" Tavi offered, her expression softening. "I can respect that. It isn't easy." She flipped the knife in her hands and offered me the handle. "Let us make breakfast together then." She found another as I stepped up to the counter next to her.

Elbow to elbow, both of us were busy cutting up vegetables and salted meat in relative silence. I couldn't help but blush at the domesticity of the situation. "Thank you", I mumbled.

"Don't mention it", she said. "What... what is that?"

"Oh, uh... a sandwich."

"A sand *what?*"

"Sandwich. It's named after someone from... uh... where I'm from."

"A witch?"

"Not quite." I chuckled. "It's complicated." I looked at my construction. I'd made a sandwich with cheese, dried tomatoes and salted pork, and then frown. It was missing something. "I wish I had mayo", I mumbled. "Maybe aioli." Another not-understanding look from Tavi. "Uh... Mayonnaise and Aioli are a kind of... flavored... sauce."

"For sand witches?"

"Well, not just that. Goes well with potatoes, too."

Octavia smiled. "I feel there's a lot we might learn from one another, Maya. I wish you'd stay a bit longer this time. I would love to learn more about the food where you're from." I looked over at what she'd made. Well, it was definitely a salad, although it did have more bread in it than the usual fare. I didn't even know I *had* mason jars. "It doesn't look like much", she added, but you keep that dry and cool, and it'll keep well." She tossed a slab of pork on top. "And *now* it's perfect", she added with a grin.

"You can eat that on the go?" I asked a little skeptically. She just nodded.

"Aye. I've had to make a lot of meals that keep on the road. Helping out on the fields with Da, there's not always time to head into the house, after all." She wrapped it all in cloth and put it back in her bag, and my sandwiches too when I handed them to her. "All done?"

I nodded. That made sense. I'd worked a very un-unionised job a few years ago that had demanded impossible hours and even more effort. I had spent a lot of 'lunches' just shoving something into my mouth before immediately heading back to the work floor to keep quotas up. "Hard work, I take it?"

Octavia nodded. "But rewarding", she said. "Ready?"

I grabbed her coat and held it out for her. "Ready", I said with a smile as she turned around. It felt strange, helping her with her coat, but weirdly pleasant. She did the same to me, like a weird pantomime we were both acting out, not quite managing to hide our amusement. I walked to the door and held it open for her, then nodded to Pan, who came running over enthusiastically.

I had fashioned something like a harness for him. He was used to it anyway, and I didn't like the idea of collaring him. He wasn't going to know how to deal with the constricting feeling, and I was worried he might hurt himself somehow. For now, it was a weird kind of sleeveless jacket I'd made out of a ripped coat I'd found, but I knew I'd have to make something more sturdy and durable at some point. Octavia laughed when she saw it.

"Your wolf is wearing clothes, now?" she chuckled.

I hooked the leash onto the harness. "Yup", I said, "it lets me keep him close by, and it doesn't hurt him." I offered it to her. "You want to walk him?" She gingerly accepted it, and held on to it, seemingly ready for Pancakes to take off running. Instead, he simply sat down next to her and curled his tail around his legs, his head held high. It was easy to see the cat in him when he posed like this. I definitely hadn't seen dogs sit like that.

"You've a particular animal", Tavi said. "That coat of his looks like it's seen better days, though." We started towards the village, and Pan walked next to us, the line slack between him and Octavia. "Maybe we can see about going by the tailor, get him something fitted?"

"Oh, that'd be awesome! I need to go see him anyway!" I said excitedly, and then slunk in on myself a bit. I didn't like exclaiming loudly. "Sorry."

"What for?" she laughed. "You're... precious, when you're excited like that. Please, continue. What did you need to see Marcus for?"

"I'm thinking of making some kind of formaldehyde solution, see if it might help with tanning. Of course, I don't have a proper distillery set up, but with what I have I might be able to work something out. The different vegetable tanning oil I... asked my cousin to bring him worked, but I think we can do better." I rubbed the back of my head. "I just... like helping where I can..." I mumbled.

"And we all appreciate you for it, Maya. You and your brother both", she nudged me as we walked down the snowy path. "We're glad he finally decided to come down from his mountain, even if it was in a snow-delirious haze. And then brought you into it, too." I couldn't help but smile.

"Thank you", I mumbled. "I've never really been... you know... part of something like this." My heart sank a bit when I realized it wasn't going to last. Well, not *really*. In a few days I'd turn back into The Witch, my 'cousin', and I'd lose the sense of comfort I'd found. I'd just have to make the best of it.

"What has you so glum, Maya?" Well, clearly my pretending-everything-was-fine skills needed some fine-tuning. I shrugged.

"I just wish this could last... longer", I said, trying not to reveal too much. The last thing I wanted was for them, for *her* to discover my true nature and drive me out for being... something like a wolf in women's clothing. "I might have to leave for a month again", I said. "But I'll be back after that!"

"I was worried about that", Tavi said. "And for what it's worth, if there's anything I can do to help you stay, say the word." She blushed again, although I couldn't tell if it was the cold or something else. "I quite enjoy having you around."

"Having a couple of Witches around can definitely be useful, I imagine", I said, "and Pan is a delight."

"I wasn't talking about Pan", Octavia said. "Or your cousin."

"Oh."

"I'd miss you if you left again."

"Oh."

She stopped and turned to me. I turned to her. She looked like a vision, her windswept hair against the snowy forest road. She reached out and tucked a stray strand of my hair behind my ear. "I suppose we'll have to make do with the time we have."

"Do... what?" I managed. She smiled, then turned back to the road with chipper playfulness.

"Well, visit Marcus the Tailor, for one!" she said. "Coming?"

13

Find My Own Completeness

Octavia leaned against the table, arms crossed and expression regretful and a bit sour. "I'm sorry the day had to go like this", she said. "I'm sure it wasn't what you expected."

"What?" I looked in her direction for a moment and stopped what I was doing. What I *had* been doing was stuffing things back into the large doctor's (or Witch's, I suppose) bag. "No! No, not at all. I mean, I kinda feel like I'm the one who let you down, you know? Like... you're the one who asked me to come into town." Pancakes sat by the door and ignored us both, cleaning his head with his paw.

She shook her head. "No, you've no need to apologize." She put a hand on my back, seemingly unaware of the shiver that sent down my spine. "In fact", she added, "I'll not let you." She smiled a bit. She was right though. Neither of us were really at fault, but our 'day in town together' had turned into me being dragged left and right to solve a whole bunch of different problems.

Apparently, people had immediately recognised me as the Witch's Cousin, and had requested my help with all manner of ailments and illnesses. Nothing major, thank god, but it still meant that Octavia and I were never really alone, let alone had the time to do anything we wanted to do. It had been clear she'd wanted to show me things, but in the end, I'd seen mostly swollen ankles and inflamed sinuses.

"Well", I blushed, "I'm not having you apologize either." I looked outside. Evening was already rapidly approaching. "Sadly, I'm afraid I've got to get going. I'd like to be home by nightfall." I gave her a sheepish smile. "Sorry."

She put a hand on my shoulder. I was acutely aware of the fact that one of her fingers grazed the skin of my neck. "You could stay the night, if you like", she said softly. "We've a spare room…" I shook my head, despite myself. Much as I wanted to, I'd just turn into a wolf, and then it would all come crashing down around me.

"I'd love to", I said, "but I can't. For one, Pancakes needs to get home and, uh…" I looked at the CatWolf, hoping he'd offer me a decent excuse. Sadly, he completely failed to manifest the capacity for speech. "Take his medication", I said. "Worms. Very gross."

"I see", Tavi said. Her smile was a little sad. "Well… if you want to…"

"I'd love to see you tomorrow", I said. She blinked like I'd thrown a towel at her, and then her face split into a wide grin. "I would very much like to come back. Again. To, uh, you." My confidence started running out of steam, and fast. "I mean, I don't have to if—"

"That'd be delightful, Maya", she said. "Come with me a moment." She started to step outside and I followed her. Pan loyally stepped out with us. "There's something I'd like you to have a look at, tomorrow. It shouldn't be any great trouble, but I still wanted to show it to you", Octavia said. "I'd be delighted if you came 'round."

"I'd love to come 'round", I said, mimicking her speech a little bit. The accusatory smile she aimed at me was powerful and disarming. I could feel my blood rush to my cheeks. "If'n you'll have me."

"Miss Maya", she said, taking a step closer, "you best not be mocking me."

I had no idea what was going through my head or what possessed me to bite my lip and glance at her from under half-closed eyelids, but I did. "Wouldn't dare", I said softly. Her eyes lingered on my mouth for a moment, before looking back up at me. Her face was close. Her eyes were all I could look at. I jolted when I felt something against my hand, and realized it was hers. The back of her fingers touching the back of mine ever so softly. I'd had people touch my hand or my arm before, so why was this caress, her finger running over my skin, so soft and gentle it was like we were barely touching at all, sending sparks up my arm, all the way to my chest?

"I'll see you t'morrow, Maya", she said softly. I very faintly felt her breath on my face.

"Ye", I squeaked and felt something against my hand again. It was wet and sniffing. Looking down, I saw Pancakes trying to see if we were secretly passing each other treats. I rubbed the top of his head. "He's getting anxious." So was I, come to think of it. I looked at the sun. It was starting to set. "I'll see you tomorrow?"

"Would you like for me to come fetch you?" Octavia asked. I thought about that for a moment, then nodded. It was a little risky, she might see me in wolf-form, but I'd just have to stay inside tonight. I wanted to avoid an incident. Tonight and tomorrow were wolf nights, and the morning after I'd wake up as The Witch again. I dreaded it a little. After all, Octavia seemed to like Maya. And it was a lot easier to… appreciate her back when I was Maya.

"I'd love that", I said, and raised my eyebrows. "Don't be late. I'll be waiting for you."

"Good", she said, and looked around. Seemingly satisfied by what she saw, she leaned forward ever so daintily and kissed me on the cheek. It was a slight, soft peck, and it blew my brains out the side of my skull like a grenade had gone off next to my head.

"Fzwl", I said as I started to walk on autopilot. I heard her giggle behind me as I reached up to touch my cheek. Where her lips had touched my skin, it burned, in the best way possible. The ticking clock on the horizon was the only thing keeping me put one foot in front of the other. I was in such a daze, I was home before I'd even realized what had happened. I was a *wolf* before I'd realized what happened.

Somehow, that night was one of the most anxious nights of my life. For the first time in both our lives, I was the one annoying and keeping Pancakes awake. I just... couldn't stay still. I found myself walking through the cabin in circles, nails clicking on the floorboards, searching for something I knew wasn't there. Even when I tried to sit still I couldn't keep my paws from tippy-tapping up and down. I had put some logs on the fire, leaving the unpleasant taste of wood in my mouth and my whiskers slightly singed, and I didn't even *care*. I was going to see her again in the morning and she'd kissed me on the cheek and it...

My heart sank. It was going to be my last time in a month, wasn't it? Because she didn't look at The Witch the same way, and I felt like I had to be more... analytical. Like it was easier to be easygoing and comfortable when I was Maya.

In the end, I managed to take a nap on the pillows and blankets that constituted the cabin's cozy corner, and Pancakes, in his infinite wisdom, tried to take one on top of me. Well, I'd at least managed to close my eyes a little. I looked outside. I was going to have to invent something close to a clock, because not knowing what time it was was slowly driving me insane.

I was in the middle of trying to use my mouth — muzzle? Maw? I had some things to study up on with regards to wolf anatomy — to feed Pan and myself using the little scoop, when I felt the effects of the full moon lessen. I finished feeding my oversized cat and then got dressed in the clothes I'd left in front of the fire. Gosh, nice and toasty. I was still flattening out my clothes, when I heard a knock on my door.

Nearly tripping over myself, I somehow managed to make it to the front door in one piece. "Hi", I said, breathlessly. Octavia beamed up at me and swept some hair out of her eyes.

"Good morning", she said, and somehow it was the most beautiful thing I'd ever heard. This was... bad. I had it bad. And she wasn't even going to like me twenty-seven days out of every thirty. I shook my brain like an Etch-A-Sketch, not in the mood for dark thoughts like that. Not when I'd be spending my time with her.

"You too", I said quietly. I looked at Pan, grabbed the scoop and gave him extra food, made sure his water bowl was full, then kneeled down next to him. "Okay, Pancakes", I whispered in his ear, "I'm gonna leave you here today, okay? Try not to destroy the house, okay? I'll be back soon. If you need to go, I *know* you know how to open the door now, I've seen you fucking with the latch." He looked up at me from his food, shoved his tongue up my nose and then went back to eating. "Alright", I coughed, "good. Glad we're in agreement. Now, Mommy's gotta go… be with Octavia." I'd whispered the last bit, and then realized I'd reflexively referred to myself as 'Mommy', which was a whole can of worms I wasn't ready to open yet. I stood up. "Ready?"

"As ever", Octavia said with a little laugh. I grabbed my coat and was about to grab the bag, but she held out her hand. "No need for that." I raised my eyebrows. I'd assumed, if we were going to be in town, I'd likely be called on. "We won't be seen by people today", she said conspiratorially, then winked. "Come on."

I eagerly joined her outside. She led me down the path to the village, but stopped me after only a few minutes of walking. Usually, the path took me around the peak of the mountain, and then down a ways to town. This time, however, Octavia led me down a path I wouldn't have noticed on my own. That was, in part, because it was covered in more than a foot of snow, and partly because I simply hadn't been looking for it, hidden as it was between a few trees. Following it up, we eventually came to the top of the mountain.

There was a tiny cabin up here. Not comparable in the least to the Witch's house, it was one, *maybe* two rooms. But it was cozy and it was remote. "Is this", I huffed as we walked the last bit up the road, "what you wanted to show me?"

"Something like that", she said as hoisted herself out of the snow and onto the porch. She held out her hand to me, and easily lifted me up to her. I stumbled a bit and bumped into her. My breath caught in my throat as she caught me easily. By putting her hands on my waist. "Careful." Her voice was a whisper, her face close to mine. Why was this setting my soul on fire like it did?

"I mean…" I felt a giggle rise up in my throat, "if I'm not, you'll catch me. That's hardly an incentive…" She smirked, but didn't let go. My breathing was shallow from the climb, but it was also hard to relax. Both of us, in fact, were still breathing heavily and blushing profusely.

"You're an enigma, Maya the Witch", she said. "You've a strange way of speaking, and a sense of awkwardness about you, but then you turn around and act like a coy *flirt*." On that last word, she'd pulled me, almost imperceptibly, closer to her. I didn't know what to do with my hands. "I do not know", Octavia continued, "how to behave around you. What you might find proper or improper. What to do or what, even, to think."

"Mood."

"There you go again", she giggled. "You're… vexing, Maya. You vex me." She closed her eyes and took a deep breath. "And if I'm to be quite honest…" Her eyes opened, and she looked at me. She was so close. All I'd have to do was reach out, but it was all I could just to let my gaze rest on her lips, hanging on her every word. "I find you completely incomprehensible." Well, that hadn't been what I expected. I turned away, but her hand reached up, found my chin, and turned me to face her. "I would comprehend you, Maya."

"Yes", I said, breathless, voice caught in my throat. Her fingers slid along my jaw.

"I would know you", she said.

"Yes."

"I would kiss you."

"Yes."

She did.

14

Clad In Black, Don't Look Back

I was lost. Lost beyond words, beyond thought, beyond myself. A second before, her face had been framed by the winter morning landscape, her hand on my cheek, loose strands of her hair brushstrokes on an already perfect canvas. Then, her lips were on mine and my heart stood still.

Every consideration I'd had for what she might think of me if she knew I was a... a werewolf, if she knew I wasn't Maya, melted away. I'd have fallen apart, turned to honey, if she hadn't wrapped an arm around her waist and pulled myself into her. I gasped. She grinned into the kiss, pushed me against the wall.

This was new, so new, but my body and Octavia both seemed to know what to do, and I let them. When her lips found my neck, I gasped, a voice that had never been mine before making sounds I would have never made that were so fantastically mine. If her ministrations on my skin hadn't sent sparks up and down my spine I would've maybe tried to stifle myself, but she was overwhelming. My heart thundered in my chest like a runaway train.

I mewled in frustration when she stopped. She took half a step back, so I took one forward. She giggled and ran a hand through my hair. "Take it easy, Miss Maya", she said. "I just... This is new, isn't it?" I nodded. All of this was new to me, in more ways than one. "Then we... should talk." She looked around and shivered. I only just now noticed I was shivering too. "Inside, though. I'd rather we didn't catch frostbite out here."

She took my hand, led me into the house. It wasn't much warmer inside, but there was a hearth. And maybe... I could impress her? I walked over to the fireplace and kneeled down in front of it, holding my hands out. Okay, so fire required... I looked around. Okay, there was one window that had light coming in through it, that was good. Then I cramped my hands like *this*, and made a kind of snorting sound like *that*, and made sure to point my hands forward...

The logs caught fire almost immediately. I wondered for a brief moment if the weird combination of things required for doing what was essentially a simple spell was responsible for spontaneous combustion. I'd read somewhere once that, very rarely, someone on a plane had spontaneously caught fire, although I had no idea if that was actually true. Regardless, it wasn't unthinkable that someone would make the noises and hand gestures I'd made in their sleep. Did that mean magic had been real back home too?

I shook my head and turned around, to a stunned looking Octavia. Her eyes wide, she was staring at the fire. I frowned only a little bit. "I thought you knew I was a Witch?" I said a little sheepishly and a little too late.

"*Ye-es*", she said, "but I thought that that meant, well, knowledge of herbology, alchemy, that sort of thing. I didn't know you could do *magic!*" I took a step back. Well, that was... something else. Maybe no werewolf reveal would be necessary. I'd just kind of assumed things would be okay, but maybe it was torches and pitchforks time already.

"I'm sorry", I said, "for— for what it's worth, there's no, like, devils involved or any-thing."

Octavia rolled her eyes. "I didn't think there were", she said, and took a step towards me and resolutely took my hand. "I was only surprised, is all. I didn't know things like this were possible, let alone that you might do them." She locked her fingers with mine. "Makes me want to see what else you can do, Miss Maya." Then her face was a lot closer again and her mouth was on mine and my breath was being ruthlessly stolen from me again.

It was like her hands were everywhere. One moment they were on my back, the next her fingers ran through my hair, then again I felt the palm of her hand against mine. We only stopped because I almost fell over. I couldn't help but giggle at my own awkwardness. "You said we should talk?" I asked. She nodded.

"Sit", she said. "I'll put the kettle on." Then she shot me a little sideways smirk. "And I'd love to hear more about this magic, too, in due time." I did as she asked and sat down at the wooden table, finally looking around the cabin a bit more thoroughly. Other than the table, which sat four, maybe six if you squeezed, there was the hearth, several cabinets which I assumed were for preparing or storing food, and a large bed in one corner.

"Do you come up here often?" I asked, and barely resisted a giggle at what I only realized afterwards was one of the oldest pick-up lines in the book. Tavi shook her head.

"Not really. Not for some time, leastways, although I did swing 'round a few days ago." She put a large kettle of water on the fire. "Just in case I might need it." She *winked*, and I choked on my embarrassment for a second. She'd *prepared* for this.

"Oh", I squeaked, my eyes water. "How nice of you." She joined me at the table and sat across from me, and put her hand on mine. Gosh. She was so soft. So pretty. I wished there was a way for me to decipher the way she looked at me, but her expression was just... wistful, like someone looking up at the clouds. "Hi", I said softly.

"Hey", she answered. "So... we ought to talk." She chewed her lip for a second with a frown on her face. "About us, I mean. And what that *means.*"

"Does it mean anything?" I asked, a little confused, until my penny dropped. "Do you, uh, want it to mean anything?" She laughed, her eyes sparking up with life and light.

"Yes, you dolt", Octavia said. "Of course I do." She squeezed my hand. "Though I must admit that it's not only — how do I put this — your personality that drew my attention, if you catch my meaning." I couldn't help but blush. I already had an idea of what I looked like when I was Maya, but having Tavi call me beautiful in the most roundabout way possible was still a blow to my lack of self esteem. "Do you?" she asked, more quietly.

I nodded. "I'd like that", I said. Although... I would be gone again before the next sunrise. Would I be able to tell her why? She squeezed my hand again.

"You're hesitant", she said. "If you're unsure, is it something we might talk of?"

"I... I don't know yet", I said, "I'm sorry. But before we get to that, was there something else that this —" I pointed between the two of us, "— y'know, meant?"

"Well." Octavia clasped her hands together. "My parents are a slight", she waved her hands through the air, "old fashioned." I nodded. While it wasn't something I'd spent a lot of time thinking about, I had remembered that medieval times were likely not the bastions of free love and identity that... oh, who was I kidding, things were still dire, but at the very least, queer people had some rights.

"I figured as much", I said. "You'd want to keep this a secret, because you can't risk getting ostracized or like, cast out, right?" She looked at me like I'd grown a second head.

"What? No! There's not a one down in that village that would come after me for being with a Witch. And if they did, I can do far worse to them that would do to me, don't you worry."

She huffed with indignation that made me want to reach across the table, grab her by the collar and drag her across it for a kiss. Sadly, she escaped what would've at least been a valiant attempt by getting up and grabbing the kettle, then pouring us both a cup of tea. I wasn't sure what was in it, but it smelled minty. "Thank you", I said quietly, carefully blew on the tea, then burned my tongue.

"Leastways", Octavia continued, "I'm only saying that it would mean that you might not be eligible to marry any of the men in town. People are quite strict about that, sadly." I choked on my tea this time. Tavi laughed as she slapped me on the back.

"Wasn't planning to", I coughed. "I'm not particularly, uhm, inclined in that direction."

"Well, if you were, if this gets out, and if it were up to me, it would, then you would have no opportunity to anymore. The occasional dalliance people will allow, but anything more serious and it's… *recommended* that one follows the relationship through." For the third time, I choked, this time on my own spit. She'd called it a relationship and she seemed to want it! With me.

Except, of course, that she didn't. Not with me. But with Maya. "I", I said, and then fell silent. I tried saying more, but my voice seemed to fail me, over and over again.

"That was the other thing, of course", Tavi said, "that is that this is all very new to you, and I want to make sure you're comfortable with everything going on." She seemed to have misunderstood my worry for hesitancy. "We can take this slowly, if you want. I do not wish to rush you into something you might not be ready for."

"It's not that, Tavi. I just think that—" How was I going to explain to her I wouldn't be here anymore tomorrow? Replaced by The Witch, while Maya just sort of existed in the background? "I might not be here again, for a while. I'll be back next month but—"

"But it's not much of a consolation", she said with a smirk. Then she stood up, walked around the table, grabbed my face in her hands, and kissed me again. Hard. Her lips pressed against mine with need. I felt her mouth part ever so slightly, her tongue touching my lips ever so slightly, before pulling away. "We'll make the time we have count, then."

I wanted to believe it was that easy. Could it be? Stealing time when we could, once a month, for only a few days, when I could be Maya? "What did you, uh, have in mind?"

She gave me an incredulous grin. "Really? You can't think of anything?" Well, that wasn't entirely true. There were lots of things I could think of, but the last thing I wanted was to make her uncomfortable or unhappy. I didn't want to come off as creepy or pushy. What I *wanted* to do…

"I would like to kiss you again", I said as I stood up and took her hands in mine. "And I think I'd very much like for you to kiss me again too." She slowly stepped backwards, and it took me a few seconds to realize she was pulling me to the bed. "Oh", I said quietly, and I felt the heat rise to my face again. "*Oh.*"

She only gave me a wolfish grin as she kissed me, her teeth on my skin as she undressed me. When she dragged me into the sheets, I was hers.

When we eventually got up, it was to both our protestations. Sadly, we *did* have to eat, the fire needed some extra logs. But we were back in bed before long, with fresh cups of tea. A lot of time was spent talking — about everything and nothing. I told her about magic and how I'd been discovering new things. She told me about the village, and where she grew up. What it had been like. What she had been like.

It was already getting dark outside when I next looked out the window. Wait, what time was it? I hopped out of bed and quickly started getting dressed. Tavi looked worried.

"You don't have to go", she said. Her voice grew softer, more quiet. "I don't want you to."

"I have to", I said under my breath. "I can't... can't." I should've kept a firmer eye on the time, but I'd been so wrapped up in, well, *her*. I'd almost been too late, and now I was completely out of time. I rushed over to her and kissed her on the forehead, and once more on the lips for good measure. "I'll see you—" I stopped. 'In a month.' It was too long. Way too long. "I'll see you soon."

I was out the door before she could stop me. My eyes hurt in the freezing evening cold, and it was only when I felt the wind sting my cheeks that I became aware of the tears running down my cheeks.

Practically running all the way home, I made it before the change happened, although I was sure I'd seen shapes through the trees. Something had been following me. When I crashed inside, I figured I had only minutes to go before I turned back into a wolf, and I'd have to say goodbye to Maya for another four weeks. Tears flowed more freely now.

Which was why I almost had a heart attack when there was a loud knock on the door behind me. I swung the door open.

Octavia stood on my porch, leaning on her knees and panting heavily. "*Heavens, Maya*", she said, out of breath. "You, really, don't, take, it, easy, do, you?" She took a quick breath between every word, leaning on my door frame.

"Tavi", I said, wiping away tears, "you can't be here... I'm not..." I wanted to drag her inside, but I also didn't want to turn into a wolf in front of her. I needed to get her out of here.

"What?" she asked, exasperated. "I already *know, Maya*."

"Wait, what?" I asked. "How?"

"You get like this once a month, and run off every evening, before the sun sets. You're not exactly *subtle*."

"But... it doesn't bother you?"

"Why would it bother me?"

"Because I'm a *werewolf!*"

"Wh— Yes, you are", she said, frowning. "I mean, of course you are. Everyone is. Wait, is that what this was about? I thought you were hiding the fact that you were really a girl."

"*What?*"

15

Kiss Your Fist And Touch The Sky

"What do you mean I was hiding the..." I frowned. This was all sideways. She wasn't supposed to have responded that way! She was supposed to, I don't know, scream, shout, get the people of the village to drive the evil werewolf witch out. Speaking of which. "Hold on, what do you mean, 'everyone is'??"

"The village!" Octavia said, waving out the door. "This is a... *how did you not know?* The pack literally lifted you out of the snow! Sorry", she rolled her eyes, "your 'cousin' out of the snow. You tried to pet me!"

"I did *what?!*" I squeaked. I must've been completely delirious at that moment, but now that she mentioned it, I did vaguely remember dreams about wolves... right before I'd woken up in her house. And... "Oh god..."

"In your defense", she said with a smile, "it was genuinely precious. Then you turned into a wolf in front of us, so we knew you were one of us. I thought you knew we knew, and it was the... Maya you were embarrassed about."

"But, wait, it wasn't full moon yet!" I protested. "How did— What d— *What?*"

"Wait, you don't know?" She cocked her head. "We can always change, Maya."

"Then what about the full moon?" I looked out the window. It wasn't going to be long now, and I wasn't ready. There wasn't enough time, I wasn't ready to stop being Maya yet, I wasn't ready to let go yet. "I don't want to go", I whispered. Octavia closed the distance between us and wiped away the tears that had started to roll down my face.

"You don't *have* to", she said quietly. "You can stay, there's nobody's making you go."

"But... I'm only Maya when the moon..." Breathing was getting harder, and I felt my-self start hyperventilating. "I don't... get... to be..." Octavia wrapped her arms around me and buried my face in her shoulder.

"You can just... be Maya", she said. "All you've to do is choose it." Her hot breath brushed my ear. Her whispers fluttered into my brain and set off every part of it like fireworks. That wasn't true, was it? I couldn't just *choose* to be Maya, that's not how it worked, because I wasn't Maya, Maya was something, someone that *happened* to me, no matter how much I wanted it to be otherwise.

"I can't just..." was all I managed before my breathing was reduced to huge, heaving sobs. She patted me softly on the back, rubbing her hand in little circles between my shoulderblades.

"You can", she said again, and very softly kissed my cheek. "But maybe you need a little... affirmation." She stepped back. "Come on, it's pretty much time." She closed the door and quickly tossed off her coat, then dropped her dress.

Even with everything happening, Tavi taking her clothes off in front of me short-circuited my brain. I would've felt awful if I'd been capable of even a single thought, but my mind was completely taken up by the beautiful, *very* naked woman in front of me. She giggled. "You'll make me blush, Maya." Suddenly she got a lot shorter, and a lot more... fluffy. The wolf, the one I'd met in the forest the other day, sat in front of me.

I heard a scrambling behind me, but as I turned around I tripped over my clothes which were now far too big for me. I scrambled backwards out of them, my own four feet getting in my way, before looking at Pancakes.

He'd woken up from the spot where he'd been asleep, and he was clearly excited at the sight of not one, but *two* large dogs for him to play with. He fell face-first off the couch, bounced up like it was nothing, and hurried over.

There was a sort of growling-hissing coming from behind me, which I realized after a second was the sound of Octavia laughing. Pancakes came over and experimentally sniffed her nose. She raised a paw and bopped him on the snout. He yelped, jumped back, jumped forward again, and then fell over and pawed at her.

"Woof", I told him reproachfully. He glared, but I wasn't having it. I nodded at the couch. He got up and went back to his spot, and I didn't know if it was my imagination or not but it looked like he was dragging his feet.

"Arf", Octavia said, winked, and turned around, nudged the door open, and ran outside. I followed her out, making sure to leave the door open just a little bit in case Pan needed to go out.

Tavi was a blur of movement through the snow, but every time she stopped, I saw the moon reflecting in her eyes. Every time she looked at me, I recognised her again. I couldn't *not* follow her. My legs moved before my mind decided to.

Tavi ran through the trees and I followed. She jumped across the stream, and I crashed into it. Not that I was going to let that stop me, of course. She let out that little chuckle-giggle again as I shook myself off. I looked up at her, and found her nose-to-nose with me. She nudged me softly, then spun on her tail and ran off again.

Where was she going? This wasn't a solution, it was just... putting things off, distracting me. But I didn't want to think about the reality of becoming the Witch again, so I decided to *let* her distract me. Maybe that was for the best.

She danced around me, weaving between the trees, and in time I found it easier to just lose myself in the game of it. Octavia. Could I call her *my* Octavia? She'd implied as much earlier, but that was before telling her The Witch and I were one and the same. On the *other* hand, did she already know that? And would she be okay with that?

Did that make me hers? As we circled around each other, both out of breath, and she shoved her nose into the fluff around my neck, I was starting to accept that, if nothing else, I *wanted* to be hers. Her Maya.

She once again led me through the snow. Up the mountain. To the little cabin we'd been at before. The sky was slowly getting brighter. There wasn't much time left anymore. We walked up to the porch, where she turned around and sat down, looking at the horizon. Time was up. The sky had draped itself in purples and reds. I was going to turn back any second now. Nonetheless, I joined her, and she moved her mouth close to my ear.

"Stay", she said. I looked at her in surprise. How was she able to speak? Nonetheless, I did as she said, and sat down on the hardwood, and looked at the horizon. "Stay here", she continued. "Stay like this. Stay you. Stay wolf." She nudged me with her forehead. "Stay Maya."

I wanted to respond with a little despondent woof. If my calculations and timetable had been correct, I had only seconds left before I'd turn back into The Witch. Into him. Not to mention naked. That was the last thing I wanted. Not in front of her. I couldn't. I *wouldn't*. "I don't know how", I said. I blinked, then tried to look at my own mouth. Next to me, the crystal-clear laugh of Octavia rang through the air.

"You look ridiculous", she said, leaned over, and nudged my nose with hers. "There. You did it."

"But... how?"

"You chose", she said with a little shrug. "That is all."

"That *can't* be it!" I protested as the sun painted her fur a warm yellow. She closed her eyes as the warm rays bathed us both in golden light. "There has to be something more to it!" She just shook her head.

"No", she said. "There's only the choice you've made. Maya was already there, love. You only had to choose to be her."

"But it can't be that *simple!* I spent *weeks* trying to figure this out, trying to understand what was going on and why I would turn into her and what made me go wolf and—" I laughed. "It's just... choosing?"

"It's just choosing", Octavia said. "Being Maya was a choice you had to make. And I know your kind." She shot me a knowing look. "You would've fretted a lifetime trying to reason things through. I only put you in a spot where a choice could be made, was all."

"You monster", I said, and sat a little closer to her. Her tail flicked mine. I flicked it back, but they got entangled. Oh well. I closed my eyes and let the warm light of the winter morning sun fall on my eyelids. "This is nice." Our tails slowly entwined.

"It is", Octavia said.

Of course, we had to head back eventually, if only to feed Pancakes. But a weight was off my chest. Maya wasn't something that happened to me. Not anymore, if she'd ever been. Maya was a choice I'd made, and now I got to be her. Back in my cabin, Octavia turned back into her human self, and carefully picked her clothes off of the ground. A part of me wanted that scene to take a more *interesting* turn, but the fire in the hearth had died and it was, frankly, too cold for those kinds of shenanigans.

Then there was me. I sat in the middle of the room. I was going to turn back. But I'd be damned if I spent another *day* as *him*. Slowly, the floor grew more distant. My limbs longer. Octavia stood in front of me, and wrapped a blanket around me when I started shivering.

"Hello", she said, and kissed me softly. I was, as always, liquid uselessness in her touch. She took my face in her hands and kissed my cheeks. My forehead. My nose. My lips. Over and over again, in a little cycle that she kept repeating, until I giggled, my voice high and beautiful and Maya and *mine*.

"What was that for?" I asked with a smile.

She grinned her teeth bare. "Because it's nice to meet you."

"It's nice to meet you too", I replied, kissed her back, then very gently bit her nose. "I'm Maya." She laughed.

"I know", she said, "and it's nice to meet you too, Maya. I'm yours."

"A", I said, as she wrapped her arms around me again. Then... I put some clothes on, because we did need to get a fire started, feed and walk Pan, and eat something, because neither of us had really eaten a lot the day before either, romantic as we wanted to be in the middle of that room.

So we made food. Together. She wrapped her arms around me from behind and kissed the back of my neck and I literally died on the spot. I returned the favor and found out that wolves can purr, too.

We spent the day talking, reading, and scratching a very spoiled Pan behind the ears. I explained the situation with The Witch to her and showed her the journals. Showed her the magic circles I'd tried to make to figure myself out.

In the next few days, weeks, I told her about where I was from. Who I'd been and what my world and life had been like, and reassured her that what I wanted more than anything in the world was to stay. With her. For as long as she'd have me.

She told me she wanted to share her life with me. So she did.

16

Epilogue

"So you knew it was me the entire time?" I asked, nudging her. The snow had all but melted, the birds were chirping, and my fingers were freezing off. "Why didn't you say anything?"

"It didn't seem my place", she said. "And 'sides, you seemed so discomforted, we thought to give you the space to come to terms with yourself." We walked down the village road, greeting and occasionally accepting gifts from people as we passed them by. Over time, I'd been fully accepted into the landscape of the town. More importantly, I'd also been fully accepted as being Octavia's, and her as mine. She was positively radiant as we went around town and I felt like I was being paraded in the best way possible. I'd never had someone be proud to be around me before, let alone to be by my side.

She'd mentioned that she didn't like possessiveness. In theory. In practice, however, she had made it very, *very* clear that she was having a hard time *not* thinking of me as hers, and that she partly wanted to claim me, even if it was only for a little bit.

"Where next?" I asked as I dropped off the last of my deliveries. Now that Spring was properly coming around, it was going to be easier — I hoped — to supply people with herbal remedies. Technically, I was still the town Witch. In practice, though, it was more like I was the town pharmacist.

Apparently, despite all of the myths and legends I'd heard of and read, werewolves did not have any kind of supernatural strength, stamina or ability to heal, so I had my work cut out for me, and I wasn't nearly as liable to isolate as my predecessor had been.

"Well", she said as she took my hand in hers, our fingers intertwining, "I was hoping we could go home and spend some time, just the two of us." She still stayed at her parents' house occasionally — they still needed her help with the farm — but most days she lived with me now. It was *exactly* as blissful as it sounded, even though we had epic nightly battles over the blankets, usually resolved through diplomatic spooning.

Now, what I wanted to say back was something suave like "Oh, what did you have in mind?" or "I aim to please." Instead, all I managed was a nervous "Hheh", and a lip-bite.

"I'll take that as a yes", she said, and kissed me. In the middle of the street. I felt the urge to wag a tail I didn't currently have. Instead, I just nodded enthusiastically. We worked our way home. When we were close, Tavi broke into a sprint. I gave chase, because it only made sense to do so. By the time we were at our front door, both of us were out of breath and laughing our butts off.

"You", I huffed, "are a *menace.*" I had to prop myself up on my knees to look at her. She giggled as she righted herself against the doorframe, giving me a cocksure grin.

She laughed, brushing hair out of her face. "And you love me for it."

"You're right about that", I said, grabbing her face in my hands and kissing her, pinning her body against the wall with mine. Immediately every desire we'd slowly built up throughout the day was letting itself out. Our hands roamed each other, and I'd forgotten all about my cold fingers.

There was only Octavia and my desire for her. Her hands and her lips and her skin and her hair and her breath and her gasps and her body against mine. We didn't even stop kissing as I pushed the door open and we practically fell into the room.

"Shall I come back another time, then?" a voice behind us said. We immediately pulled away to look at the intruder.

"Tavi", I said.

"Yes, love."

"There's a woman in our living room."

"So there is."

"That's a dog by her feet."

"So it is."

"She's got quite a large hat."

"So she does."

"I think she might be a witch."

"I reckon you're right, love."

The woman put her hands on her hips and raised an eyebrow. She seemed familiar, clad in all black. That's when I realized she was wearing *modern* clothing, although her Witch's hat seemed to have been made a little less professionally. She had a bag slung over her shoulder, which she was rooting around in. Against the far wall, the wolf-like shape of Pancakes was standing on his tiptoes, his back arched. He made a sort of wheezing sound I could only imagine was an attempt at hissing. "You must be Octavia", she said. "I seen you down at the village."

"Excuse me?" Tavi replied. "Who are you? Why are you in our house? And how do you know me?" She marched across the wood floor to the woman, who just crossed her arms defiantly. The dog at her feet, some kind of Lab or Retriever, growled as Octavia approached, but she wasn't the least bit intimidated.

"Don't speak to me like that in my own house, girl", the woman said. She glared past Tavi and at me. "Though I suppose under the circumstances I understand your misgivings." The penny dropped, realization set in, horror crept up. I'd recognized the witch, because she looked... well, a lot like I had. Before I'd come here. Only more like... my own sister. The jawline was there. The rough frame. But the eyes were more alert than mine had ever been. The hair was long and well kept. The eyebrows groomed. The eyeliner *razor* sharp.

"No way", I mumbled, and walked up. "You're... you're the original Witch?"

"Yes", she said. "And I see you've had more success with that body than I did."

"Wait, so you were trying to..." I nodded. It made a degree of sense. There had been a ritual, after all, for a witch who didn't go in with magic. "Wait, if that's what you were trying to do that night, why am *I* here?"

"Because magic is unreliable, frustrating, and makes no sense", she huffed, her hands on her hips. "Though I'm lucky to say that medicinal remedies in your world have proven to be more reliable. Considering your —" she waved to Octavia and myself, "— activities, I'll assume you're quite happy with the changes."

"I am", I said with a little smile, and found myself standing next to Octavia again. Partly because I wanted to protect her. Partly because I wanted her to protect me. "So you're on... uh, hold on, Hormone Replacement Therapy?"

"Yes", she said. "I am. Not as fast as I'd like, faster than I could've hoped for when resorting to... horse extract." She scrunched her nose up. "But I feel things could be improved, so I decided to try my hand at magics again to find my notebooks." She held up one of the journals with an accusing glare. "*Though I found someone else has been writing notes in the byline.*"

"Listen!" I retorted, "I didn't know if you'd be back, some of this stuff is more useful than other stuff, and I needed to make sense of some of your *scribbles!* Your handwriting is *abominable!*"

"I had other things on my mind, I'll have you know!" she said, slapping the palm of her hand with the journal for emphasis. "Not to mention the fact that it is, in fact, quite hard to concentrate on something as inconsequential as handwriting when your body feels *wrong.*"

"Well, I can relate to that at least", I said, shrugging. "Alright, fair, you can take the journals with you. Oh! Could you leave the ones about animal husbandry though?" I nodded at a stack near the cozy corner. "You had some really interesting ideas about calves and I know Tavi's Da has a cow that's probably going to have a difficult pregnancy and—"

"Yes, yes", The Witch said, waving her hand dismissively, but I could see a smile playing around her lips. "I get the feeling they aren't in… the worst hands imaginable." She put the journal in her bag.

"Who's, uh, the dog?" I looked down. The dog looked up. It looked smarter than any dog I'd ever seen.

"Clarus", The Witch said. "Though he used to look like that." She pointed her thumb over her shoulder at the still-hissing Pan. "I attempted to give him a body that conformed somewhat to the image he had of himself. This was the best I could do, but he seems happy enough." She put her hand on his head and I could see his tail begin to wag ever so slightly. Still a dog, then.

"And your name?" Octavia asked. "We all just called you 'The Witch' down in the village." She was a little less combative now that she knew who the intruder was.

"Well, what my name used to be, I suppose, no longer matters", she said. "Call me what you like." She looked at me. "Oh, if you're intending for us to trade places again, you'll have to get your name changed from Morgan. Although I would warn you that, if you do, I *will* resist you."

The thought of fighting her seemed so absurd, the casualness with which she'd uttered the possibility so ridiculous, I just laughed. "No", I said, "I don't think I will. I'm quite happy here. I take it you are, too?"

Morgan nodded as she walked around the room and grabbed more of her journals. "Yes. Though the world seems to have some trouble accepting the existence of magic and witchcraft, and I'm hardly the best person to show them. Nonetheless, I think great strides are being made."

"Excuse me? You just… announced it?"

"Yes", she said with another nod. "It seemed prudent. There's some systems in place that make change too gradual and easy to resist by those in authority. It seems to be helping." She scratched her dog behind the ears. "Now, I believe I should start heading back. I'll be 'round some other time in case I've forgotten something. I detest this kind of magic, and there's always a possibility of damaging reality or some such nonsense."

"Wait!" I said. "There's so much I still want to ask you! What's the world like now? What are you going to do next? How did you first manage when you got there?" The idea of a Witch in our world, casually mucking things up, overturning established rules of reality and society almost casually was… well, I wanted to know more. But the Witch didn't seem particularly interested in telling me about it.

"Suffice it to say that I've done well for myself. Should you need something more concrete than stories, tell me now, and I'll attempt to provide it when next I visit." She looked at where she'd appeared. There were slight scorch marks on the floor, and for the first time, she looked a little sheepish. "I'll… try to aim for the front porch, that time."

I looked at Octavia, to see if there was something she could think of, but she just shook her head. I turned to the witch and smirked. "Could you bring me some different cookbooks?" I asked. "I miss some of the cooking from back home. Different cuisines, and all that."

"I can do that", Morgan said. She looked behind her. "Anything you want me to do about the cat?" I thought about that for a moment. Pancakes had always been a relaxed cat, and that hadn't really changed now that he was a wolf. He was still happy, still kind of dumb, still easygoing. I shook my head.

"I don't think so", I said. "I think he likes it this way."

"Very well", The Witch nodded at both of us. "I bid you both a good day. And I apologize for the... interruption." Morgan raised her hands and started to weave symbols in the air. She opened her mouth, eyes fixed straight ahead, clearly ready to speak the incantations that would take her back to my — well, *her* — world, but then paused. She looked at Tavi. "Congratulations on the baby." Then, with a guttural word and a flash of nothing, she was gone.

I turned to Octavia like a glacier on an afternoon stroll. "The bwh?"

She bit her lip. "I was going to surprise you later", she said.

Well... I just *had* to kiss her again.

Book II

Mutually Assured Seduction

1

The Duel

"I hate him so much, Kat."

"Oh my holy fuck", Kat sighed with exasperation. "Let it *go*." She flopped backwards in the grass and stared angrily at the clouds. She squinted and one of them dissipated with a satisfying 'pop' Next to her, Mark fumed over the sheet in his hand. He was staring at his name, halfway down the page. Just above it was the name of the offender.

Roland Mayweather.

"I can't let it go, Kat!" Mark Rose said through gritted teeth. "He beat me! Again!" He waved the piece of paper as if it would make a difference, as if shaking it enough could scramble the words into an order he'd be more satisfied with. Kat groaned.

"That's just one class, Mark. Don't be an asshole. Besides, you beat him in Calculus and Abjuration", she said, remembering only because Mark hadn't shut up about it for a week after his results had come in.

"Yeah, but he had a higher score in Evocation, and everyone knows that's the most important school they teach here, anyway", Mark grumbled, but her attempts at soothing his ego had worked. A little bit.

"Coolest, you mean. Just because you don't throw fireballs as well...besides, that makes you tied, doesn't it?"

Mark shook his head. "He was higher on Transfiguration."

"Who even *cares*, Mark? There's five hundred students in our class and half of them are better than you. Why are you so obsessed with this Roland character?"

"Because!" Mark lashed out, and then sighed, mumbling a sorry. Kat knew he got upset about Roland easily, but she wasn't going to let him get away with verbally abusing her. "Because", he said, calmer this time, "he's a rich boy who's only lucky to get as far as he has because of his dad's money. I've had to work harder than him my entire life. He shouldn't get to coast like he does."

"And", Kat added, clearly angling for an honorary psych degree, "if you beat him, you prove you're good enough despite your lack of money?"

"Shut up, Kat", Mark said, but his tone made her smile. She'd gotten through his defenses. He was honestly a good friend, when he wasn't obsessing over his classmate.

"If I recall correctly", Kat said, pressing on, "you had the same score on Transfiguration, didn't you?"

"Well", Mark said, "sort of."

"What do you mean, sort of? Either you did or you didn't." Kat propped herself up on her elbows and looked at Mark, who fished a different paper out of his back and handed it to her.

"We got the same score, but he's ranked higher", Mark said, pointing out the spot.

"That's because it's first alphabetically, dumbass. Let it go", she said, but he wasn't listening.

"I wonder if I could change my last name", he said. "It'd be definitive proof I'm the better warlock."

"I literally don't have words for how stupid of an idea that is", Kat said, executing a perfect facepalm. "Why don't you challenge him to a duel? Last man standing is the best, and if he kills you, I don't have to listen to you *whine* anymore", she joked.

"That's a great idea!" Mark said, perking up.

"Wait, no."

He jumped up and slung his backpack over his shoulder. "I'm going to go find him right now!"

"Mark, please." Kat was trying to get up fast enough to stop him, maybe tackle her dumbass friend to the ground to get him to keep from getting his head blown off, but he was already on his feet and running away.

"Thanks, Kat!" Mark yelled over his shoulder as he ran towards the campus building. Kat finally got up and with a resigned, frustrated groan, she grabbed her own bag and followed him in the same direction. With any luck, he'd be a pink stain on the atrium floor before she got there. She wasn't in the mood to defend her dumbass of a best friend. It was *Friday*. She wanted to go home and watch television.

She made her way to the main faculty building, partly because that seemed to be the most likely place where she'd find Mark, but mostly because she was still half a mile away and she could swear she already heard yelling. Boy howdy, Mark was an exhausting friend. But he'd been there for her when she needed it, so the least she could do was scoop up his remains and hand them to his family in a bucket if this all went sideways.

A small crowd had gathered around the yelling figures. She already recognized one of the voices, much as she wished she didn't, and she assumed the other one was Roland.

They were yelling the way only teenage boys can; that is to say that they both tried to sound intimidating while having shrill, cracking voices. It was awful. She pushed her way through the crowd and found herself at the front of the ring of people surrounding Roland and Mark.

"You're a second-rate Warlock, Rose, and you're just jealous because I'm *better* than you." Roland sounded snobby, but the fact that he was shaking betrayed that he was upset, more than anything. Roland was a head taller than Mark, who didn't exactly stand very tall at a 'meager'—compared to Roland, anyway—five foot and eight inches. Roland also had a chiseled jaw, piercing blue eyes and short, grayish-blonde hair that looked tactically disheveled. He was, Kat had to admit, handsome, if on the lanky side, the way only teenagers managed to be. He looked like he'd one day be athletic and beautiful, but right now he moved like he was all elbows and knees.

Mark, by comparison, was positively frumpled. His clothing was second-hand, compared to Roland's brand clothing, and he had a light stubble on his chin that made his pale skin look even grayer. His brown eyes and brown hair made him look positively unremarkable and, while she couldn't be sure, Kat assumed there was an element of envy to Mark's dislike of Roland. "The *only* reason you're higher than me on Transfiguration is because of your last name!" Mark said angrily. "You were born with everything, and you just take it all for granted! Even your name helps you out!"

"Shut up! I work *just* as hard as the rest of you! Do you think I *like* the way—where—who I was born as? Fuck you!" Roland's voice kept breaking and Kat wondered if he was going to cry. Mark didn't seem to notice, however, because he was just as upset.

"Then—Then—" Mark stammered, and fished his tome out of his backpack. The crowd around them gasped. The Grimoire was unique to each student, the culmination of their studies, and the most powerful focus any of them would ever have. It was not to be wielded lightly. "I challenge you, Roland! I'll prove to you that I'm *better!*" He waved his Grimoire around. It was a small but thick tome, bound in dark leather with only a few sigils on it. It wasn't going to ward off any demons any time soon, but it was clearly used well. For all his bluster, Mark did study hard, even if he wasn't, yknow, *good*.

Roland stood there shaking for a second and Kat was now *certain* he was on the verge of tears. But he mirrored Mark's display and produced his own Grimoire. It was a beautiful red book, inscribed with gold lettering, the best money could buy. He'd probably received it as a gift from his parents. "Fine. I get to choose the school of magic." *Hoo boy,* Kat thought. *Here we go.* Kat assumed that Roland would pick Evocation and then pelt Mark with fireballs until either one of the teachers intervened, or Mark could be served Well Done. "I choose...Transfiguration!" Roland shouted. *Huh.* "I'll prove to you that I can defeat you in a duel, Mark Rose, and then you'll know it's not just my *name* that got me this far!"

"Deal!" Mark opened his grimoire to a page. On it were scrawled the infernal and arcane symbols that had, for Mark, worked best to transfigure reality. They would be useless to anyone else. "What are we transfiguring?" He sounded like he was trying to figure out what they were actually going to do while still sounding angry and combative.

"We—" Ronald paused, thinking. "We transfigure...*each other!*"

"What?!"

"In...in a shape that means you can still talk, and you can still attend class! Whoever can keep up the spell the longest is the *better* warlock! And the first to *ask* to be changed back", Roland grinned, " automatically forfeits."

Mark glowered at Roland. Kat knew he was suppressing a smile. He wasn't great at deeply complex changing magic, but he knew he had great magical stamina. Whatever Roland threw at him, Kat knew that Mark was sure he could endure it longer than Roland could keep up the spell, and that *he* could keep up the spell longer than his rival could withstand the horror he'd be turned into.

"Ready?" Mark said. "Before the teachers get here!"

"You're bluffing, Mark. I'm going to prove once and for all that you're all talk."

Both of them started incanting, quickly, their tomes glowing as they activated the magic sigils on the pages, the words almost visible in the air as they changed reality to suit their whims. Both, Kat knew, would probably turn the other into the most heinous thing they could think of, and they'd both probably be punished for causing a ruckus on campus. But there were no actual rules against using non-lethal magic on another person if they consented, so the teachers wouldn't be able to force them to turn back.

Mark was the first to finish his spell and stretched out his arm, a little awkwardly, at Roland, and the magic, a beam of reds and purples, flickering and flashing, flowed through him and into his opponent. Just as it hit, Roland did the same thing and a beam of blues and greens flowed directly back into Mark. Both of them made noises that sounded like they were trying *not* to scream out, like they were trying to keep their cool, both in front of each other and in front of the gathered crowd.

This, Kat thought, was probably better than the alternative. Combat duels, contrary to transfiguration magic, were expressly prohibited on campus because of the damage they could do. Students were known to blow themselves up in their dorm rooms and because of this, most campus buildings had wards against Evocation and similarly destructive schools of magic. But Transfiguration was, all things considered, mostly harmless. It turned thing A into thing B and required a constant stream of magic to keep the thing in that state. When the Warlock turned off the stream of magic, it would, like an elastic band, snap back into shape A. Occasionally, things would stay in shape B, but, Kat remembered, that applied only to inorganic material, so she wasn't worried. Worst case scenario, she figured, she'd have to carry around her friend as a talking tree frog or something for a month. And his books, she realized, and sighed. She hoped Roland would have a measure of mercy. Maybe the worst thing he could think of turning Mark into would have hands. That would be ideal.

The magic exploded and threw both of the teenagers backwards in a cloud of red and blue smoke. It was easy enough for Kat to figure out where Mark had landed, all she had to do was follow the trail of magical vapor in the air that indicated his trajectory. It was almost comical how far they'd both flown, and she hoped that the residual energy would protect them both, to a certain extent, from the impact. Not that she really cared about Roland. In fact, she nothing'd him. She didn't give two shits about him. He was another student in class and she most certainly did not share Mark's obsession with him, despite the fact that he was handsome. Kat simply wasn't interested in guys like that.

She followed the trail all the way to a beautiful arrangement of, ironically, rose bushes, where she heard groaning coming from a hole in the wall of thornless branches. Some poor gardener was going to be real upset when he found out what had happened. "Mark?" she asked, and was greeted with another groan. She stuck her hand in the bush and found something to grab onto and pulled. Mark came stumbling out and Kat froze in place. Her eyes were wide and she couldn't help but stare.

"What is it?" Mark said. "You look taller. What did he turn me into? How bad is it?"

"Well, It could definitely be worse", Kat said as she moved some of Mark's hair out of his face. "You make a pretty cute girl."

2

Meeting Girls

"That bastard", Mark fumed as he dusted himself off, patting down his new anatomy with trepidation. Kat grinned. She couldn't help but grin. Of all the horrible things Roland could have done to her friend, this stuck out to her as positively benign. It didn't exactly color her perception of Roland in a positive light, if he looked down on the possibility of being a woman so much he'd consider it a curse, but this was, at least, doable. At least Mark still had a reasonable number of limbs.

"Oh, calm down, Mark. Being a girl isn't so bad", she said, and patted him on the back. That earned her a withering glance, and she could tell Mark didn't find this nearly as amusing as she did. Her friend's eyes were red like he was ready to cry. "Hey, are you okay?"

"I just hope my incantation hit him too", Mark said, his new, soft voice shaking a little bit. He was clearly trying to keep it together, but not really doing a great job of it. Not sure how to feel about this development, Kat crossed her arms and frowned. Maybe Roland hadn't been the problem here; maybe the Mayweather kid had simply known Mark secretly thought women were a curse.

"You challenged him, remember?" she said. "Why are you so upset about this?" Mark looked at her, his eyes bloodshot. She barely managed to prevent herself from taking a step back. Her friend seemed genuinely upset. He grabbed his bag and started walking back toward the little plaza where they'd had their fight without saying another word.

Kat glared daggers at his back, but waited until Mark was out of earshot to let out a frustrated yelp before jogging after him. He was *so frustrating*. But she felt sorry for him.

And this was partly her fault for suggesting it, though she would probably only admit it under threat of torture. *Maybe.* Her friend was more than a little susceptible to her (terrible) ideas, and she had on more than one occasion considered the possibility that Mark looked up to her. Now he was easily three inches shorter than her, so he had no other choice than looking up. She grinned to herself.

There was still a small crowd in the plaza. That was odd. She'd expected it to disperse after the two antagonisers had ejected in opposite directions. But clearly, Roland had already returned, because a new circle had formed itself around him. She didn't know who else it could be. Mark was trying to wrestle himself to the center of the crowd, but people didn't recognize him, and he didn't have quite the musculature he had before. Kat followed suit, dispersing the crowd a lot easier than Mark could. Mark glared up at her, but she didn't dignify that with anything more than sticking out her tongue at him. "Just say thanks, dillweed", she said, loud enough that he could hear it, but it was in vain, because they'd reached the center of the circle. Kat frowned and looked back and forth between Mark and Roland, not sure who to slap first.

Mark, looking like a short girl with mousy hair, stared in triumph at Roland. Kat only knew it was Roland because of the girl kneeling next to him. A lot of rumors had gone around regarding Roland and Millicent, but Kat had taken them as seriously as she had Millicent's name, and clearly 'Millie' had felt much the same way, sparing at most a single elegantly raised finger at people who jeered or whistled. Millie was cool, in that torn-jeans leather-jacket kind of way, and she *owned* 'Millie' Right now, however, there was no consideration of looking cool, largely because Roland was in a bad way.

He was sitting on the ground, sobbing into his hands. Kat hazarded a guess and assumed it was because Roland was now a leggy blonde, still easily six foot tall, but with beautiful golden hair cascading down his back, and Millie was carefully rubbing his back. When Kat and Mark approached, she looked up. Kat immediately threw up her hands defensively, but Millie looked concerned, rather than angry. However, she clearly recognized Kat and extrapolated from that who the seething girl by her side was, and shot Mark a glare.

"Him too, huh?" Kat said, kneeling down. Where Mark had been close to crying but focused on his Righteous Vengeance, Roland had clearly collapsed under the *agonizing* weight of femininity, something Kat was going to have to learn not to hold against him. She'd managed all her life; why was it such a hassle for him? However, the jeering from their fellow classmates wasn't, in her opinion, warranted.

"Yeah", Millie said. "That Mark?" She nodded at Kat's smug-looking friend. Kat nodded. "You're his friend, right?" Another nod. "I want to be mad at him for what he did to Roland, but uh..."

"Yeah", Kat said. "Same." There was a sniggering from the crowd. Some of the larger guys were looking down on the two girls with contempt. Kat wasn't in the mood for this. She raised herself up to her full height (which, granted, wasn't spectacular, but still) and held up her hands. Warlocks often used grimoires, tomes in which they collected the knowledge of the 'infernal' (hah) magic they conjured up. Witches found it easier to connect to a plane of existence where the magic they sought knew itself. Sure, they had to do studying, but they were, for all intents and purposes, wildly different ways of approaching magic. Most boys chose to become warlocks and most girls chose to become witches, but that was probably as much a result of branding and outdated gender roles as it was practicality. But it also meant she could pull a stunt like this.

"Everyone but the four of us *leave* or I'm testing out my new Brown Note Incantation." For effect, a few muddy looking symbols appeared in the air, and the gathering of students dissipated after that. Now that things were more quiet, Roland's soft sobbing was more easily heard. Kat couldn't help but feel sorry for him. Mark still stood grinning over them until Kat shot him a look. For all of the attempts at foul glances he shot at Kat, a single one of hers brought him, in this case literally, to his knees. A small part of her smiled at the knowledge that her opinion of him mattered that much to him. A bigger part of her wanted to smack him. So she did.

"Ow! What? Ow?!"

"Why, pray tell", Kat said, waving a finger in front of his face, which he had to go cross-eyed to look at, "do you think being a *woman* is such a punishment, *hmmm?*" Kat hissed between her teeth. She wanted to do the same thing at Roland, but she couldn't slap a crying girl. Although, going by the thick tears rolling down Mark's face seemingly out of nowhere, it looked like she had, inadvertently anyway. "Oh, what the fuck", Kat mumbled, and she looked at Millie for...something? Support, probably. Millie could only shrug and keep one arm over Roland's softly hiccuping form.

Roland slowly raised his head. When he and Mark made eye contact, it was like hearing a powerline go live. There was electricity in the air. Kat rolled her eyes again. They could be so damn dramatic. Slowly, a smile spread across Roland's face. Comparing the two of them, Roland was what could be called more "classically" pretty. Roland's new face was sharp, his already handsome face now positively angelic. In comparison, Mark was...well, Kat wasn't one to judge, to her all girls were pretty. But Mark looked more like he ought to be wearing an oversized sweater and sipping hot cocoa in front of an open fire. Kat shook that little fantasy out of her head. That was no way to think about her best friend. She turned to Millie and found not fantasizing about the cute punk girl just as hard. She groaned internally at the horror that was her life, suddenly surrounded by beautiful women.

"Both of you", Millie said. "Chill your shit. You've got your little bet. Congrats. Now what?" Mark and Roland shot a look at each other.

"I'm not giving up", Roland said, undercutting his bravado with a sniffle and a wipe of his nose. "Not unless *Mark* is." Mark shook his head with what Kat assumed he thought was bravery.

"You *wish*", Mark said, and just a cursory glance between the two of them confirmed to Kat that they *both* wished they hadn't taken it this far. But she also knew they were both too stubborn and too proud to walk any of this back. She knew Mark well enough for that, and knew boys in general well enough to come to a similar conclusion with regards to Roland. "I'm going all the way", Mark said, and Kat knew in her heart of hearts that he thought he sounded cool. "I bet you can't even last a month."

"You're on", Roland said. "And we're making this *interesting*." The way he said that made the hair on Kat's neck stand up, and she looked at Millie, hoping the cute punk girl would do or say something to make her friend shut up, but she was just as stunned as Kat. "And no asking the teachers for help. You have to *be* your new form until you give up."

Mark took only a second to consider this until he nodded his head vigorously. "Deal! You're going *down*, Ro—wait, no. You need to use a *girl's* name, don't you?" he said, his voice dripping with malicious glee. Roland, however, seemed completely ready for that.

"So do you, but it looks like you already have one, don't you, *Rose?*"

Mark shook his head, and Kat almost expected him to tut. "Tssk, no, if we're doing this, I'm going to choose your name *for* you."

"And I'm choosing yours?"

"That seems only fair", Mark said.

"Alright then, *Violet*, you're on."

"*Violet Rose?*" Mark-now-Violet balked. "*Really?*"

Roland grinned, a tiny victory won with much more satisfaction than was clearly appropriate. But this ridiculous battle of tiny wills wasn't over yet. Violet took a step forward.

"One last condition", Violet said, and Kat was so close to tackling this idiot to the ground. However, a morbid part of her brain told her to hold off, to see where this was going to go. If things got out of hand, she could always tell a teacher, right? Violet kneeled in front of Roland. "I'm not going to bother with any of that he or him stuff. You're a girl now, after all. Aren't you, *April?*"

"April Mayweather?!" April seethed. Violet grinned. "Deal." They shook on it. Kat and Millie made eye contact with a resigned sigh. Their friends were idiots, and Kat and Millie knew it. But at least they agreed on something. It was, well, *something*. Then, both the newly christened April and Violet both went their own way. Both of them looked at their respective best friends, but Kat shook her head.

"You go on ahead. We've got stuff to talk about."

Violet and April both shrugged and left. April, she assumed, would be going home to her parents for the weekend. 'Violet' would probably be staying in her dorm. Although it was entirely possible that she would be assigned a new room as a girl. She wasn't actually sure yet. Whatever, it wasn't her problem right now.

"I'm Kat", she said.

"Millie. That turnip is your friend?"

Kat nodded. "The tall hot one is yours?"

Millie raised an eyebrow. "Hot one?"

Kat shrugged. "You saw her." Millie relented with a nod and a smile.

"Yeah, Roland and I go way back. Sorry, April."

"Now what?" Kat asked.

"No clue. Let's just try to keep them from doing anything dumb and killing each other?"

"Deal. Although..." Kat wondered aloud.

"Hmm?"

"Well, I think we should strategize. Meet once a week, see how well they're doing. I don't trust Ma—uh, Violet, not to do something stupid if she gets desperate. If you and I stay in touch, we can keep them from imploding or something."

"Does hhhhh-she ever talk about April?"

"*All the time,*" Kat said with a resigned sigh.

"Same here. Never shuts up about her."

"Well, wanna meet up in the cafeteria on Monday? We can talk strategy then."

Millie raised an eyebrow and Kat could swear there was an invisible little grin playing around her lips. "Alright, Kat. Good to meet you. Glad your idiot of a boyfriend bothered my best friend."

Kat laughed so loud it upset a nearby set of pigeons. "You could have just asked, Millie. 'Violet' isn't my boyfriend. Or my girlfriend, for that matter." They shook hands. Kat was acutely aware of the fact that they held hands just a second too long. Millie's fingers were slender, cool and very soft, and, trying to save face, she winked. "I'll see you Monday."

"It's a date", Millie grinned, and walked off too, leaving Kat to overthink the entire encounter.

3

Geography and a Cup of Coffee

"How was your weekend?" Millie stirred a big mug of tea casually, looking over at Kat. Kat was not in a space to do anything casually, holding on to her espresso for dear life. On-campus off-brand coffee had been a godsend, but only having access to it at noon was exactly three hours too late. Or, she considered, nine in the morning was three hours too early to start classes. Mornings were for other people. Noon was Kat's morning, and she was having her 'morning' coffee.

"I'm alive", Kat said with a forced smile. Millie cracked up at her pained expression, and Kat's constructed smirk became a real one. Millie was wearing her leather jacket, her black nail polish flaking and her black lipstick was smeared, and all of it looked entirely deliberate. Kat was trying very hard not to be into it. Millie, meanwhile, caught her staring, and only raised an eyebrow. Kat cleared her throat. "Ahem", she said. "How was yours?"

Millie shrugged and leaned back, carefully sipping her tea and burning her tongue. "It was all right. Was up too late yesterday", she said. She didn't look it, but Kat assumed she was one of those people who rolled out of bed looking perfect anyway. Kat shot her an inquisitive glance, and Millie shrugged again. "I've been trying to get a can of spray paint to tag on its own. It's...going. Slowly."

"Enchanting *is*, as they say, a bitch", Kat agreed. Her specialty, which she was never going to admit to the cute goth-slash-punk girl opposite her, was actually botany. Part of her wished it wasn't, but then she was elbow-deep in dirt and she could feel the earth talking to her and everything felt right. Of course, right after she'd have to pretend that it meant nothing to her. Indifference was exhausting, but a necessary part of school life. "Though this morning was a damn wash regardless of what class we were going to get."

"Ugh", Millie agreed. "Dickstrap is the *worst.*" Kat couldn't help but scrunch her face a bit. Derek 'Dickstrap' Dykstra was their geography teacher, and he hadn't actually been considered a terrible teacher for a long time, until a few years ago people had found out he tended to think a little old school. For a teacher who didn't actually teach magic, he apparently had some outdated ideas on who could be witches and who could be warlocks, and his tenure had actually been under review after he'd made some disparaging comments to the female students, but it had been just tame enough for nothing to have come of it. But it had gotten him a new nickname. And he'd lived up to it this morning.

"You know", Kat said, "I was so ready to spend the entire week trying to talk Violet out of this whole stupid bet, but with Dickstrap's whole thing..."

"Yeah", Millie said, "I feel you." Her eyes seemed to bore into Kat, and it was hard for her not to feel self-conscious under so much scrutiny. Considering how much time her best friend usually spent in their own head, focused on their own obsessions, feeling awkward was normal. She wasn't used to being listened to like this. She wasn't sure if she hated it yet, especially considering who was doing the looking. "At this rate, I just want both of them to make it through the month, even if it's just to prove the old bastard wrong."

"Word", Kat said, the events of the morning coming back to her. It had been...unpleasant. When they'd all walked into the auditorium, April and Violet had both walked to the front of the class to present themselves, and explain why they'd be responding to different names during roll call. It...had not gone well. Dykstra had looked at the two of them and, for a moment, Kat thought he might have broken into laughter, mocking them both. That might have been better, because then everyone in the class would have been on their side. Instead, it had been a lot more painful.

Millie and Kat had shot each other a glance from across the auditorium, both of them worried about their friends and neither of them able to really do anything. Yelling at a teacher was a great way to get themselves suspended. All they could do was watch as Dykstra raised his back and looked at the two students.

"I don't care about your bet", Dykstra had said. That wasn't the worst thing in the world. But it had been April and Violet's response that had been so painful. They'd both cried out in protest, but Dykstra had raised a hand and looked at them both with a look of utter condescension. "As far as I'm concerned, the both of you are two of my most mediocre students." He paused and looked at Violet. "As far as I'm concerned, you're Mark Rose", he said, and turned to April, "and you're Roland Mayweather. It doesn't matter how much you change your name or appearance. Take a seat, boys."

The two warlocks had protested again, but Dykstra had shut them both up with detention and extra homework. When Violet had sat down, Kat wanted to ask if everything was okay, but the look on Violet's face had made her change her mind. Kat had expected her friend to look angry, but Violet's eyes were red, like she was close to crying. Sure, Kat felt like her friend was taking the whole bet too seriously, asking her several times to use girl's pronouns for her and call her Violet exclusively, but she also didn't like seeing Violet hurt.

The rest of the class, Dykstra had called on Violet and April over and over again, using the names of Mark and Roland with a careless glee. It had been especially jarring considering he otherwise exclusively used last names. Every single time, it had seemed to sting Violet like the personal insult it was. Kat had wanted to reach out and comfort her friend, but she also knew that the teacher was just as likely to up his bullying if he spotted another weakness. After class, Violet had returned to her dorm room without another word.

"How is yours doing?" Kat asked Millie. She'd been mostly busy worrying about her friend, but as far as she was concerned, April was just another student. Kat held her no ill will, and she'd enjoyed spending time with Millie. Someone who had friends like that couldn't be the worst person.

Millie sighed. "April's had a rough weekend", she said, and finished her tea. Kat followed her example, and after a minute both of them walked outside. They both still had half an hour before classes resumed, the weather was lovely, and neither of them had their best friend to take care of. "She told her parents", Millie continued while they looked for a spot on the campus lawn. They sat down under the shade of a tree and Kat did her best not to feel like this was a date, focusing on what Millie was saying. "They thought it was hilarious, and they're encouraging her to engage in healthy competition."

"That's...good, isn't it?" Kat said, wrapping her arms around her legs as she leaned against the trunk of the tree, closing her eyes and enjoying the soft warmth of the summer heat.

"Well, yes and no", Millie said. "April's parents are...difficult." She paused. "You sure you wanna hear this? I don't want to bore you." Kat opened one eye and peeked at her.

"Are you kidding me? I could listen to you talk *all* day", she said, and only after grinning smugly did she realize just how gay that had sounded. She realized there was no taking it back, and the only refuge was in audacity. Millie didn't seem too bothered by it, which was even more intimidating to Kat.

"Well, that goes both ways, Kat", Millie smiled, and laid down with her hands under her head. "Anyway, yeah, April's parents have always pushed her. That's how we met, actually. They picked the students with the highest score and set up playdates." Millie smiled sheepishly as Kat raised an eyebrow. "Listen...I was a bookish kid. And it didn't work, April was never going to be a model student. Anyway I'm worried they won't take it well if this doesn't turn out to be 'proof' that she's finally becoming the promised son they've always wanted."

"What do you mean?"

"This bet of theirs", Millie said, playing with a flower in the grass, "this isn't going to prove anything."

"Mmm", Kat said.

"They're just...acting out. Neither of them is going to get better at magic because of it."

"True."

"And April's parents are going to go mental if they think this negatively impacted her grades. She's been stressing all weekend, and this morning was...well, it wasn't the final straw, but it was definitely an *extra* straw", Millie said, sighing.

"Where is she now?" Kat asked. Rich kids didn't always go home during lunch, but it wasn't unheard of.

"Having lunch alone. She needed time. I take it Violet is doing much the same?"

Kat nodded. "She's in her dorm room. She pretty much lives on campus."

"Oh", Millie said. It was an 'oh' with implications and assumptions.

"Her parents are fine, really", Kat said. "Just...don't have a lot. She's on a grant, and it's cheaper if she stays in the dorm."

"Oh", Millie repeated, an 'oh' of understanding this time.

"She's actually got a pretty big room. It's practically an apartment. It's a lot bigger than her room back home."

This time it was Millie's turn to raise an eyebrow. "You've been to her room often?"

"Pfft", Kat said. "Not like that. We grew up on the same street. Mark was the cool kid who collected rocks and I was the dumbass who kept the other kids from throwing more of them at him." She paused. "Her", she corrected herself. "Is it him or her when we're talking about them in the past tense? I'm trying to be respectful of how seriously they're taking this, but they're not making it exactly easy."

"Ehh", Millie said. "I've got a cousin who did that. You get used to it. I just try to think of her as a girl, and I'll switch back after the month is over."

"Just like that?"

"Your friend is still your friend, boy or girl." Millie paused. "Fuck Dickstrap."

"*Fuck* him", Kat concurred.

"You're cool", Millie said, looking up at the clouds. "I was worried you'd be like Violet."

"What do you mean?" Kat asked, trying, on the one hand, not to be offended for her friend. On the other, she desperately wanted Millie to say more nice things.

"Violet and April are so hyper-focused on each other, on those numbers. I was worried you'd be like them. But you're chill", she said, and stuck a flower by the stem between her teeth. "I was worried you were just a pretty face."

Kat froze and her eyes shot open. She'd hoped that Millie hadn't noticed, but the goth girl was looking right at her. When she caught Kat's eye, Millie winked, causing her heart-rate to double.

"How dare you", Kat managed, but it came out a little more high-pitched than she intended to. "Judge me by my looks when you go around looking all..."

"Hmm?" Millie hummed a question, her eyes closed with all the confidence in the world.

"You know..."

"I know, I just want to hear you say it."

"You're the worst", Kat smirked. "How did April put up with you for that long?"

"Well", Millie said, took the flower out of her mouth, and lazily looked over to Kat again. "I'm free next week on Friday. Why don't you find out over dinner?"

"Fucking hell", Kat laughed. "Alright. It's a date."

"Yeah, it is."

The break couldn't last forever, however, and Kat and Millie went to separate classes. Kat found Violet as they walked into the botanical gardens. She walked a little faster to match pace with her friend. Violet looked a little better than she had after class, but only a little.

"Are you okay?" Kat asked.

"Yeah", Violet snapped, and then took a deep breath. "Yeah", she repeated, softer this time. "I just...want today to be over, you know? I want to go back to my dorm and just not think about anything."

"I get you. But hey, they say botanical witchcraft is easier if you're in touch with your feminine side, so at least class won't be the worst, right?" Kat said. She hoped that this might cheer up her friend. It failed.

"Ugh, don't remind me. This might be harder than I thought it would be, Kat. I wasn't expecting, you know, pushback."

"Well, I'm here for you regardless. Are you sure you want me to keep calling you Violet?" she asked, as they walked down the rows of potted plants to the small auditorium.

Her friend nodded. "It makes it easier, knowing you're taking it seriously too. Right now, calling me Mark would feel, I don't know, wrong. I think I'd want to quit sooner."

"All right. But you keep me in the loop, okay?"

"Fine. Dork."

"Nerd."

"Ass."

Kat smiled, happy she could still talk to her friend the way she had before, and remembered what Millie had told her. Thinking of her friend as a girl wasn't too hard, she realized, and she smiled.

"You'll be all right, Violet."

"Thanks." Violet smiled and took a deep breath, and tried to focus on botany the way Kat had suggested. As it turned out, being turned into a girl hadn't made a lick of difference, and she was as rubbish with plants as ever. Kat poked fun at her, and she pretended to be annoyed. When Violet finally went back to her dorm, Kat could tell she was in a much better mood and went home smiling.

She panicked only three times when she realized all of a sudden that she had a date the week after.

4

Butterfly Hisses

In the following week, Kat had several brushes with Millie. Technically, April and Violet had been there too, but she was a little preoccupied by the goth girl. She wasn't completely oblivious to her friend's seething, of course. She did what was required, holding Violet's arm while the latter pretended to need holding back to keep from fighting April. Millie did the same thing, but both of them couldn't help but make eye contact while this happened.

On Wednesday, they had lunch together again, this time on the roof of the main campus building, having sandwiches while they talked about absolutely nothing and everything, both of them stealing glances at each other while they thought the other wasn't looking (wrong, every time) and smiling when they caught a glimpse. Their position high up also allowed them to keep an eye on their wards, which turned out to be necessary when Violet and April seemingly ended up in a screaming match in the center of the campus grounds for no reason. To give each other the strength necessary, to make sure neither of them failed, they held hands during the levitation spell as they descended, and that was the *only* reason they held hands. That Kat's skin tingled for the rest of the day was purely coincidence.

The screaming match was easily broken up, largely because April's voice kept cracking and Violet seemed to be on the verge of tears. Both of them blamed the other for their difficulties, Kat noticed, but seemed largely unable to really pin down what those difficulties were.

"It's your fault that...that...You're cheating!" April screamed, and she seemed to be rooting around in her book bag for her grimoire, unable to find it, ready to start slinging hexes at Violet without a moment's notice. She wasn't aware of the fact that she'd almost forgotten it in class, and that it currently resided in Millie's backpack. Instead, April found an apple and chucked it at Violet—badly. It only succeeded in scaring off a pigeon that had been around to have a curious ogle at the two noisemakers.

"M-my fault? I...I can do this, Mayweather! If you think I'm not strong enough to do this without cheating I—I'll..." Violet, realizing what April was looking for, also started digging around in her backpack, but she didn't succeed in pulling out her own grimoire, because Kat walked up behind her and put her hands on the now-smaller-girl's shoulders, which Violet pretended to be shocked and annoyed by, but Kat knew she was secretly grateful for the interruption. Violet had been on a hair trigger at every interaction.

On Friday, it almost came to a head again when they'd both sat down in the cafeteria and one unfortunate student getting up revealed that they were sitting opposite one another with only a single table between them. They stared at each other all through lunch, trying to eat menacingly at the other. Millie and Kat had spotted their friend staring, followed the line of fire to the other table, and waved at each other sheepishly, and then both sat down opposite their respective best friends to break line of sight. This also meant sitting with their backs to each other.

"I hate her so much, Kat."

"Shhhh", Kat said, and ate her mashed potatoes. They were *good* mashed potatoes, she noticed with pride as her friend visibly seethed. She couldn't bring it up, of course, but she was actually top of her class in botany, and she'd been helping the school's kitchen staff with growing their own vegetables. It was cheaper, and considered good practice for the promising students.

"You know, I thought the hardest thing about this challenge would be the fact that I would have to be something else for a month, but I didn't think..." Violet paused, probably looking for a way to phrase their next sentence in a way that didn't sound like a compliment. "I didn't think it'd be so hard to look my arch-rival in the *face*", she finally said.

"Oh?" Kat wondered out loud. She probably shouldn't have. She knew better than to encourage her friend's obsessive rambling, but she had been curious to find out why Violet and April's relationship had become even more testy as of late.

"She's just...I mean...look at her!" Violet pointed at the other table with her fork, but Kat refused to give her the satisfaction of looking around. Besides, she'd only be looking longingly at the back of Millie's head, and that wouldn't have benefited anyone. "As Roland, she was already, you know, the typical 'oh-ho-ho look at me, I'm tall and attractive' jock type", Violet said. Kat disagreed—internally—with that assessment, strongly. April had been tall, sure, but never a jock. And for personal reasons, she hadn't really given the girl a lot of consideration as to attractiveness. Not pre-transformation, anyway. "But now she's all...she's like the queen bee, you know?! I didn't think it'd be so hard to look at her, but it's like she's sculpted!"

Kat raised an eyebrow. "Are you saying the challenge is harder because you made your opponent *too pretty?*" she asked, trying not to laugh. This was, of course, exactly the kind of thing Violet would do, up to and including complaining about her own hubris. She wasn't going to give her friend the benefit of pretending like it wasn't. Violet angrily shut down and ate the rest of the better-than-expected meatloaf.

The next Monday, Kat and Millie had another sneaky lunch at noon, sitting back to back by the small brook that ran through the campus grounds, listening to the quacking of ducks while they both tried to focus on studying. After a while, consciously or otherwise, they had synchronized their breathing, and they were both acutely aware of the other shifting behind them. Millie had taken off her leather jacket —it was too hot in the sun anyway—and the black top she wore was of a thin fabric. So thin, in fact, that Kat was acutely aware of the fact that the other girl apparently went braless, something she was terrified of bringing up but could in no way, shape or form put out of her head. They compared notes about class, sitting shoulder to shoulder, and Kat tried not to be aware of how Millie smelled like old books and lilacs. She didn't know that Millie was trying not to memorize what she smelled like, either. If she'd known, she might have made a noise, and she was already blushing heavily, though she lied to herself that it was because of the sun.

That afternoon, she had botany with Violet again. She'd been working with the teacher more to grow magically-enhanced vegetables, something she'd been getting exceedingly good at. It also didn't annoy or bore her to be doing the same thing over and over again, getting slightly better every time. It was just very satisfying work, for her, and whispering soft magic into the roots of glowing plants and *feeling* their gratitude was all the encouragement she needed. This was in stark contrast to Violet, who was having trouble keeping a succulent from bursting into flames.

Kat had rushed over before the teacher could see the smoldering leaves and pinched out the little embers. "What the hell did you do?" Kat asked, a little incredulously.

"I was thinking about April", Violet replied. Her face was stoic, but her voice betrayed the fact that she clearly felt guilty for having been caught.

"Plants don't catch on fire when I think about people", Kat reprimanded, and blew a little life into the plant. Not enough to give Violet a good grade, mind, but enough to keep her from blowing the class.

"I'm just so angry at her! And Dykstra was being a Dickstrap in class again, and he doesn't even understand what we're trying to do! And she looked so sad that I felt sorry for her. I felt sorry for my arch-rival, Kat!" Violet frowned as she recalled the events of class. It had, indeed, been a shit-show again. Dykstra had done his thing again, but seemed to have chosen to single out April this time, calling her Roland over and over again, calling her to the blackboard several times, scoffing at her inability to answer questions that, Kat knew, were too advanced for them. She wondered who she would have to report that too.

"I get being mad at Dickstrap", Kat said, "but what did April do?"

"She's just...she keeps saying I'm cheating and I hate it because this is actually really hard! And the accusations just make it harder, because she clearly thinks I'm not good enough, and it's all that entitlement all over again. Spoiled brat."

Kat's head spun trying to keep up with the mental acrobatics going on, but she did her best, for her friend's sake. "You're saying you're mad at her for—from where I'm sitting—being envious of you?"

"Yes! No! It's the *accusation*! I'm having a hard time and I hate it when people tell me I didn't get here on my own merits." Violet paused. "Oh my god, do you think she's taking pity on me?"

Kat remembered their latest interaction, which had resulted in the two girls almost fist-fighting in the halls again, foreheads pressed together. Kat could have sworn she'd heard the sound of cats hissing as they mumbled insults at each other. "No, no I don't. Try not to kill your plant again, Vi, I'm not going to keep saving your ass every time."

"What did you call me?" Violet asked, her frown dissolving like snow in the sun as she looked at Kat.

"Vi? Short for Violet?"

"Oh", Violet said, and smiled a little bit. "I like that. It's...ah...uh...cute."

"Yeah", Kat said, trying not to smirk as she looked at her smaller friend. "It is."

The next day, she and Violet ended up re-studying their notes near the trees where they usually sat. Exams weren't *close*, but they both knew that Violet wasn't exactly a model student and could use all the help she could get, and Kat was a good enough student that she could afford to take the time out of her day to help her friend out. In Violet's defense, she always paid Kat back with lunch desserts, something Kat had tried to resist for four months before she'd relented. Violet was clearly very grateful, especially lately, since her practical magic had been suffering, probably from the constant distractions she was suffering.

Violet sat up against the tree, going over Kat's notes and comparing them to her own, when she heard April's voice behind her. Even before, Violet had complained about April's frustratingly charismatic voice, but now that she was blonde and beautiful, it had apparently been exacerbated. April's voice was low and husky, like she was at all times recovering from a cold, and even Kat had to admit that it was a *very* attractive voice. "Studying hard, Rose? I know you need it."

Violet didn't look behind her, instead focusing on trying to look smug. "I'm only trying to stay ahead of *you*, April Mayweather. Not that it's *hard*."

"Taking new classes for witches only is a brave choice, Violet Rose, but trying to get your bad grades away from me won't work", April replied, walking closer.

"Oh, I know, I saw that you enrolled in the same ones I did. It's brave, but foolish. I'm just doing it to prove that even as a witch I can beat y—" Violet's voice caught in her throat as she turned to face her rival.

April was dressed in a beautiful summer dress, her hair was loose and blowing softly in the warm afternoon breeze, and a lot of time in the sun had apparently blessed her with freckles. She looked, Kat admitted to herself and nobody else, gorgeous. She noticed that Violet was blushing furiously, and she wondered if this was her being angry again, at the fact that she was finding it really difficult to be angry with the pretty girl in front of her. Not that she could blame Vi; she couldn't find herself even thinking angry thoughts about April when she looked like this.

"W-why are you looking at me like that, Rose?" April demanded, self-consciously tucking her hair behind her ear and raising her book-bag in front of herself like a shield. "What are you planning?"

"I—what? I'm not planning anything! Why are you...You're doing this to distract me, aren't you?" Violet stammered.

"I'm not trying to distract you! But maybe I should!" April began to raise her voice, though probably unintentionally. "You're cheating again!"

"What do you mean, I'm cheating?! You're the one who looks b—g—ridiculous!" Violet demanded, and began to get up, but April already stormed off in a huff, her cute flats kicking up little tufts of grass, and Kat and Violet both found it really hard not to keep looking at her until she was out of sight.

"What the hell was that about?" Kat mumbled, and looked over at Violet, who was pretending not to cry and failing, in large part because she was getting teardrops on Kat's notes, and Kat was preoccupied with comforting her friend for the rest of the day.

5

First and Fourth Dates

It was Friday and Kat was freaking out. This was her first-ever date, not counting the one time in grade school when Kevin had asked her to have dinner with him and then thrown up due to a bad reaction to spoiled milk. Not that she'd been interested in him to begin with, being nine years old and gay as a maypole, but it had definitely killed any interest she'd had in the boy to begin with. But it had also left her completely unequipped to deal with the fact that she was about to have her first ever date with a beautiful girl, and she didn't know what to do. What was she going to say? Was she supposed to say anything? What did people even *do* on dates? Did they wear something different? She was sure they did, but her Sunday best would look ridiculous.

She'd been stressing out most of Thursday, including the fifteen minutes they'd spent before class mumbling good-mornings at each other and complaining about it being too early, and then most of Friday as well. She wondered if Millie felt the same way. Friday had been a day off, so they'd agreed to meet in the early afternoon. Kat had, for the first free day in a while, completely failed to sleep in. She'd tried to, but she'd woken up at eight AM sharp, staring at the ceiling, going from deep slumber to wide awake in the span of half a second. She'd tried to study in the morning, but that hadn't happened either. So instead, she'd been stressing.

In the end, she'd decided on wearing a loose-fitting sweater and jeans, something she could be comfortable in, and easily take off if...if it got too warm because of the weather. She wore her favorite top underneath it, the softest shirt she owned.

She'd told her mom she was meeting a friend for mid-afternoon studying and dinner, but when her mom had asked if it was Violet—Kat had informed her mom of her friend's bet at the first opportunity, if just to make things easier on herself—Kat had dodged the question, earning her a raised eyebrow. With a "Be safe" and a pat on the head, her mom had let her go, however, and she'd taken the bus to school, where they'd agreed to meet.

Kat got off at the bus stop across the street and already saw Millie sitting on a bench in front of the school, seemingly completely relaxed, legs crossed and one arm tossed over the back of the bench. Gosh, she was so cool. But it had taken Kat a second to recognize her, because Millie was dressed entirely differently than she was used to. Instead of the usual leather-goth-punk look, Millie wore a red dress, in a fifties rockabilly style, her hair even done up in a cute jet-black bob. She absolutely rocked the look, and Kat had to swallow and take a deep breath before she could even consider crossing the street, knowing she'd have a hard time keeping her cool around the cool-as-shit and now also hot-as-fuck girl. Not that Kat didn't usually feel that way about Millie lately, it was just going to be a lot harder to pretend otherwise when Millie was dressed like that. Another deep breath and, looking both ways, Kat crossed the street and waved at Millie, who gave her a smile so wide and warm it gave Kat an almost painful case of butterflies.

"Heya", Millie said, and got up a little too fast. Kat only noticed because the other girl also immediately tried to straighten her dress. It struck Kat only then that, maybe, Millie was a little nervous too. It helped, in a sense, knowing she wasn't the only one screaming internally, even if this was a special occasion.

"Hey you", she said, trying to sound nonchalant and failing miserably.

Millie laughed softly, nervously, and scratched the back of her head, looking down at her dress. "Do, uh, you like it?" she asked.

Kat almost screamed. Not out of anger or frustration, but because Millie looked *adorable*. This was the first time she'd seen Millie look vulnerable and less-than-utterly sure of herself, and it was a precious sight, especially on top of the wonderful outfit. She was utterly and completely honest when she smiled warmly and looked Millie up and down. "You look gorgeous", she said. This elicited a blush from Millie, which was another first.

"Hey! No fair, catching me on the back foot. Besides", she said, "you look beautiful too." Now it was Kat's turn to be bashful. They stood there awkwardly for a moment, Kat almost hiding behind her purse, feeling self conscious about even bringing it, until Millie finally broke the silence again. "Shall we?"

Kat nodded gratefully, and they began walking side by side, Kat trusting Millie to lead the way to wherever they were going. Quickly, when they'd both stopped thinking about just each other for a moment, conversation came easy. They talked about class, about the weather, and found more genuine ways to complement each other, both in clothing and, once the accolades and praise had become a playful game of pin-the-blush-on-the-girl, each other's personalities.

"Where are we going, anyway?" Kat asked as they went down a side-street into a suburban neighborhood after a few minutes. She vaguely recognized the area, just behind the school.

"My place", Millie said matter-of-factly, looking straight ahead, navigating the two of them across the street. Because of that, she didn't see Kat's mouth fall open and her beet-red cheeks.

"O-oh", was all Kat managed, before Millie walked up to a house that looked largely identical to most others in the street, and opened the door. For some reason, Kat had expected Millie to live in a house that was somehow different. Maybe a four-story mansion, or a creepy ghost house. A two-story suburban house hadn't occurred to her, but now that the beautiful girl was holding open the door for her in a pretty red dress straight out of the fifties, it seemed to fit her perfectly.

"Well?" Millie asked, and Kat realized she'd been staring. She stammered a nothing and went inside, Millie softly closing the door behind her before leading her on a tour of the house. Apparently she lived there with her parents and two younger siblings. All of them were out for the day. It was, after all, a Friday. The house wasn't big, per se, but it wasn't small, either. They had to have enough room for five people to coexist and it definitely seemed like they did.

Finally, Millie took her to a dining table and suggested she sit down for a moment. Kat looked up at her with a question in her eyes, and Millie was happy to answer.

"I just have a little bit more work for dinner", Millie said sheepishly. "I thought I'd be ready in time. Can I get you something to drink? Mom said it was okay if we had some wine." It was strange for Kat to hear Millie talk about her mom in such a domestic setting. Part of her saw Millie as having an eldritch abomination as a mother, or possibly Morticia Adams (or both), but going by the house, Millie's family was perfectly wholesome.

Kat nodded, and then had a quick change of mind. "Y-yes, but only if you let me help you with cooking." It was a bold move, but she was about to find out if it would work. Besides, she wasn't going to spend the next half hour or however long sitting awkwardly by herself. Even if it was in silence, she preferred to be doing something with her hands.

Millie smiled and nodded. She guided Kat to the spacious kitchen and poured them both a small glass of white wine, and got to work. Apparently 'a little bit more work' meant quite a bit more, as the vegetables still needed cutting and cooking, and the meat hadn't even marinated yet. Not that Kat minded; she was happy to be spending time with Millie in whatever setting. She got to work chopping bell peppers for what seemed to be a healthy stir-fry, lost in thought, occasionally looking over to Millie, who was a little less self-assured in the kitchen than she was anywhere else, and couldn't help but smile. When Millie caught her, she quickly looked away with a smile.

She was so caught up in what she was doing, she was shocked out of her reverie when two arms wrapped around her waist and she felt a soft breath that made her skin tingle. Then a pair of lips softly kissed the back of her neck and she almost cried out, so completely unsure of what to do or how to respond. What came out of her mouth was a deep sigh. After a few seconds or possibly a century and a half—Kat had lost all track of time—Millie pulled away again.

"W-what was that for?" Kat stammered. Millie looked as bashful as she felt.

"I—Didn't you—"

"N-no, I loved it! I just...I don't know where that—I mean...I didn't know we were, yknow..."

"I thought...I know you're taking it slow, but..."

"What do you mean?" Kat asked.

"Well, after a few dates..."

"Wait, what?"

"Isn't this, like, our fourth date?"

"I thought it was our first!" Kat said, her eyes wide but smiling.

Millie laughed and took a step forward. "Am I going too fast?"

Kat thought about that for a moment. "No, it just took me by surprise, that's all. I wasn't even sure you, you know, liked me."

Millie rolled her eyes. "Yeah, that's why I've been spending as much of my free time as possible with you. Because I think you're just okay." She looked Kat in the eyes and every fiber of Kat's being wanted to fling herself out the window. "I like you, Kat, that's why I invited you over to my place for dinner." She took Kat's hands in her own and Kat was acutely aware of the short distance between them. "Is that okay?"

Kat nodded and decided that, since she'd been the useless one all this time, it was time to change the roles, even if it was only for a few minutes. She wasn't sure how long she'd be able to keep thinking straight like this, so she decided to make a move while she still had a few brain cells operating at minimum capacity. She pulled Millie closer and the other girl stumbled forward with a soft, almost inaudible 'oh' until they were pressed against each other against the kitchen counter. Kat felt her breath on her face, and her underbelly was doing the butterfly thing again. Their fingers interlaced and they looked each other in the eyes, flicking left to right, as if looking for something, trying to get a read on each other.

"You sure?" Millie asked breathlessly, and Kat kissed her. It was passionate and real, and Kat's very first kiss. She was so drunk on the other girl that, even if it was for just a moment, she stopped worrying, stressing, thinking altogether, completely absorbed in the softness of Millie's lips. They stood like that for an eternity, albeit a short one, neither wanting to pull away, until their inexperience forced them to breathe. When the kiss finally ended, it ended with the satisfying *sound* of a good kiss. It had been, all in all, a proper smooch.

Neither knew what to say, and went back to making food, both now terribly distracted. Kat failed to chop a single cucumber with any consistency, constantly biting her lip, and stealing glances over at Millie, the other girl's lipstick still on her own lips.

When dinner was finally done, they ate it in the living room as they watched a movie together. They didn't say much more. Some barriers had been broken and, at least for that day, no more words were needed. They ended up cuddling, Millie in Kat's arms, as they watched the screen. If afterwards anyone had asked them to say a single thing about the movie, they'd both have been utterly unable to recall a single detail. They could have written a book about the other's eyes, the softness of their lips, and gentleness of their embrace, however.

When it started to get dark, Kat had to get ready to go home. There was a bus stop nearby, so that wasn't going to be a problem.

"I-I had a great time today, Millie", Kat said, blushing. She had trouble looking Millie in the eyes. Every time she did her voice got caught in her throat, and she wanted to kiss the other girl. Suddenly, she realized that she could, took a step forward and gave her a peck on the lips. Millie smiled with surprise, a smile that became a wide, happy grin.

"I did too, Kat. I'd...really like to see you again."

Knowing full well she didn't mean 'at school on Monday' Kat nodded. "I'd like that too. I have to go, I'm going to miss my bus."

"I'll see you soon?" Millie asked, and Kat noticed she looked a little nervous, so she took the other girl's hand, squeezed it, and then gave Millie another kiss, this one softer and more intense. It took both of their breaths away.

"Very soon. I'll call you."

The ride home went by in a flash. When Kat came home, her mom was about to ask her something when she saw Kat's blissful expression and couldn't help but burst out laughing.

"That good, huh?"

"Aaa!" Kat said, and shuffled off to her room to scream into her pillow.

6

Battle Of The Herbos

Monday didn't come nearly soon enough. Of course, Kat had spent the entire weekend trying not to overthink things, trying to figure out the exact correct length of time to wait between texts so as not to seem too eager. As always, Millie was infuriatingly confident, and Kat couldn't help but blurt out the occasional groan of frustration as she tried to find the right answer to the various flirts Millie bowled her way. In the end, she felt like she'd held her own. Barely.

Katastrophe: I had a great time yesterday :)
Millieficent: I know ;)
Millieficent: and don't worry
Millieficent: I did too
Katastrophe: and thank you for making dinner! it was d e l i c i o u s
Millieficent: meh
Katastrophe: ??
Millieficent: the appetizer was better ;)
Katastrophe: !
Millieficent: you're so cute
Katastrophe: !!!
Katastrophe: First of all how dare you
Millieficent: come here and stop me
Katastrophe: ughhhh I want to
Millieficent: same thing again next week?

Katastrophe: definitely
Katastrophe: I'll bring snacks this time!
Millieficent: eeeeexcellent
Millieficent: I've been craving a kitkat
Katastrophe: omg
Katastrophe: that was so corny
Millieficent: do you want me to stop?
Katastrophe: uhhhh no
Millieficent: good girl
Katastrophe: o///_///o
Katastrophe: you are evil
Millieficent: you know you can't trust witches
Millieficent: they'll put a spell on you
Katastrophe: are you like this with everyone???
Millieficent: not at all
Millieficent: only with girls I can't stop myself from looking at
Katastrophe: !!
Millieficent: you know, the ones that take my breath away
Millieficent: the ones who make me think about kisses all damn day.
Katastrophe: you're going to be the death of me
Millieficient: worth
Katastrophe: hell yea

She'd done what she could to keep her useless brain from screaming, from making every response an onomatopoeic scream. She'd managed, somehow, but it had been hard. Still, getting consistent confirmation from Millie that she felt much the same way had been very comforting. Sure, Millie's confidence was very attractive, but it was also more than a little scary. It had made her seem like this was something less...intense, like this didn't matter as much to Millie as it did to Kat. Or maybe Kat was just terrible at reading signals. But getting written confirmation from her date had gone a long way to alleviate her fears.

When Monday rolled around, she was practically vibrating with positive energy. Even though she knew Dykstra's class was coming up, she was keeping in good spirits and was completely ready to support her friend regardless of how the Dickstrap was going to treat her. It seemed the teacher had once again decided to focus on April, clearly finding her to be the more pleasant target. He kept asking her questions that were not yet covered by the material, and then chided her for her lack of preparedness, constantly using her boy-name. The lack of respect, the fact that a teacher, an adult in a position of authority was so willing to disregard her wishes, was clearly getting to her, as only halfway through the lesson, Kat could tell she was on the verge of breaking down, her eyes already red.

When April then shot Violet a look, it took Kat by surprise, for the simple fact that it was such a pained, such an angry look. It clearly hadn't gone unnoticed to Dykstra, who misinterpreted it completely and switched targets, demanding Violet come up to the board several times over.

When class was finally over, both of the transformed warlocks were visibly shaking, and by now several students were muttering to each other. Sure, at first, to a lot of them anyway, it had seemed a little funny that these two loud-mouths had gone after each other that way, and having a teacher like Dykstra go after someone else meant he wasn't coming after you. But many were starting to feel like he was going too far, leaning into bullying. Kat couldn't agree more, of course, but she was too busy comforting Violet to concern herself with gossip. When Violet went to her room to take a nap again, Kat met up with Millie for lunch. April joined them. Kat didn't mind. She realized she'd never actually had a conversation with her before, and though she would much prefer to spend the entire lunch break trading witty, blushy banter with Millie, some things could wait.

"How are you holding up?" Kat asked, sitting down opposite from the two of them. Her leg rested softly against Millie's under the table, the gentle pressure a reminder of what they had (not that Kat had any idea of what that was, but it was comforting nonetheless). They weren't ready to talk to Violet and April about the results of their date(s) yet, not while nerves were this raw.

"Why do you care?" April snapped. Millie nudged her and shot her an unimpressed frown. "Sorry", April said. "I just...I hate him so much."

"Violet?" Millie asked.

"No. I mean...no, I mean Dykstra. I don't..." She had to take deep breaths to keep herself from crying. Kat could tell she was on the edge of that precipice where a stray thought or a wrong word would have you sobbing and useless for the next thirty minutes. She didn't envy the poor girl. "It's just not *fair*."

"What's not fair?" Kat asked. "You keep mentioning something about Violet cheating..."

April looked up at her with teary eyes, seemingly trying to gauge her reaction. "Would you even tell me? You're on her side, right?"

Kat rubbed her face and tried not to sound too frustrated when she looked the teary-eyed blonde in the eyes. "April, I barely know you, but I can tell you're hurting. That matters more to me than your stupid bet. No, Violet isn't cheating, as far as I'm aware. How do you even think she's cheating?"

April shook her head. "I don't know. She just...seems to have so much of an easier time of it. I should have turned her into something else. I don't know why it occurred to me that turning her into a girl would have worked. It's like...it comes so naturally to her, you know?" Kat raised an eyebrow. That was *not* the impression she'd gotten herself, but clearly April was just as good at misreading situations as Violet was. Regardless, she stayed quiet to let April speak. "I just...It's *so hard*! And it's so effortless for her!"

"What is?"

"Being a girl! It's like, she fits into it without trying", she said wrongly. "I tried to wear a dress last week, to try and get in the right headspace. I'm just...I'm trying. But I felt so fake and gross, and then Violet told me I looked ridiculous and she's *right* and I just..." She was interrupted by her own sobbing. Kat resisted the urge to find Violet and yell some sense into her.

"She was wrong, April", Kat said. Millie nodded enthusiastically. They'd both seen her in the summer dress. She'd looked stunning. "You looked stunning", Kat said, hoping to get through to April's sobbing. "Violet was...I think she was projecting, honestly."

April looked up confused. "W-what do y-you mean?" She wiped her nose.

"She's been having just as hard of a time with this as you have, April. If I had to guess, I'd say she was jealous. Of how pretty you are."

"Jealous? Why would she be jealous?" She paused, and then her face turned sour. "Of course. Just because I'm taller..." She got up, got her phone out and walked off while ignoring Millie and Kat's exasperated 'Wait, no's. They looked at each other and then at the door.

"Were you ever *that* dense?" Millie asked.

Kat shook her head. "No, and I can be really dense."

Millie grinned like a Cheshire cat, and reached across the table to squeeze Kat's hand. "Yeah, you can. But you look really cute doing it."

"H-hey!" Kat blushed. "Don't you...Hrmpf", she grumbled playfully, and then got up. "Come on, let's keep these two turnips from killing each other."

Millie got up too, but faked a frown. "Five more minutes?"

Kat pulled her in close and gave her a very quick smooch, not really caring who else in the cafeteria could see them. "Later."

"Yay!" Millie said with exaggerated jubilation as they went outside, looking for their two dumbasses. It didn't take long to find them. Like last time, it was a matter of following the screaming.

Kat and Millie came up on the pair. Instead of looking like they were about to start scratching each other's eyes out, Violet and April yelled at each other from a short distance, both of them already having their grimoires out. They meant business. As all rules went for schoolyard fights, nobody was going to involve teachers. In fact, several students were already weaving charms that would obscure the fight, and whatever noises might come from it, from outside observers, creating a shimmering dome around the two combatants.

"We should do something", Kat said.

"I don't know", Millie said. "I don't think either of them is really competent enough to hurt the other. And, you know, worst case scenario, half of the kids here study some form of Restoration."

"True, true", Kat said, and decided to, like Millie, stay as an observer for now. She might still intervene later, she figured, but for now, maybe it was best to let this play out. It had been building up for almost three weeks, and these two had some issues to work out.

"I can't believe you think I'm...I'm *envious* of you!" Violet screamed. She was holding up a magical barrier. As good as April was at destructive magic—which was better than Violet—Violet was just as good at defending herself. As if to prove the point, a fireball fizzled out against the shield.

"Of course you are! You've wanted what I had for so long and now you're mad at me just because you think I'm...I'm pretty!" April shouted back, hurling fireball after fireball at the shield to no real effect, though the impressive fireworks display did elicit some ooh's and aah's from the gathered audience.

"I...I don't", Violet began. "Of course I think you're pretty! I...Look at you! But that's not...I mean you've always been...Shut up!" No longer wanting to be on the back foot, Violet pulled some of the cobblestones out of the ground with a wave of telekinesis, and sent them hurtling at April, who blasted them out of the air with beams of heat.

"And now you're *lying* on top of *cheating!*" she said as she walked closer, trading fireballs for the incoming stones, neither of them getting through to each other. "You...Being like this is *so easy* for you! And then you...you have the *gall* to be mad at *me*. I can't even *look in the mirror* without feeling like a fraud! You *cheated!*"

Violet was crying now, confused, scared and angry, and Kat was wondering if she should step forward, but decided against it. She looked at Millie, who was a lot more relaxed.

"You know, the way she's throwing that stone, maybe April should have called her Violent Rose", Millie said with a smirk.

"Boo", Kat responded. "That's *terrible*."

"True. And, yknow, April May still win."

"Oh my god."

"They'll be fine, Kat. I think this is going to be a good thing."

"I hope so", Kat said, trusting Millie, and her best friend. She looked at the girl and couldn't help but lose focus for a second. She saw Millie in a new light, now that she knew what she looked like up *real* close, what she felt like to kiss. Her breath caught in her throat. She was pulled from her reverie when Millie pointed.

"Does Violet know how to use a sword?" she asked nonchalantly.

"Uh", Kat said. "No. Does April?"

"Not even a little bit", Millie replied. "This'll be interesting."

The two lady warlocks had both given up the attempt at defeating each other with magic, too well matched for each other, and had summoned large, ethereal swords. Violet seemed to currently have the upper hand, if only because she was relentlessly attacking April over and over again. The other girl could only hold up her sword to try and deflect the uncoordinated strikes.

"Why. Can't. You. Just. Let. Me. Have. This?" Violet cried out, every word accentuated by a slash from her sword. She paused for a moment, clearly out of breath, and April used the break to return the attack. Violet only barely managed to raise her own weapon in time, and Kat gasped as she briefly imagined her friend getting skewered. But clearly, in this too, they were basically equals. Equally inept. April failed a swing and left an opening, which Violet looked like she was about to take advantage of. Seemingly changing her mind at the last moment, she spun with a beautiful lack of elegance, which got her awkwardly kicked in the shin and pushed back on the defensive.

"None of this would have happened if it wasn't for you!" April yelled. "And you just...You look so good and so *right* and then you have the audacity to...to be envious of *me!*"

Violet deflected the blade and they clashed in the middle, their faces pressed close together. Neither of them had the rage on their faces they'd started the fight with. Both of them wore a mask of anguish, of pain and tears. "I just...Why do you...I just...Stop being *better* than me! I'm...Gah!" She clearly had a lot of trouble keeping herself together as tears streaked down her cheeks. "I'm good enough!"

"I...What did I do to you?" April said. Kat could tell that both of them were running out of energy. The strength drained from their pose with every passing second. "I just wanted to be...and now you showed me this...and it's hard and I don't...I don't understand...You could have just left me alone and I...I never would have felt like this!"

"I just...You look...I just wanted to..." Violet began, but she was out of words and her sword began to drop, not out of defeat but simply because she didn't have the strength to keep the weapon raised anymore.

"You were good enough without me, you *idiot*", April said, lowering her weapon too, clearly only enough strength left to be angry. She leaned in close to Violet, their foreheads almost touching. "And now you get to be *beautiful* and it's so *effortless* and I wish I could just be like—"

April had tried to stop herself, but it was too late. She'd said the quiet thing out loud. The two of them stood there, panting, barely catching their breath, and then Violet looked at her, their noses an inch away from each other, and a look of understanding washed over her.

"Y—I—Wh—" Violet stammered.

Pause.

"You too?"

"Oh", April said.

There was a silence for a moment as everyone inside the dome seemed to hold their breath.

"Hey Kat?" Millie asked.

"Yeah?" Kat replied.

"Are they kissing?"

"I think so."

"I'm confused."

"I feel like I *shouldn't* be."

April had grabbed Violet by her stupid, cute face and kissed her. They stood in the middle of a circle of students, many of whom were going 'Awwww' Many others just gawked, dumbfounded and confused, while April and Violet cried and kissed.

"I guess it's a draw", Millie said, and took Kat's hand in her own.

"Yeah", Kat said. "And you were right."

"Hmm?"

Kat looked at her best friend who looked up at April, currently wiping the taller girl's tears while trying to blink away her own, and saw that both of them had gone through something real and come out the other side with...each other, perhaps. "They'll be alright."

7

Aftermathematics

The crowd dissipated, albeit slowly. There were some gawkers, and a few students even helped out repairing the destroyed yard floor. Kat had no idea whether or not they did it because of their indomitable community spirit, or because they feared a school-wide reprimand, and she didn't really care. After ten minutes, it looked as if the fight had never taken place, with one exception. Violet and April, now sitting down in the middle of the yard, were still holding hands, foreheads pressed together, whispering softly. Kat and Millie sat down in the grass looking at their two friends.

"You know, when they're not being obnoxious as all hell, they're actually really cute together", Millie said, holding Kat's hand.

"In a puppy-love kind of way", Kat said with a bit of a smirk. She was trying to focus on banter, but the feeling of Millie gently caressing Kat's hand with her thumb was proving to be something of a distraction. Butterflies came and went in waves and her brain was clicking on and off like a laptop with a loose battery. Still, she could appreciate the absurdity of the situation a lot more now that she wasn't worried about her friend's physical health. A little voice in the back of her head reminded her that Violet had never dated anyone in her life, and that, for all intents and purposes, it was now her emotional health on the line. She told the voice to shut the heck up and enjoy the moment, even if it was just for a little bit.

And what a moment it was, now that she thought about it. She was holding hands with a really cute girl, lying in the grass on a warm summer-noon, free to be as gay as the daisies in May, while her best friend was having her first ever kiss a little ways away, probably happier than she'd been in a while. She averted her eyes from the two inexperienced kissers—what Violet and April lacked in knowledge they made up for in enthusiasm—and turned to look at Millie, just to appreciate her face in the midday sun.

Millie leaned over and kissed Kat gently on the nose. "You're very cute too, you know that?" she said, flustering Kat all over again, and then smiling happily at the effect she'd had. Kat was putty in her hands, and Millie knew it, pulling her in close until their faces were only inches away from each other. Kat thought she couldn't blush any harder, but Millie was determined to prove her wrong. Another kiss on the nose. "This way I can feel your heart beat faster", Millie said. Kat squeaked.

"Kat?"

Kat pulled her love-drunk head out of the cloud of butterflies it had been floating in, blinked a few times, and managed to focus on Violet, who was standing a few feet away. Her friend was holding hands with April, Kat noticed, and shifting her weight from one foot to the other. "Yah?" she managed. It was hard to focus. Millie had *not* turned to face Violet and instead planted a very soft kiss on Kat's ear.

"You alright there?" Violet asked. Through the many, many, *many* feelings and sensations she was experiencing, she managed to notice that Violet was trying to seem confident, but she only shuffled her feet like that if she was nervous.

"Yeahhh", Kat sighed, still not entirely present. It was all Millie's fault.

"That looks pretty gay, Kat", Violet said without a shred of judgment.

"Pot calling kettle. Come in kettle", Kat said, looking at the two girls holding hands. "I see you've uh...had a fight, Vi. Wanna talk about it?" Millie had finally turned to look her own friend in the eyes. April looked a little guilty, but not nearly enough to hide the fact that she seemed to be mostly giddy. Millie just nodded approvingly, causing April to blush, smile, and nod back.

"Uh", Violet said. "I uh..."

"Thought so. Sit down, twerp", Kat said. Violet and April did as commanded, plopping down on the grass next to Kat and Millie. There was a moment of silence, but between the distant sounds of shouting and talking teenagers and the warm breeze, there was no real need for words for a while. Millie and Kat laid down with their eyes closed, Kat's head on Millie's shoulder.

Finally, Millie spoke up. "So you two calling off the bet, then?" Kat felt like Millie wasn't saying something, but she couldn't quite put her finger on it. Kat had assumed that Violet and April, now that their rivalry was over, wouldn't be in a hurry to keep up their challenge, so why did Millie sound like she knew something?

"Of course not", Violet said. Well, that was Kat proven wrong real quick. "It's just for the rest of the week. And I'm still going to prove to April that I...That I can do this." She didn't sound as sure as she had at first. Now that there wasn't an aspect of aggressive competition, Kat figured, her resolve had probably taken something of a hit.

"Yeah", April mumbled. "Me too."

"Good luck", Millie said, and Kat saw her subtle smile.

They stayed in the grass a bit longer, Kat and Millie snuggling while April and Violet simply enjoyed holding hands. It seemed that, after their initial makeout session that had immediately followed a magical duel, they were completely drained, simply enjoying resting against each other. Now that all the fighting was done, not many people gave them a second glance. The school tended to have a very liberal stance on affection between students, especially those eighteen and up, and regular anti-discrimination campaigns meant that the only looks the four of them got were from younger students. Mostly envy from those who didn't yet realize that being a girl in love with another girl was allowed.

Sadly, all good things had to come to an end and the bell rang, signifying the end of their break. The rest of class that day went by with somewhat strange feelings for Kat, who wanted to spend more time with Millie, while at the same time wanting to make sure her friend was okay. Violet, on her part, had her head in the clouds, which was probably for the best, because the Botanical Gardens were filled with the murmuring of students, passing on the gossip to those who hadn't heard it yet, and embellishing it for those who had. But Violet didn't care. Violet was too busy being in lesbians with April.

Kat's attention was pulled away from her friend by the teacher, Ms. Richards, a stern, older woman with a hard face and kind eyes, who pulled her aside.

"Have I...done anything wrong?" Kat asked, not understanding. She'd been a model student, and her grades had been excellent. Usually, a teacher wanting to talk to someone was bad news for the student in question.

"Not at all, dear", Ms. Richards was quick to reassure her. "I'm only worried about your classmate."

"You mean Violet", Kat said. On the outside, she kept a straight face. Inside, she rolled her eyes and groaned, because she had to *somewhere*. She could barely dare to dread what shenanigans Violet had gotten up to again.

"Y-es", Ms. Richards said, uncertainly. "Ms. Rose hasn't always been a great student. And I know you've helped her with her homework projects." Before Kat could object, the teacher raised a hand. "Don't bother denying it, dear. But don't worry, I can recognize enough of her own handiwork in the...creations she brings to class for her to pass. No, I'm just worried...these past few days...her magical applications and ability have dropped off significantly, but she seems to be doing better everywhere else." She paused. "They've been keeping up those transformation spells for a long time."

"I don't..." Kat began, and then trailed off, confused.

The teacher paused again and took a deep breath. "I get that she's happier lately. I'm glad to see she's in a better place and that it's improving her grades, but what she's doing can be dangerous. Her reserves are going to run out soon." Kat nodded. She had seen the improvement in Violet's mood lately, too. It had made sense; she'd never had a girl friend before and it had obviously done wonders for her, improving not only her mood but her self-esteem, too. Ms. Richards took another tactful pause. "Look...she's doing better, but if she keeps this up she might hurt herself. I'd rather she talk to a teacher about this. If she wants to officially change her name, she can always talk to the school counselor. Ms. Lopez is a friend of mine; she might be able to help your friend find the resources she needs, so she doesn't have to rely on transformation charms anymore."

"I...okay, thank you", Kat said, a little overwhelmed. She had no idea the school supported contests like the one between Violet and April. It seemed irresponsible. "I think I know what you mean. I don't think it'll be a problem for much longer, but I'll keep it in mind", she said. The contest would be over soon, and their reserves would have time to fill back up after that. "She'll be okay", Kat added with a reassuring smile.

"Well...I'll take your word for it, then." She took one last deep breath and was about to head back to do a round of the gardens, to see how the other students were doing, when she turned halfway around to face Kat again. "By the way, if you want to submit a thesis idea, you can already. Your grades are...well, I think you know." The teacher smiled proudly. "I'm happy to have a student like you here, so make sure you challenge yourself."

With that, she left Kat to shuffle off back to her plot of soil next to Violet's quietly. She had a lot to think about. She was worried for Violet, but her friend was quietly and happily humming to herself as she was working. There was also the thesis to consider. Starting on it a year early wasn't something she should have worried about, but she'd signed up anyway after getting her Botany grades in, and accepting that it was something she was both good at *and* passionate about.

The rest of the week went by in relative quiet. The four of them, Violet, April, Millie and Kat, had lunch together on most days. Now that the barriers had been demolished, aggressively and with lots of kisses, they all got along well. Violet and April were still figuring a lot of things out. Kat and Millie had both recommended to their respective wards to take things slowly. They were both new to relationships, and they were both a little prone to miscommunications, but with Kat and Millie there as a buffer to help them talk about their feelings in a healthier way than what they were used to, things seemed to be going well. Before, Violet probably would have never listened to Kat on this stuff, but she had no idea how to do *anything as a girl*

Not that she would have to for much longer, anymore. Friday was rapidly approaching, at which point their bet would run out of time, and it'd be a draw, and they'd end their mutual curses. Both Violet and April seemed to be anxious whenever Millie or Kat brought it up, clinging to a veneer of bravado every time. Kat was a little miffed that they were still so hung up on the bet, but she respected her friend's decision to keep up with it. Still, there was a limit to stubbornness and they were about to crash directly into it.

They decided that they'd be meeting up after school on Friday, so that it would have been exactly four weeks. That seemed fair, April and Violet agreed, both slightly shakily. In class, Kat caught Violet staring at the clock intensely, and she nudged her friend.

"Either you win or it'll be a draw, Vi. You can hold on a little longer. And then you won't have to worry about it anymore, alright?"

"Haha, yeah", Violet said with *no* conviction whatsoever. Kat took a deep breath and rubbed her friend's back.

"You'll be fine, Vi", Kat said, and couldn't help but feel like she was lying to her friend.

8

There and Back Again

Friday rolled around like an uninvited guest, texting only to let you know that they were definitely showing up. Kat could pick up on April and Violet's discomfort easily, but she still didn't really grasp why they were both so upset about the thought of the bet ending. It wasn't until they'd made plans to meet at Millie's house after classes—it was closest to school—that she had a vague idea. She realized during lunch, when she caught Violet staring wistfully at April. At least Vi had the good sense to blush furiously when Kat nudged her. That's when it occurred to Kat that it was entirely possible that Violet was scared for their relationship. That maybe what had worked between April and Violet as girls wouldn't work between them as Roland and Mark. That Violet was scared April wouldn't like her anymore, and vice versa.

As the bell rang, signifying the start of the weekend, she could tell that Violet was visibly shaking from time to time, her breathing shallow and uneven. April wasn't doing much better, even with Millie nudging her and trying to keep her distracted as they walked down the street on the way to Millie's place. Her parents would be out for the weekend and had approved a sleepover.

"Your parents are…very chill, Mills", Kat said, hooking her arm through Millie's. She wasn't trying to pry, not really, but she was a little worried that the girl she'd been starting to think of as her girlfriend might have been, well, neglected. Millie shrugged.

"They work a lot, especially on weekends, so they're okay with me having people over so long as I make sure everything is clean by Monday." Millie looked at her, and caught the look. "You're cute when you fuss over me, Kat", she said, and kissed her on the nose before she could object.

"That's gay", April said with a snicker from behind them. Kat looked behind her and stuck out her tongue.

"You're one to talk", Millie said with a wide grin. The joke didn't seem to land as well as she wanted to. Violet hadn't registered it, but April clamped her mouth shut at Millie's words. Kat and Millie shared a glance, but decided not to press the issue, as they crossed the street to Millie's house.

Once inside, everyone threw their backpacks in the corner. Studying was for later, today was Friday. While, sure, that meant no homework, usually that also meant relaxing. But Kat knew neither Violet nor April wouldn't be relaxing any time soon. They both looked like they were dying of nerves, and Kat wanted to just scoop them both up in hugs and tell them it was going to be okay. Realizing that there wasn't anything actually stopping her from doing so, she did. April breathed deeply, and Violet made a noise that could have been a sob, but could also be easily denied and claimed to be a hiccup. Millie went into the kitchen to make tea.

Kat and Millie sat down on the sofa in the living room, while April and Violet stood opposite each other. The trepidation was palpable. Their hands, both holding their grimoires, were shaking, though both seemed to be trying—badly—to hide that fact.

"So", Violet said.

"So", April agreed.

"It looks like you managed to last the whole month, huh?"

"You did too."

"Yeah."

"So I guess we call it a draw", April said.

"I guess so", Violet said.

"So do we want to dispel the magic at the same time?"

"If you think that's best", Violet mumbled. Kat felt like they were playing for time. They might well have been. Or it could have just been nerves. Whatever it was, it was infectious. There was a pit in her stomach, and while she wanted to say something to reassure them both, she couldn't find any words that would feel right. She didn't know what to say. She didn't know what they needed to hear.

Violet and April both opened their tomes and took a deep breath, looking each other in the eye. Kat and Millie had looked over their written spells, making sure the results wouldn't be as violently explosive as they had been the first time around. They'd cleaned up a stray syllable here, a squiggly line there. Violet's fragile voice cracked as she began to cant the words, and April was on the verge of tears as she spoke the magic into being. Violet's red and purple clashed with April's blue and green, and then they both relaxed and the magic flowed past any barriers they had, and flowed around and into them. Kat was sure she saw tears on both their faces as their bodies were engulfed in a white light as they seemed to glow from the inside.

When the magic subsided, they were both standing in the same spot they had been before. Violet was only a little bit taller than she had been just before, and her hair was a little longer than it had been a month ago, but her features were undeniably masculine. The same went for April, who was no longer a leggy blonde but tall, athletic, a handsome face with strong cheekbones. Both of them looked miserable. They both looked at each other while the clock in the room slowly ticked away the seconds. Neither of them looked away from the other for a second.

"D—I need..." April began.

"I—You—" Violet tried to say, and then both of them burst into tears. Kat and Millie looked back and forth between them. Kat felt like her fears had been realized. It seemed obvious that Violet and April —or rather, Mark and Roland, she corrected herself— couldn't imagine themselves in a relationship with the other. Millie, however, seemed to be a bit more relaxed.

"Do you want to..." Mark began, and didn't have to say anything more. Roland nodded vigorously. Before Kat could say anything, ask them any questions, they both immediately began to chant again, casting magic at each other. Swirling colors appeared in the air above and around them as they said the words quickly but carefully, making sure not to miss a single word, not to mispronounce anything. But as they spoke, Kat saw the energy flicker in and out of sight, and both spells fizzled out into nothing.

Roland was the first to notice, and tears began rolling down his face. He immediately started over again, and again the magic began to take shape and then faded away. He turned to Millie as if demanding an answer. Mark soon joined him.

"It's not working", Mark said. "Why isn't it working?!"

Millie sighed and hugged her knees. She still seemed a little unbothered to Kat. "You've been keeping each others' quote-unquote 'curses' up for a whole month", she said, miming quotation marks to emphasize her point, "and it takes a lot of energy to cast something like this. You're probably just drained."

"But—But—" Mark began and then looked at Roland. "I don't want to...I can't..."

"I'm so sorry", Roland sobbed. "I'm not...I can't be..."

Millie looked between the two of them intently, as if she was watching a game of chess being played.

"I was pretty", Mark said with the smallest possible voice. Tears rolled down his cheeks. "I was Violet." Roland looked at Millie, who shot back a glance that Kat couldn't read. But it looked like Roland could.

April turned back. "You still are", she said. Before the other could respond and ask what she meant, April gently took Violet's face in her hands and kissed her. Millie exhaled like she'd been holding her breath the entire time. Kat frowned, not understanding. Millie just wrapped her arm around Kat.

"I don't get it", Kat said quietly.

"Just watch", she whispered, as April and Violet kissed softly. They were both whispering 'I'm sorry's to each other and then chiding the other for apologizing.

"I think I love you, April", Violet said softly.

"I love you too, Violet", April returned. Both of them hearing each other say their name sent them crying again.

"Even when I look like—"

"I don't give a fuck what you look like", April said. "We'll figure something out."

"Cough", Millie said. She even held her hand in front of her mouth like that hadn't just been the most telegraphed fake cough ever elicited by a person. April and Violet both turned to her, their faces wet with tears. "I'm pretty sure", Millie said, "Kat and I can redo those spells for you while we figure out a way to make things permanent." The two girls looked at them with wide eyes, like it hadn't even occurred to them. "Now, unless you want to wait, say, a week, for your reserves to build back up so you can do the spells yourselves and risk blowing yourselves up, let a couple of witches do it for you, okay?"

"kay", April squeaked and took a step back as Millie hopped out of the couch and pulled Kat upright.

"I still don't get it", Kat said. Millie kissed her on the nose with a smile.

"Kat", Millie said, "I'd like you to meet April and Violet." Kat frowned and looked back and forth between them. Realization was beginning to dawn. Millie pushed a little more. "Your best friend and mine are Violet and April, regardless of what they look like."

"Oh!" Kat said, her face splitting in a wide smile. It had taken her a good minute, but she was finally arriving at the right conclusion.

Millie grinned. "There it is." She turned to the others. "Alright, step apart, you two. Kat, you take on Violet, I'll do April. Shouldn't be too hard, they did all the prep work." She stuck out her hand to April's grimoire. "Gimme." April sheepishly handed her the book, then reached over to Violet, and squeezed her hand. The two girls smiled at each other for a moment, before stepping several feet apart. Millie looked at the book for a moment, and then at Kat, who was similarly leafing through the tome she'd gotten from Violet, and they swapped books.

Kat and Millie both began chanting. Warlock magic was different from their witchcraft, but both of them were accomplished magic users regardless, and with their help, April and Violet's spells had been prepared to perfection. It wasn't long before brightly coloured rainbows of pure ethereal light swirled around them, then flowed from them into the other two girls. Again, they seemed to shine from the inside. There was a sound. There was the absence of a sound, like not just every person, but everything held its breath for a moment. Then there was another sound, like a thunderclap but very small, and Violet and April stood in the exact same spot. April ran her hands through her long, blonde hair, touched her face with an incredulous smile. Violet honked one of her own boobs.

"It worked!" Violet said with elation.

"Well, duh", Millie said smugly, but it fell on deaf ears as April and Violet wrapped themselves around each other, smothering each other in kisses as they were both hit by waves of euphoria. After a few seconds, they fell over on top of each other on the sofa.

"I think we should give them some space", Kat said.

"This is my house", Millie protested. Kat just interlaced her fingers with Millie's, and pulled her away.

"Thank you!" Violet and April both managed, before turning their attention to each other again, mumbling little declarations of love at each other in between kisses.

Millie rolled her eyes playfully, and was about to say something glib, when Kat dragged her out of the room, closed the door and kissed her. "You did good", Kat said. "I wouldn't have figured them out. You're amazing." Before Millie could say anything back, Kat barreled on. "You're amazing, and I love you", she said, and Millie's brain switched from wisecrack to gay mode, barely able to mumble a 'same' before they both lost themselves in each other.

9

Meet The Parents

"Are you sure you're up to this?" Kat asked. She looked over to her friend on the seat next to her. Violet was fidgeting a little, though it was hard for Kat to be sure if it was nerves or the general jostling of the bus. She didn't want to make any assumptions, but she was, for obvious reasons, worried for her friend. Violet took a deep breath, and nodded. She opened and closed her mouth a few times like she was going to say something, and then just nodded again. Kat glared.

"I'm…I'm as fine as I can be, Kat. Are you sure you want to be there too? You don't have to…" she trailed off. Kat would probably, after some prodding, be willing to admit that she wasn't always the best at reading people, but even she picked up on the fact that Violet was low-key begging her to be there.

"I offered because I want to be there for you, dumbass", she chided playfully, but when Violet shrank away, she wrapped an arm around her best friend. "Hey, I'm sorry. I genuinely want you to be okay, okay?" She felt a bit guilty for making Violet feel insecure, especially with how vulnerable she was. "I'm here", she added.

Violet rested her head on Kat's shoulder, which was giving Kat some complicated feelings, which she was ignoring for now, focusing on her friend and the difficult step she was about to take. Violet had decided that she couldn't pretend to not be Violet. She hadn't been home in the past month—her parents both worked several full-time jobs, and there wasn't much for her to do at home alone—so this would be the first time they'd see her as Vi. Kat squeezed Violet softly. She was going to be there for her, of course. She'd decided as much as soon as the idea of officially coming out had been uttered. It wasn't that she was necessarily worried, because Violet's parents were good, kind people, but Violet had a tendency to lose herself in her own head and Kat figured she could do some good being there with her.

The bus approached their stop, and Kat nudged Violet out of the seat with a playful hip-bump, trying to keep the mood light. "C'mon, we're here."

"I live here, Kat, I know", Violet joked, but it was clear she was forcing herself to seem a bit more cheerful than she was.

"It'll be fine, Vi", Kat said as they got off the bus and made their way to the front door of Violet's house, a convenient stone's throw from the stop. Violet stopped in front of the house, taking deep breaths. After a few seconds, Kat realized that she was trying to psych herself up and that it wasn't working. She spun her friend around and pulled her in for a hug. "It will be fine", Kat repeated, as she pulled away and pressed the doorbell for her friend. She gave Violet's arm an encouraging squeeze. A few seconds of nothing happening intensely passed by. Then a few more. "Are you sure they're h—" Kat began, and then the door opened.

Christopher—Chris to his friends—was a fairly short man who had clearly attempted to stay in shape until well into his thirties, at which point he must've lost track of things. He had since acquired a layer of what might be best described as padding, giving him a self-assured but eminently huggable presence. This was further amplified by the jovial, friendly smile on his face, marred only by the bags under his eyes. He looked tired but determined to enjoy his Saturday.

"Oh, hello, Katherine", he said, his eyes darting between the two girls on his doorstep. "I thought Mark would be coming home today; he didn't mention bringing any friends." Kat could feel Violet shrinking into herself next to her at the use of her old name. It had only been a month, but she'd been violently opposed to even considering switching back to her old name. She'd made that very, *very* clear. They'd rehearsed some of the stuff that had to be said on the way there, though, and at some point the name would've had to be said. Kat was going to be the one to do it. She doubted Violet could even get the name past her lips at this point.

"Heya, Mister R. I'm actually here on...their behalf. Is their —is your wife home? It's a little important", Kat said. Chris looked concerned.

"Uh, yeah, she is. Is everything okay with Mark?" he asked as he stepped aside to allow Kat and Violet to come in. Kat nodded as she walked past.

"Yeah, it's just...something that needs to be talked about, I guess", she said as she walked the familiar route to the living room, where Violet's mom was curled up and reading a book. They'd both taken the weekend off, which was why Violet had chosen this particular day to come out to them.

Laura looked about as tired as her husband, but she looked incredibly comfortable, a large iced tea on the little table next to her as she was clearly buried deep in a book. She had enough of a presence of mind to look up as they walked in, and her face split into a smile as wide and full of hospitality as Christopher's.

"Hello, Kat. It's good to see you!" She looked at Violet for a moment, and then looked behind them, looking for her son. "I thought Mark was going to be with you?"

Kat nodded as Chris walked past her and sat down on the sofa next to his wife. "What's up, Katherine?"

Kat took a deep breath, about to start the conversation, but it seemed that Vi had regained some of her courage as she was the first to speak up. Kat looked at her friend with proud surprise, and took a step back to allow her to do what might well be the bravest and most difficult thing she'd ever done, but not so far that she was out of Violet's zone of safety, available for a comforting hug or hand squeeze when necessary.

"How it happened doesn't really matter", Violet began. "But I'm...I was turned into this", she said, waving generally at herself. Her parents frowned and leaned forward, confused as to what this new girl, this stranger was telling them.

"I'm sorry", Laura said. "I'm not sure I caught your name. Who are you, exactly?"

Deep breath. Kat put a hand on Violet's back, and the simple touch seemed to give her the encouragement she needed. "You gave me...my name when I was born. M-Mark." She paused to let what she said sink in. Laura blinked a few times. Chris leaned back, his eyebrows raised.

"Mark?" Laura asked, squinting.

Violet shook her head. "Not anymore. I...I prefer being this way. It's taken me a while to figure out, but...Mom. Dad. I'm a girl."

Laura rubbed her face. Chris chewed his tongue for a second. Then he looked at Laura. Back at Violet. "You know", he said. "She does kind of look like you when you were younger." Laura cocked her head and nodded. Chris leaned forward and clasped his hands together thoughtfully. "I..." he paused, and looked at Kat. "This isn't a joke, is it? If it is, it isn't very funny." Kat shook her head. "Well, in that case..." He looked Violet in the eyes. "I think I speak for both of us when I say...hi, girl, I'm Dad."

"Chris!" Laura said, barking a laugh, and she playfully slapped his shoulder. When she turned to Violet, her expression softened. "It's really you, isn't it? I see it in your eyes. I'd recognize my baby anywhere."

Violet, throughout all of this, had been frozen, Kat realized. She had been completely immobile like her entire body had been spooled up and wound tight. She might even have been holding her breath. But when Laura got up and smiled, Violet broke down. Tears started rolling down her face and Laura immediately stepped forward and hugged her newfound daughter.

"Hey", Vi's mom said. "It's okay. Your dad and I always told you you could tell us anything, and that's never not been true. Gracious, your hair is soft." Her little non-sequitur eased some of the tension out of the room. She held her daughter for a few more moments and then stepped back, holding Violet by the shoulders. "It *really* is you. I —oh!" she exclaimed. "I can't believe we still don't have an answer yet."

"", Violet said.

"What's your name, dear?"

"I'm Violet", Violet said.

"Violet Rose?" Laura raised an eyebrow and looked over to Chris, who was grinning like he'd just won the lottery. "She really is yours." She turned back to Violet. "It's good to finally meet you, Violet." She turned to Chris a second time. "Darling, good news. We have a daughter!"

—

Milliefcent: oh my god that sounds amazing

Katastrophe: Right? They were _so_ nice

Katastrophe: Vi is still hugging it out with them

Katastrophe: Got invited over for dinner :)

Katastrophe: home now

Milliefcent: i'm so glad to hear that

Milliefcent: about the parents being good I mean

Milliefcent: tbh i have no idea what i had to expect. glad the girl has supportive parents

Katastrophe: as opposed to?

Milliefcent: i'm a lil worried about April. her parents aren't the most eh...

Katastrophe: accepting?

Milliefcent: i was gonna say chill

Milliefcent: her big brother is a pilot, apparently, and so the pressure on her has been high to also do well

Katastrophe: poor thing

Katastrophe: took my parents a while to be okay with me too tbh

Katastrophe: made it clear to them that they didn't get to decide how gay or not I was

Katastrophe: only whether or not i was gonna be in their life

Milliefcent: :o

Milliefcent: you're hot when you take charge

Katastrophe: o////o

Katastrophe: how absolutely _dare_ you

Milliefcent: are you blushing?

Katastrophe: no! >:#C

Milliefcent: cutie

Katastrophe: aaa

Milliefcent: are you free tomorrow?

Katastrophe: aaaaaabutalso yes i should be. what's up?

Milliefcent: so there's two things

Milliefcent: first off, i wanna talk to you about like, them at school. you mentioned something about a counselor?

Katastrophe: ms Lopez, yea

Millieficent: i wanna strategize a bit there
Katastrophe: probably a good idea
Katastrophe: what's the other thing?
*Millieficent: i haven't kissed you in _hours_*
Millieficent: it's downright criminal
Katastrophe: aaa
Katastrophe: okay :3
Millieficent: you're cute when you aaa
Millieficent: i wanna see what other noises i can make you make

Kat threw her phone across the bed with a squeal and hid her face under the pillow. Millie was much, *much* too powerful for her own good, and Kat had no reasonable defenses against it. Not that she really wanted to defend herself. To a certain extent, it was liberating to feel so...vulnerable to someone she trusted not to hurt her. But good golly did the girl ever know how to turn her into a useless puddle.

She did have one final trump card, something she'd been saving up for the right moment, where she'd be the one in control, where *she* would be the one melting Millie instead of the other way around. She crawled across the bed looking for the phone while she thought of Millie. Officially, while they'd been dating, they weren't *together* together yet. It was an important step, of course, and one not to be taken too lightly. But at some point, she realized, she was going to want to call Millie her girlfriend. Well, she was going to want to do so out loud. It wouldn't change anything between them, she knew, but there was something magical about having a girlfriend. About *being* a girlfriend. A warm sense of belonging. Belonging with.

She found her phone again when it dinged with a new message.

Millieficent: still there, kitkat?
Katastrophe: kitkat? :o
Millieficent: don't like it?
Katastrophe: i like it coming from you :)
Katastrophe: hey Mills?
Millieficent: ya?
Katastrophe: I love you
Millieficent: i love you too
Millieficent: dang, it's just not the same when i can't whisper it in your ear
Katastrophe: you'll have plenty of opportunities tomorrow :3
Millieficent: parents aren't home again. wanna do another sleepover? without vi and april this time?
Katastrophe: o///o
Katastrophe: aaa
Katastrophe: yes
Katastrophe: aaa

Millieficent: good girl
The phone bounced across the bed again as Kat yote it in a panic.

10

Scared And A Little Hopeful

Monday rolled around like it always did. Once upon a time, Kat had dreaded Mondays. She never found herself comfortable in groups of people, and integrating into an existing group had always been an uncomfortable experience for everyone involved, like mandatory team-building exercises. But now it meant spending time with a best friend who had actually found herself, who was learning to enjoy life (and how to be a girl), as well as sharing lunch with April, who she'd grown fond of, in a big-sister-kind-of-way, and Millie, who she'd grown fond of in a decidedly un-sibling-like way. Sunday had been very wonderful, a little scary, and mostly breathless. She'd been learning a lot about herself, even though the two of them were taking things slow.

Geography was, as always, a frustrating ordeal, however. Dykstra found it once again necessary to single out Violet and April, but found them not nearly the ideal victims they'd been only a week earlier. They bore his use of their old names and pronouns with dignity, even though Kat could see Violet tense up every time. Coming out to themselves had renewed their strength, but it was still an uncomfortable situation, being targeted by someone in a position of power.

But Millie and Kat had considered that the day before. Today, after class, they'd take the girls to the school counselor's office, and help them not only come out to the faculty, but Kat and Millie would serve as eyewitnesses to Dykstra's behavior, hopefully reprimanding him and getting him to stop harassing the two girls. Millie especially could name four other students who would be willing to back them up. Over the past month, and especially the last week, the general opinion on Violet and April had shifted from an eye-rolling amusement at the two more unpopular kids having a go at each other to a low-level indignation. Sure, April and Violet weren't very popular, but in the end they were fellow students and a bully was a bully, no matter how high up the food chain. If there were no teachers (or snitches) around, there were plenty of their classmates who had begun to voice their frustration.

After class, Millie and Kat dragged their counterparts to Ms. Lopez's office. They'd made an appointment and everything. Rather than being connected to the rest of the faculty building, the school counselor's office was just around the corner from the cafeteria, allowing a student with a more private matter to slip away quickly without being seen going directly to the teachers. It was a clever solution, and especially now, Violet and April seemed grateful for it. They looked nervous. Sure, they were out, to a certain extent, but officializing their new status was still a scary prospect.

A little light shone green next to the door, indicating that Ms. Lopez was free and available for them to come in without knocking. Millie held the door open, and Violet and April slipped inside like they were committing a B&E, almost hunched over as they scurried into the office. Kat stole a quick kiss from Millie as she walked in behind them. The school didn't outright ban displays of affection, but they did try to keep it somewhat subtle when they were on campus grounds, so any excuse to get a quick smooch in was a good one.

Through the second door, and they were in Ms. Lopez's office. It was not big. The school counselor had a lot of work—teenagers throughout history aren't exactly known for their mental and emotional stability —but she could clearly do with a larger office, a bigger staff, and perhaps even a budget. She sat behind a desk that had seen better times, although only oral tradition went that far back, her small, half-rimmed glasses teetering on the edge of her nose. It was *hot* in the room too, even with two windows open, and the counselor looked like what she needed was a fan and a hot drink. Instead, she'd bunched up her black hair in a messy bun that had several pencils shoved into it, and rolled up her sleeves.

She looked up from the page she'd been writing when the four of them came in. She gave the best impression of a 'No, you're not disturbing me at all' kind of smile. "This is...Rose and Mayweather?" She looked at her watch. "How is it four already??" A polite cough and she gestured for them to sit down on the two chairs. Millie and Kat stood behind them, content to stay standing. There wasn't enough room in the office for two additional chairs. Ms. Lopez shot them a questioning glance.

"Emotional support", Millie summarized. Ms. Lopez shrugged.

"So how can I help the two of you?" She looked between Violet and April. She'd likely seen their student file, so she probably hadn't expected two girls showing up, but she wasn't drawing attention to it. Violet began to explain the situation, starting at the beginning, thankfully leaving out the fact that it had been Kat's idea to begin with. She focused mostly on how she'd felt during the past month, how she'd slowly begun to dread the end of it. April chimed in with confirmations and the occasional 'same' Their hands were entwined next to them, probably hoping the counselor couldn't see it. From where Kat was standing, she knew Ms. Lopez could most definitely see them holding hands, but again refrained from saying anything.

"Last week...we realized we couldn't go back", Violet concluded. "I can never be...I'm Violet, I *feel* that."

"I'm April", April said, quietly.

Ms. Lopez pushed her glasses back up her nose—in the heat, they kept sliding down—and sucked her teeth for a moment. "Well", she said, "we have several transgender students on campus, so the process isn't exactly arcane." She opened a drawer, took out a binder and began to retrieve several coloured forms. "You're going to have to fill these out. They're mostly 'Do you swear under threat of perjury' nonsense, but it allows us to protect you in the case of harassment and discrimination." She looked between the two of them. "Now, normally, I'd ask if you're sure, but you spent the past month switching pronouns and presenting. Unless you have doubts, of course?" April and Violet both shook their heads aggressively. Ms. Lopez smiled. "Thought so."

"Eh, Ms. Lopez?" Kat interjected.

"Maria, please", Ms. Lopez said, holding up her hand. "I feel old enough as it is. Yes?"

"Well, we wanted to talk to you about that harassment", she said, a little less cocksure now that the attention was on her. Maria Lopez's brown eyes were very intense when they were pointed at you.

"Oh? Has someone already given you—well, your friends—any grief? We take bullying quite seriously", she said, her mouth a thin line. Kat knew that the school took bullying seriously. She also figured that Ms. Lopez was probably dreading actually doing anything, because the school had been sued before by rich parents refusing to accept that their little angels were actually shit-flinging turdgibbons in disguise.

"It's...not a student", Millie jumped in, Kat's knight in shining armor. Ms. Lopez leaned back and crossed her arms. She looked extremely stern and even Millie's usually relaxed demeanor stiffened up. "Mr...Dick-Dykstra...he's been targeting the two of them. Even after they explained that they'd prefer to use other names."

Maria Lopez took a deep breath with her eyes closed. "If you came forward to him and requested to use different names and pronouns, he should have brought that to the faculty—which I know for a fact he didn't—instead of denying you outright." She retrieved a small book and wrote down some things in it. The only sound in the room, other than the faint sounds of life happening outside the window, was the soft scratching of pen on paper. Then Ms. Lopez looked up again. "I'll be honest, girls. This isn't the first time Mr. Dykstra has needed a reprimand. That's why we don't usually tell him—" She stopped and interrupted herself, squeezing her eyes shut. "Probably shouldn't have told you that. Anyway, it's nothing you should concern yourselves with." She wrote some more in the small booklet and closed it. It was almost full, and Kat just barely managed to read the small sticker on the front that said 'Dykstra.' Maria wasn't kidding.

"Now, with regards to your transition", she said, changing the subject. "You're not the first to use transfiguration to make yourselves more comfortable in your own skin, but I think you're also aware it's not permanent?" Violet and April nodded, and Kat noticed that they squeezed each other's hand a little tighter. "Now, the school has several programs for low-income students." Kat saw Violet stiffen up, but Maria went on without mentioning that Violet was a recipient of a program like that. "We offer a lot of support, but the medical treatments that usually go with this sort of thing are a little outside of our scope." She paused. "That means budget, honestly. You're both eighteen?" They nodded. "That does help somewhat. Still, you'll likely have to approach your parents if you want to begin medically transitioning."

Kat saw Violet's shoulders droop. She'd talked about it with her parents. Both of them were neck-deep in debt, and finding well-paying work had been difficult. They simply couldn't afford any kind of treatment for Violet right now. Maria immediately saw the shift in Violet's pose and took off her glasses, which decreased how stern she looked by a factor of ten.

"I'm very sorry, Violet. It's just not something we can afford to do he—" She paused again as the high-speed bumper car that was her brain bounced in a new direction. "Actually, I have some questions to ask a colleague of mine before I go any further", she said, writing something down on a post-it note. "I have an idea, but I need to ask around about legal stuff. I don't want to give you any false hope, Violet, but there might be something. What about you, April? Do you think your parents can help out?"

"I'm not out to them yet", April mumbled.

"Ah", Maria said. "Well, I have some materials here." She looked around the room, its cupboards full and boxes everywhere. ".. somewhere. For relatives of transgender people, explaining things. If you think that'll help."

"Yes, please." April nodded.

"And if they're being difficult or not understanding, they are also always welcome to come to school with you. I can talk to them separately or with you in the room and explain things." That seemed to satisfy April, who nodded again, forcing a smile. "Now, is there anything else I can help you all with? I have a lot of research to do and I want to make sure I do it well." They all shook their heads. "Very well then. I would also like to add, of course, that everything said here was said in the strictest confidence until you sign those papers and hand them in, at which point I'll inform the faculty of your official name change." And then, like flipping a switch, her expression turned from kind and reassuring to angry thundercloud. "And I'll talk to Mr. Dykstra."

Other than the obvious reasons, Kat was, in that moment, very grateful she was *not* Mr. Dykstra. Despite Maria Lopez's kindness towards the girls, Kat got the feeling that the woman was a hellion when she got into an argument. A part of her wanted to be a fly on the wall when she confronted ol'Dickstrap. With a murmur of thank-you's, they all shuffled out of the office again.

"How are you feeling?" Millie asked Violet and April once they were outside.

"Scared", Violet said. "And a little hopeful."

"Mostly scared", April said quietly. "I'm going to tell my parents tonight." Kat saw Millie lean forward, ready to pull her friend into a hug, but Violet was quicker, wrapping her arms around April.

"I'm here for you, April", Kat heard Violet mumble softly. "No matter what happens."

Kat and Millie decided to give them some space, taking each other's hand in their own. The future was uncertain for their friends, but they weren't going to be without love and caring any time soon.

11

Unexpected Visits

Kat sat on Violet's bed shoving handfuls of peanuts into her mouth. Elegance, she had once decided, was situational and subjective, and therefore not applicable to large chunks of her life. Helping her friend figure out advanced magical theory just a few weeks before cramming for exams began in earnest while simultaneously doing research on her own thesis was one of those situations where being ladylike had to take a backseat to stuffing her face with peanuts. Priorities, she felt, had to be kept straight. She had three separate books in front of her. Two of which were her own notebooks, and the third was one on warlock-to-witchcraft spell conversion.

While technically warlocks and witches were gender-neutral professions, many people tended to choose the one that, historically, fit them the best from a presentation perspective. Especially since a recently popularized show had ruined the masculine word for 'witch.' A lot of the guys at school who'd decided to pursue witchcraft had been pretty miffed about that. Similarly, feminine warlocks existed but were exceedingly rare, which Kat blamed on gender-roles. A little voice in the back of her head piped up, reminding her that she, too, was a witch, but she squashed it by pointing out that that was only because the coursework was much more in her ballpark.

And now Violet wanted to switch to witchcraft, which Kat couldn't blame her for. Wanting to feel validated in her newly-accepted femininity by pursuing feminine hobbies wasn't necessarily ideal, but especially early on, every last crumb of euphoria was one she was willing to grant her friend. Her happiness was already positively impacting her grades, and now that she was no longer draining herself by keeping up an enchantment, she was likely to do even better. Kat wouldn't be able to hold up the spell herself indefinitely, either, but she liked to think her use of magic was a lot more refined, and her grasp of the actual mechanics a lot stronger. The strain on Kat wouldn't be too high, and hopefully they'd find a more permanent solution soon.

But in the meantime, there was some conversion to do. Switching courses happened—teenagers had a tendency to experiment—so they weren't exactly breaking new ground here. Witches tended to lean on the more practical, physical aspect of magic use, while warlocks leaned heavily towards the more theoretical and, Kat felt, *flashy* parts of the arcane. Ask a warlock to build a fence and they were likely to draw glowing circles in the air, crafting the fence from the very foundations of reality itself. A witch, by contrast, might ask her neighbor to do it in return for an ointment that helped with the shoulder that had been hurting. Warlocks got things done quicker and more explosively. Witches had a tendency to live longer.

Some books had been written on the subject, and Violet had been studying them, so in between the flying crumbs of peanut, Kat tested her on the basics of applied empathetic psychology and its relation to animal husbandry. To Violet's credit, she was doing quite well. She'd never been a great warlock, and she'd probably never be a great witch either, but the more grounded nature of witchcraft was a good way to get her out of her own head, which she needed right now.

Violet had been worrying about April, and probably with reason. April was supposed to come out to her parents tonight, and so far, Vi hadn't heard from her. Millie was apparently out to dinner and a movie with her parents, so she wasn't available to be on standby. So Vi tried not to check her phone every five minutes while she recited the literature, and Kat tried not to worry too much about her friend while she figured out if offering to grow levitating potatoes—levitatoes—would get her chased out of her teacher's office. It was raining softly outside, and the sound of rain against the window was helping them both concentrate a great deal. She'd cracked open a window ever so slightly to let the earthy smell of petrichor in.

Violet's dorm room was quite large, one of the perks of being an 'officially' low-income student. It was a traditional two-person room converted for a single person, including a very small kitchenette. It wasn't much, but Vi didn't *need* much. She wasn't sure yet how the administration would deal with her transition, and whether she'd be moved to an all-girl dorm, and for right now, she wasn't too worried about it too much. For the most part, the other kids in the dorm tended to keep to themselves, not usually disturbing each other. Kat was washing down her last industrial load of salted nuts with an energy drink when someone knocked on the door. Unusual, but not impossible.

Kat raised her eyebrows at Violet, who had been starting to get up, and shook her head, and then nodded at the books. Violet took a deep breath. Rather than open the door physically, or do something as crude as to use full-on-manifested magic to open the door, Kat wanted her to use a branch of magic almost unused by warlocks, that almost every witch had access to. She hadn't exactly mastered it herself, she was barely a novice, but Vi needed to train herself in the witchy art of Dramatic Magic.

Violet raised her hand, and snapped her fingers. For a second, nothing happened. Then, quite dramatically, the door clicked out of the lock and slowly swung open. Kat was about to congratulate Violet when they both saw April standing in the doorway. She was soaking wet, her beautiful blonde hair clinging to her face. Even with her rained-down appearance, it was clear she'd also been crying. She didn't say anything, just standing in the doorway with bloodshot eyes, shivering slightly. Violet was the first to respond, jumping up and running towards her, worry easily visible on her face.

"What happened?" Violet demanded as she gently pulled April inside. The poor girl was dripping onto the carpeted floor, and her bookbag almost slid off of her without her doing anything. She opened her mouth to say something, closed it again, and began to cry. Kat had also gotten up, but felt like she would be getting in the way. Luckily, Vi had already wrapped April into a big hug, not caring one bit about how wet her own clothes were getting. April was starting to sag through her knees and Violet held her as she descended, rather than letting her crash her knees on the floor.

April cried for a bit, while Kat sat on the edge of the bed, ready to jump in if necessary. Finally, April took a deep breath and leaned back a bit. "I ran away", she said quietly.

"Fuck", Kat said diplomatically.

"Yeah", April agreed.

"What happened?" Violet asked again, quieter this time, taking April's hands in her own. "Oh, fuck, you're freezing!" She began to quickly help April take off her jacket, and then seemed to realize she was practically stripping her girlfriend and leaned back, blushing. "Y-you should get out of those clothes", she mumbled. April smiled at her bashfulness, which was a definite plus, and she complied, taking off her jacket and sweater.

Violet quickly scrounged for a skirt—which was technically a skirt Kat had lent her—and offered it to April, who seemed unaware of the fact that there were other people in the room. Kat turned around with a blush before April could flash her, and she noticed that Violet had done the same.

"Why are you turned around?" she asked Violet. "She's your girlfriend!"

"I—because—shut up!" Vi whispered back.

"I'm decent", April said quietly behind them, and they turned around again, Violet immediately running forward to hold April again. This time, Kat felt it was appropriate for her to do the same thing, pulling in both of them. She briefly wondered if them smelling nice had been a side effect of the magic, and then shooed away that thought. Finally, April pulled away again and sat down on the bed, Violet right next to her. Kat crossed her legs on Vi's desk chair. "They didn't take it well", April said, holding Violet's hand as if her life depended on it.

"Mom was quiet. I told her first, when I got home. She was listening and asking questions, but like, the hard ones. 'Are you sure?' 'Where did you pick this up?' I didn't want to make her upset or turn her against me, so I was just trying to be honest, that the contest had just made me realize things that I'd always repressed, and she did a lot of pacing. I think she was starting to accept things when Dad got home." Something about the way she'd said that last part made Kat dread what she'd say next.

"Dad was mad. Really mad. He—he thought the idea of the bet was hilarious, but when I told him I wanted to stay that way he was furious. It was just yelling at first, a—about—about—" April was starting to breathe more and more heavily, and Kat could tell she was starting to have a panic attack, so she got up and knelt in front of her.

"Hey, it's okay. You're safe", she said. "Did he hurt you?"

April shook her head, and then seemed to hesitate. "Well...n-not really..." She paused again. "He s-said I was his son w-whether I liked it or not, that he wasn't going to let me throw away my future. Then Mom started to cry and said she didn't want to lose her b-baby boy and—and —" April began to cry again and Violet held her close as the tears ran freely. Kat was carefully squashing down the bubbling rage inside of her. She'd find an outlet for it later. Right now was time for comforting. April took a breath and Kat gritted her teeth. There was *more*. "D-dad, he started shaking me", April said. "He was yelling and I didn't understand all of it. Then Mom pushed him and told him to stop and he yelled at her too and I ran out the door." She lowered her head. "I never even took off my backpack. I—I hope Mom is okay."

Violet and Kat made eye contact for a moment. Kat nodded. Violet nodded back. She didn't know what they'd both agreed to, but they'd agreed to it together, and right now, that was what mattered.

"You can stay with me for now, April", Violet said. "I'll...I'll prep the couch", she added sheepishly. Kat repressed a faint smile. April only responded by leaning against Violet again.

"I'll see if we can talk to the counselor tomorrow", Kat added. "I'm sure other queer kids at school have...well, I'm sure she can help."

"Okay", April said quietly. "Thank you." Violet reached up and squeezed April's hand.

"Of course. Girls have to look out for each other, you know." That earned her another little smile. "Do you want me to message Millie or are you gonna?"

"Dad took my phone", April said meekly. Kat was just about ready to turn a motherfucker into a frog. It was a bit of a faux pas and leaning a bit too heavily into the stereotype, but some motherfuckers gotta be turned into frogs.

"All right, don't worry too much about it. I'll let her know." She turned away to grab her phone, and also to hide the look of fury and rage that had crept its way up to her face and that was becoming too hard to hide. Maybe she should have signed up for after-school kickboxing after all. The urge to kick the absolute shit out of a bag of sand was tangible.

April turned back to Violet and whispered another "Thank you." Violet made it clear to her that she had nothing to thank her for, and comforted her. She didn't use words to do so, although Kat saw very clearly, before she turned away blushing again, that Violet most definitely used her lips to soothe April.

12

Double Dates

"I—I don't know, Mills", April said. She sat on the edge of Violet's bed while her girl-friend was in the shower. It was noon and it had been two days since she'd left her house. From what Kat had picked up, her parents had been flaking on making sure she was okay. There had been a demand for her to come home, but the fact that she was a legal adult made it so the school couldn't just hand her over. When Ms. Lopez had been informed of what had happened she had nodded stoically. She'd then given April a dinky old backup phone, asked them all to come back next week, and had then shuffled them out of her office while she took care of some business. They'd heard her yelling into her phone through the double doors. An hour later, April had received a text from Ms. Lopez on her 'new' phone that she was legally allowed to stay on school grounds until a permanent solution was found.

But now they had to wait until Friday, and April had been spending most of the past few days crying. Despite their awful response, she still cared deeply about her family and being rejected so thoroughly had been a stab to the heart. Kat, Millie and Violet had taken turns making sure she was okay, making sure she was washed and dressed and dragging her to classes. After two days, she seemed to be doing a little bit better, and while Kat would've liked to claim partial credit, it was pretty clear that sleeping in the same bed as Violet had given her something tangible, literally and metaphorically, to hold on to. But Millie and Kat had decided that she needed something extra. They were barely adults, but being on her own was forcing April to be an adult very quickly, and the others had decided that normalcy and companionship away from her parents' home was an option. Violet, who saw her parents only from time to time, agreed.

So they'd scheduled a double date. "It'll be like starting a new tradition", Kat had said optimistically. "Just the four of us, we go get dinner, watch a movie, have drinks after. It'll be cozy and you'll be among friends." Millie had squeezed her hand, and the smile she'd shot Kat had made the girl blush. "A-and besides, you need to get away from campus. We have the rest of the afternoon off. So why don't we take you two shopping and then grab something to eat?" April wasn't so sure, but even she'd agreed that there was nothing wrong with *trying* to feel better, and upgrading her wardrobe wasn't the worst prospect in the world.

Just then Violet had come back in wearing a towel. After a month, she'd figured out how to tie it together so it didn't slip off. She'd gotten dressed behind a room divider and came out from behind it looking suitably ruffled, wearing a summer dress that made her look like a snack. Kat had shot her a smile that was full of sharp teeth. "And then *you* can give me back my bras, Vi." Vi looked a little guilty, but she met Kat's gaze and stuck out her tongue. She'd gotten some hand-me-down clothes from her mom and some emergency underwear, but half of it had been on loan from Kat.

"You offered, nerd."

"How dare you use the truth against me", Kat returned. She saw April smile in the corner of her eye. It was good to see her perk up a bit, and it wasn't long before they'd managed to get her dressed enough to go shopping. Once she was out of the building and off-campus, her mood seemed to brighten up even more.

They sat in pairs on the bus. Kat, as ever, was still a little overwhelmed by the fact that Millie was holding her hand. Her hands were warm, but dry and soft. They shared a quick kiss, Millie nudging Kat's nose with her own a few times, playfully teasing her. Kat resisted making a noise of protest in public, but only barely. After a few seconds, she nodded at Violet and April. They'd be on the bus for another twenty minutes, and April had already fallen asleep with her head on Violet's shoulder.

"I'm... proud", Millie whispered. Kat understood why. They'd found themselves and each other in a very short amount of time, and they'd both...Kat couldn't find the right word. 'Relaxed' wasn't quite right, because they still had a lot to worry about, especially now. But where they'd both been not only wound tight but had seemingly experienced the world almost reluctantly, there now seemed to be things, positive things, small things, that could cheer them up and make them smile. They both smiled now, and it was beautiful to see.

"I am too", she answered Millie. "They look good together. If a bit clumsy." She grinned. They'd done a lot of practicing, but the girls still occasionally knocked their heads together when they both went in for a kiss. They'd also tried to tease each other once in a while, and it had always gone hilariously.

April had made a mistake on an exercise the day before while studying, and, as she was leaving the room to get snacks from the kitchen, Violet had blown her a kiss. "That's why you're the cute one", she'd blurted out as she'd rounded the corner. A few seconds later, Violet had stormed back in, murmuring "Sorry!" over and over again while kissing April's entire face. It was cute seeing them try to figure out how to relationship, but for the most part, they were being honest with each other about their feelings, considering each other, and being affectionate. All things considered, Kat thought, they were doing very well. She looked at Millie. Millie looked back.

"I love you", she said.

"I love you too", Millie returned.

"I think we look pretty good together too", Kat said. For a second, she was confused, because Millie didn't answer. Instead, she went through her purse, and retrieved her blackest lipstick and applied it. When she finally made eye contact with Kat again, it was that sideways glance that made Kat feel like she was being preyed on by a large cat.

"Babe", Millie said, and kissed Kat softly and deeply, passing on the lipstick. She pulled away and cleaned up the smudges around the now-stunned Kat's lips with a finger. "We look amazing", she concluded. Kat squeaked in unison with the brakes on the bus, and Millie took her hand to guide her out the door. Violet and April followed closely behind them, also holding hands. Kat would probably have found the whole thing adorable, but her brain was still stuck booting up.

Shopping for clothes was something Kat had often found bothersome, and when Millie had first come to her with the idea, she'd scrunched up her face in a way that Millie had called adorable. It had earned Kat a kiss on the nose too, and while she'd been blushing, Millie had explained to her that some things were a lot more fun if you took your time and, more importantly, your partner and friends. "You can sit on the floor of your living room, roll an egg back and forth with your friends and it'll still be fun", she'd said. Kat couldn't bring up any objections to that. And, after all, this was more for April's benefit than her own.

And they had a pretty good time, all things considered. Initially, April had some trouble relaxing. She'd clearly been stuck in her own head, but after a while of actually getting to be excited about dresses, she had slowly started to thaw somewhat. She and Violet had been hesitant to spend money, for obvious reasons, but this had all been in the name of cheering up, so Kat and Millie fronted some of the cost for essentials and for the most part, they had enjoyed playing dress-up in stores until dirty looks by the staff had forced them to move on.

Kat had been happy to see her best friend try out new styles. When she'd first been transformed, Violet's style would have been most easily described as post-bargain-bin hoodiecore. But now that she'd had a chance to try new things, it was clear that she was beginning to veer more towards a sundresses-and-big-hats aesthetic, the effective cuteness of which was exacerbated by the fact that she was shorter than the others. By contrast, April had gravitated towards a combo of jeans and jackets that seemed to play off Millie a little bit, though nobody had mentioned it. Kat and Millie had shared a meaningful glance, but the advantage of meaningful glances, Kat had learned, was that they were easily disguised as gay ones.

After a lot of shopping, banter, teasing and gay nonsense, they sat down in the food court, putting down a few bags. They weren't full, but they did have some clothes Millie and Kat had insisted on buying for the two girls, and some accessories they'd tried to secretly buy for each other.

"How are you feeling?" Millie said with a smile, managing to look cool and relaxed even when eating a burger, a feat not many people could pull off. Millie and Violet looked at each other and the smile that bounced between them warmed Kat's heart.

"I needed this", April confessed, and she took Violet's hand. "Thank you. All of you." She made a show of looking around the table.

"Of course", Kat said, and she knew she looked silly, trying to smile reassuringly while shoving too many fries in her mouth at the same time. She was pretty sure it got the message across, regardless. "This was more fun than I thought it was going to be, I'll be honest."

"Told you", Millie said, giving her a greasy kiss on the cheek. "There's going to be time to worry tomorrow. But if we can't do anything today, we might as well make the best of the time we have, right?"

"Thank you, Gandalf", Violet said, bowing her head dramatically, and Millie threw a curly fry at her.

They decided against catching a movie at the mall theater. April had clearly ran out of energy to be around random strangers, and Kat squeezed Millie's arm to draw her attention to the slowly deflating girl. Kat and Millie both pretended to be tired, and after a few minutes they were on the bus again on their way to campus, sitting a little closer together. It meant not being able to be as openly affectionate —Kat didn't want to make the others uncomfortable—but it did allow her to make sure the other two were okay. Violet and April hadn't been out in the open as much in the past month, and though they'd clearly managed to focus on getting to be girls-out-shopping-together, that clearly wasn't going to last forever. April was already dozed off on Violet's shoulder again, and Violet needed the occasional nudge against the knee not to lose herself in her own head.

Kat and Millie dragged the two depleted girls to their dorm room. The summer sun had gently begun to set, and Violet and April were both almost sleepwalking, and needed the occasional steering to keep from bumping into benches or other students. No school-wide announcement had been made—and if it was up to Ms. Lopez, none would be. The fact that the two girls had decided to *stay* girls after the end of the bet had spread throughout the school. Other than the occasional glare from some misguided, exclusionary soul, their fellow students had picked up what they'd been putting down. They were much more accepting of someone trying to find themselves than they'd been about two loud-mouths trying to one-up each other. Especially if those two were also very cute together.

Kat briefly considered putting on a movie in the room, but decided against it. She wanted to be around April and Violet, making sure they were okay, that they didn't spiral into self-doubt and fears, but they were so tired they were most likely to pass out as soon as their heads hit the pillow, so she and Millie got them to the dorm room and then quietly closed the door behind them as they left.

Millie took Kat's hand as they walked across the now-mostly-quiet campus. Kat looked at her. Millie looked back. "I had a great time today", Kat said. "I was wondering if you'd like to...Y'know..."

Millie smiled warmly and squeezed her hand. "I'd love to", she said, and they didn't say anything more as they walked to Kat's room.

13

Even More Confidential

"So, Miss Mayweather", Maria Lopez said, going over the daunting stack of papers in front of her, "good news, bad news or great news?" The little office was sweltering, and the open windows did very little to reduce the heat. Kat wondered briefly why Maria didn't have a fan, but then she realized that, considering the loose stacks of paper all over the place, it would probably do more harm than good. So they sat in uncomfortable sweatiness while Maria prepared several pages of legal documents.

"Uhh, bad news first? How much worse can it get?" April said, and Kat wanted to wap her over the head with a rolled-up magazine. Of all the things to say...She briefly considered rapping her knuckles on the girl's skull, because it might as well have been made of wood.

Maria seemed mildly amused. "Luckily for you, Miss Mayweather, not that much", she said, and took a drink from a glass that had up to a minute ago contained several cubes of ice. They'd never stood a chance, melting visibly within seconds. "You're already eighteen. Here, that's the age of majority. From a legal standpoint, you're an adult. That means that, legally, we can't force your parents to take you back in." She looked at a piece of paper that, even from where Kat was standing, was covered with horrifying legalese. She'd seen tomes of infernal Knowledge That Mankind Was Not Meant To Lay Its Eyes Upon and she'd been less scared of that than she was of the language used by lawyers.

"I mean, I'm the one who ran away..." April mumbled. Violet squeezed her hand and smiled reassuringly at her. They held the eye contact for a second longer than was strictly necessary, but Maria didn't seem to notice.

"The problem, Miss Mayweather, is that we've already received word from your parents. You don't appear to have a home to go back to, and you would have had to have to figure out income, insurance and taxes in a very short amount of time..." She looked at April over her glasses. "I believe our curriculum is lacking in teaching you a lot of the minutiae of finances, so that would've been...problematic."

"Would have been?" Millie asked before April could start freaking out. Kat had noticed it too. Maria Lopez didn't seem like she was very worried, but, all things considered, she looked like she wasn't the type of person who was ever worried. Counselor Lopez, Kat surmised, probably only had two speeds: Motherly Compassion and Seething Rage Against the Ineffective Machine.

"Yes. That's the good news. Or the great news, depending on your point of view, I suppose. I don't presume you've heard of Maslow's pyramid of...never mind." She pushed her glasses back up the bridge of her nose. "Not important. Point is is that I wasn't just *saying* things when I mentioned that this school had systems in place to care for our...vulnerable students. While, again, we can't pay for any medical treatments, we have the facilities to house you." April blinked a few times, trying to parse what was being said. "It won't be...I know who your parents are, Miss Mayweather. Unless they have a change of heart—which, considering the way they spoke on the phone, I can not guarantee in any way, shape or form—you will not have the life you had. But we can offer you shelter, and cover your tuition fees until you graduate." She paused and chewed on a pen. "And if you are willing to sign a few documents confirming your status as a protected minority, that would include your graduate degree", she said, a little more thoughtfully. "Though we might have to move you around a little bit. I'll have to figure that bit out. 'Hem.'

April squirmed a bit in her seat. "This is a lot to take in..." she said, and Millie put a hand on her shoulder. April relaxed a bit and scooted almost imperceptibly closer to Violet. Kat was glad the girl didn't have to do all this alone. She was clearly overwhelmed.

"I know, Miss Mayweather. But I feel it's important you have this information first. Lastly, you'll be mostly tax-exempt as you're still a student, and we can cover your bare-minimum insurance, but if you want, well, medical treatment to transition or, god forbid, a car, that's not something we can cover. Medical bills in this bloody country are too high as it is; it would bankrupt the school if we did." Ms. Lopez put the papers down. "But, well, long story short is that you can stay here, Miss Mayweather. You'll be assigned a dorm room, and you can keep going to classes. If your parents change their mind, you'll be free to go home, but if not..." She looked at April and smiled. "You're not alone. There's more people in your corner than you think."

"Thank you", April said softly. She was clearly a little overwhelmed, but Kat hoped April was experiencing at least a bit of the relief she herself felt. This was, all things considered, wonderful news. She hadn't expected April's parents to retroactively kick her out, but from what she'd been told, it hadn't been entirely out of character.

"I have *more* good news, and a lot less technical", Maria continued. "It concerns the both of you." She looked at Violet and April. "Well, all of you, really." She got up from behind her desk, taking a moment to pick up several binders, which she tucked under her arm. She waved at the others to make their way to the door. "Walk with me." Kat and Millie shuffled out of the door first, the logistics of the tiny office demanding that they leave the room in a strict order or risk getting stuck against the furniture. Once they were out in the hall, Maria led the way. "So, unofficially—that means you keep this to yourself until things have proceeded—Professor Dykstra is getting a full reprimand. Including a possible loss of tenure. We've cross-referenced what you've all reported with other students and complaints from teachers, and his behavior has been..." She paused for a moment as some students passed in the other direction, then continued, walking the four girls towards the campus gardens. "..unacceptable", she finished.

Kat and Millie looked at each other with excitement. It wasn't often that they had an adult they could rely on, but it seemed that, for once, there was someone they could not only trust but who was on their side, wanting to help, and able to do so. Even if Dykstra wouldn't be fired, he'd be a lot more hesitant to pull his shenanigans if his position was threatened. It meant that they wouldn't have to sit idly by while their friends were being treated like dirt.

"Don't pass this information on to anyone else", Maria said. "This is strictly confidential, but I thought it'd be something that might lift your spirits come Monday." She smiled again at the girls as she reached the entrance to the botanical gardens. "Now, the final bit of news", she continued as she entered the gardens, "is...how do I put this...even more confidential? Just...don't mention it to people and you'll be fine. It's not...illegal, as such..." she said, and Kat couldn't help but feel that the definition of 'legal' was probably being stretched to its absolute limits here.

"Hey, girls." Ms. Richards waved as the girls entered the gardens. She was standing by a desk covered in what appeared to be lab equipment and various potatoes and yams. Kat frowned. A lot of the material was stuff she'd been considering using, if she'd ever settled on a thesis subject. April and Violet looked up at Ms. Lopez with confusion, but returned the botany professor's enthusiastic greeting.

Maria just smiled. "It'll make sense in a moment", she said, and guided the four of them to the table. "So..." she looked at Violet and April, "we cannot cover your medical bills. That much is clear. The treatment you need is expensive." The two girls nodded. That much had been made abundantly clear.

Ms. Richards was the one to continue. "The medication you need isn't...*too* hard to replicate through botanical witchcraft", the teacher said, choosing her words carefully. "It's just...illegal for institutions like ours to do so." She paused and looked at Ms. Lopez, who nodded. "The patents are protected fiercely, but..." She looked at the two girls and then at Kat. "If, say, a student wanted to...*study* this field...and maybe do a thesis on the subject...she might be allowed to do so." Ms. Richards chewed her tongue. "If that student had *willing* volunteers to test the efficacy of the *practical* application of her thesis statement, *legally* that would be allowed, if this was not, well, *advertised*." She enunciated one in every few words carefully, raising her eyebrows for emphasis, making eye contact with Kat that was as subtle as a brick to the face, but Kat was already picking up what was being put down. April and Violet's sharp intake of breath indicated that they weren't as slow on the uptake when it came to this as they had been about each other. "That is, you know, *if* such a student, who is gifted in the field of botany and just so *happens* to want to pursue a thesis with regards to *Solanum Tuberosum*, which *appears* to be the most likely candidate when it comes to this...*experiment*." Ms. Richards' eyebrows danced up and down with so much vigor Kat was worried briefly they'd bounce off her forehead.

Kat looked up at Ms. Lopez, who nodded, carefully. "All of this", Maria said, "is purely hypothetical, of course. Officially, this hypothetical student could do a thesis on ethical creation of cheap medication with a physical trial to go with it. Unofficially, of course", she looked at all of them and smiled, "I think you can help your friends. I *must* stress that you keep this quiet. We're...exploring the boundaries of legality, here, but as long as you don't advertise, sell or involve the faculty beyond checking up with Ms. Richards, who will, of course, monitor your progress to keep the experiment *safe*, well..." She looked at Violet and April. "I think we have found ourselves a loophole."

Kat had the feeling that the rules here weren't so much being bent as straight up tied, twisted and knotted into a pretzel of Olympic proportions, but she also trusted Ms. Lopez not to put them in danger. And if she could combine her academic ambitions and help her friends with what was obviously one of the most important changes in their lives, she wasn't going to hesitate for a moment. She tried, for a moment, to find a way to sound as diplomatic and careful as the adults had been. If this situation was really as precarious as they'd made it seem, she felt she was probably going to have to get used to using doublespeak. "Ms. Richards", she said, "I think I have an idea of what I want to do my thesis on."

Ms. Richards grinned from ear to ear, and Maria Lopez chuckled softly. "Now, I have no idea what you're talking about", Maria said, "but just in case it becomes relevant, I have several waivers right here." She put a binder on the table, in between three kinds of potatoes. "If *anyone* would be willing to sign up for a kind of trial of sorts that involved your thesis, that would be the exact kind of document you would have to sign with them. You know, hypothetically." She pulled her hand away from the binder quickly, partly because Violet and April looked at it the same way cats look at their food bowl being filled with fresh fish.

Millie wrapped her arms around Kat's neck and kissed her cheek. "I'm proud of you, baby", she whispered, and Kat tried not to blush. Everyone else pretended not to see her go beet red.

Violet turned to the teachers and then finally to Kat. There were tears in her eyes, and April was looking pretty sniffly too. "This is real?" she asked. Ms. Lopez nodded. Violet took Kat's hand and looked at her friend. Her cheeks were lined with wet streaks. "Thank you, Kat."

"Of course, you dumbass", Kat said. "You're my best friend."

Ms. Lopez and Ms. Richards scooted them out of the botanical gardens, legal papers stuffed in Kat's arms, and they spent the rest of the day signing documents, crying at each other and cuddling the two girls who, despite everything else, had hope for the future.

14

New Beginnings

It had been several weeks. Kat's head rested on Millie's lap, trying not to doze off, but it was hard work. She wanted to be as in the moment as possible, enjoying Millie's fingers running through her hair, but she was just so dang comfy. Millie was reading a book that hovered just in front of her, more for the exercise than because she was really interested in the material. Kat liked to think she was also a pretty good distraction. She felt sleep creep up on her again so she opened her eyes, looking up at Millie's face, scrunched up as the girl tried to keep the book afloat.

"You're pretty when you're concentrating, you know", Kat said with uncharacteristic confidence. They'd been together for some time now, but she still had trouble staying calm when she was trying to compliment Millie. Drowsy calm probably contributed to her ability to fawn over her girlfriend with a 'straight' face. Millie's concentration was broken, and the book dropped down. Kat didn't even blink as her girlfriend caught the book in mid-air. She had full confidence in Millie.

"Babe", Millie said with an exasperated smile, "that could have hurt you." She wiped some hair out of Kat's face, and kissed her forehead.

"Are you saying I got to you?" Kat grinned. It earned her another small kiss, this time on the nose.

"I'm saying you're a distraction and you know it."

"Distraction and proud", Kat smiled. They both smiled contentedly for a moment. Kat saw Millie look up and followed her gaze to the two girls approaching them. Hand in hand, Violet and April were talking to each other about this and that, their bare feet in the warm grass as they twirled around each other.

Over the past few weeks, their 'volunteer work' for Kat's thesis had been a tremendous success. It had taken Kat some time, with Ms. Richards' help, to get the dosage exactly safe and right, but it had been only a matter of days. Now, Violet and April were forced to eat some combination of yams and potatoes twice a day, but Kat didn't think she'd ever heard either of them complain for even a second.

Sure, the four of them still took turns casting the transfiguration charms on Violet and April once a week. But in those few moments where the spell wore off they had already seen immense progress. Where normal medication could take weeks or months to effect change, they'd seen distinct progress, months' worth, within the first week. The difference between their transfigured selves and the person underneath was getting smaller every week, and it had reflected on the two girls in the best way. Kat had never seen either of them so happy, so joyful. It warmed her heart.

It had been reflected in their grades, too. Sure, they spent about half the time still keeping the spells intact, but they were just so much *happier* it was easier for both of them to focus on studying. It didn't hurt that they made pretty good study buddies, and spending all of their time together made it inevitable that they'd spend at least *some* of their time studying together.

April's parents hadn't come around. Well, not *really*. They'd extended a poisoned olive branch. "We love you", her mom had said. "Please come home. Why are you hurting us like this?" And then her father had appended the "And give up this whole 'girl' business. We miss our Roland", cementing April's decision. With help from the others, April had made a very clear and concise statement in a letter.

"Whether I'm in your life or not is up to you. But only as April. Take it or leave it." April had been worried it was too curt, too aggressive, but Millie had insisted, that they'd keep asking for more, that they'd keep moving goal posts under the guise of love and family until she'd be forced to pretend to be a boy for the rest of her life. That had made sense to April, who was more than a little familiar with her family's insistence on conflict-averse optics. April's mother seemed to be somewhat willing to reach out. The last time they'd had contact, it had been Millie, going over to the Mayweathers' house to get some of April's stuff. According to her, the parents barely spoke to each other, and if they did it was snide and cutting, so perhaps April could hope to one day be reunited with *some* of her family.

Kat smiled at the two. April was showing Violet how her new summer dress went spinny, and Violet was just staring dreamily. It was hard to tell from this distance, but Kat was pretty sure she saw the short girl bite her lip. "Useless", she sighed. Mille chuckled. "You know", Kat said, "I've been wondering."

"Hmm?" Millie returned her hand to softly running her fingers through Kat's hair as they both looked at their friends.

"Why did they *both* have a sword summon prepared?" Kat asked. "It's a hard spell, not one I'd imagined either of them knowing, let alone be able to perform."

"I think it's a lesbian thing", Millie mused, softly running her nails over the top of Kat's scalp, eliciting an approving purr.

"That doesn't make sense", Kat mumbled. "Why would that be—"

"Do you know it?" Millie interrupted.

"Well, yes, but that's not...oh..."

Millie chuckled again. "Maybe we should spar some time." She looked down at her girlfriend. "I'm sure you'd look really hot with a sword."

"H—hey", Kat stammered. "I don't even know how to fight well! I just thought it was...you know...You'd just win anyway!"

Millie kissed her forehead again. "Are you implying that you wouldn't want me to win, Kitkat? That you don't want to be forced to your knees, your chin tilted up by the point of a sword?"

"Hhh", Kat said eloquently. "Maybe. No. Yes. Shut up."

"Good girl", Millie said and kissed her softly on the lips, silencing any upcoming protest. Kat's grumble turned into a soft contented moan.

"That's gay", Violet said happily as she and April joined the other two beneath the tree. They had finally made it all the way over, despite constantly being distracted by each other.

"Your face is gay", Kat mumbled from under Millie.

"Hell yeah, it is", April said and kissed Violet on the cheek. Millie finally sat upright again, leaving a slightly disheveled Kat to smile contentedly up at the sky. "How's things?" April asked.

"Pretty good", Millie said. "I'm still figuring out where I wanna go with my studies, to be honest." She levitated the book up. "I'm considering taking some Warlock courses next year. See what fits. Kat's been doing great, though."

"Full marks!" Kat added, raising a triumphant fist. "With bonus credit for 'exemplary behavior in ensuring the safety and wellbeing of a fellow student or students.'That means you two." She grinned at Violet and April, who grinned back. "If I can actually publish what we're doing here, I could probably pursue this indefinitely."

"That's awesome, Kat", Violet said with a warm smile. "I'm glad you've finally stopped pretending you don't like being up to your elbows in filth. It really is your calling."

"Fuck off", Kat said lovingly. "What about you two?"

"Taking things one day at a time", Violet said, leaning back in the grass. "We both have a lot of stuff to figure out. Who do we want to be, all that stuff." Kat raised an eyebrow. Violet looked at her girlfriend, and for a split second her brain was lost in that pink gay fog that made her eyes go glassy before she continued. "I can't speak for April, but I never figured I'd be a girl. That I'd *get* to be one. So now that I'm here I have no clue where to go from here. I know I love April", she said, and April rewarded her candor with a little kiss, "and I know I'm a girl. But beyond that? Not. A. Clue."

"Same", April said, the quintessence of eloquence. "Besides, we've got some big stuff coming up.

"Right", Millie said. "I heard they're finally giving you a room of your own?" Millie was referring to the fact that April, for the past two weeks, had been staying in a smaller, provisional dorm room in the girl's dormitories. While it had apparently been very validating, and she'd gotten lots of tips on how to do her make-up, the room was very small, especially if she was going to be living in it for the foreseeable future. Considering her financial situation, the school had elected to present her with one of the larger rooms, in the same building as Violet's.

"Yeah", April nodded. "Across the hall from Vi."

"Pfft", Kat scoffed. "Why even give you an extra room, then? Like you'll be spending *any* time not wrapped around each other over summer break."

"Listen", Violet said. "I... "She paused. "I was really hoping a valid counterpoint would present itself by the time I got to the end of this sentence, but nah, I got nothing."

"I'm not complaining", April shrugged. "Can't hurt to have my own living area, right?"

"I was just teasing", Kat said. "Everyone needs space. It's healthy." She took a breath. "Still nothing from your parents on that front? I can imagine it's kinda hard to go from, well, where you came from to pretty much nothing."

April shrugged again. "I'm eating a lot more rice and pasta, that's for sure. But I'm okay, really. I don't need much. Dad always complained I wasn't ambitious enough." She chewed her lip for a moment. "I don't know, if I'm honest. Haven't heard from Mom and Dad, but my brother says they're fighting a lot." Thankfully, April's brother had been mostly accepting of her, after a while, and while he hadn't burned all his social credit with them by actively fighting them, he had been trying to advocate for her to some extent. "I don't know what the future looks like, but...I don't know. It's not like I don't have family anymore. Mom and Dad...they're...It's complicated." April smiled softly as Violet squeezed her hand. "I'll figure it out."

"We'll figure it out", Millie said reassuringly. Kat nodded and Violet made an affirmative noise. April hadn't been wrong, Kat realized. She might have been referring to her brother or another relative who had accepted her. Kat had the sneaking suspicion, however, that to April, the three people who sat here in the grass with her were the people closest to her. It had been a hell of a journey for Violet and April, and Kat was secretly proud of them both. Violet had gone from a vindictive little turd of a best friend to a young woman who was trying to figure herself out, find her place in the world. April had been a mostly self-absorbed privileged rich kid, and now she was a proud young woman who was embracing her newfound family, and her identity with it.

Kat hadn't known Millie, of course, not really, but she was immensely grateful that Violet and April had picked their fight. Kat had never been this content before. She spent a lot of time with Millie—and a lot of time at her house—figuring out what it meant to be in a relationship with a girl, and so far she'd loved every moment of it, and Millie had made it abundantly clear that the feeling was mutual.

Her biggest issue right now was the fact that Violet and April were both incredibly cute. Her best friend had always been a distraction, but now Violet had the power to make her blush. She had diligently pushed down any and all feelings in that direction because of everything going on, but it was really hard to ignore the eye contact that *felt* like it was meaningful and held just a little too long, and again she tried not to think about it. Those were feelings for *later*. Right now, she wanted to enjoy the moment without making things even more complicated.

"I love you", Kat said happily, and made sure to look all three of them in the eye. She got three 'I love you's and a kiss back, and she smiled in the summer sun. It had been a very strange few months, but she wouldn't have changed it for the world. In each other, she waxed poetically to herself, they'd found a small family, and it was one she was going to treasure for a long time.

Book III

Part-Time Monster

1

Time Out

"Oh my god Damien, you fuck!"

"Should have been quicker, bish", Damien grinned. He frantically worked the controller, not really caring about his own score anymore and straining his hands to steal every kill he could. It was driving Alli crazy, and that was fine by him.

"You just have the best character, ass." Allyssa's pretend anger was marred strongly by the big goofy grin on her face. She'd missed hanging out with her best friend. Damien had been a lot more difficult to get a hold of since his sixteenth birthday, two years ago. She tried not to think too much about the illness that kept him at home three days a week. Allyssa hoped it wasn't something too terrible, but he didn't like talking about it. He'd reassured her it wasn't terminal and he wasn't like, in too much pain or anything. But he needed to be home on time and manage his energy levels. Days like this had become a rarity, but it felt good to game like they did in the good old days. Even if he was insufferable, playing as the Amazon Barbarian character, the most mobile character in the game.

"You're just jealous because you have to play as a dude", Damien shot back. He wasn't wrong, she thought. The Amazon was the only aesthetically pleasant character, and she couldn't blame him for preferring to play as her. She'd never tell him, but she was scared for his illness, which is why she always let him pick first. She wanted him to be comfortable and happy for the time they could spend together. She tried to keep the smile on her face as she found herself consistently outmaneuvered by Damien's tall and muscular avatar.

"I just didn't want to see you constantly get your ass handed to you, Damien."

"Yuh-huh. Keep telling yourself that. I could run circles around y—"

The alarm cut through his sentence, through the room, like a razor. The rest of his sentence hung bisected in his throat. Damien immediately became sullen. He paused the game and put his controller down on the sofa, and turned off the alarm on his phone.

"I have to go."

Allyssa felt her heart break, seeing her friend like this. He looked so hurt, so sad, and she couldn't do much. But she could do this. She put her own controller down, and hugged him. He stood there stiffly. She tried not to cry, to be strong for him. He'd never returned her hugs, but he'd made it clear he enjoyed them. Still, she found it hard not to be a little hurt that he seemed...repulsed? Damien had been touch-averse since they'd met in grade school, but he'd found himself comfortable enough for these small displays of affection, even if he couldn't return them.

"Come back soon, okay? We've got loads of time now."

He nodded mechanically. She unwrapped herself from around him and sniffed. Damnit.

"I'll see you soon, Alli. I really have to get home."

She nodded again. He lived close enough, so he could visit whenever. The opposite wasn't an option, sadly. His parents didn't allow visitors for fear of contaminating his sterile area, he'd said. Besides, during his treatments he wasn't worth much, apparently. Couldn't see visitors, let alone entertain them.

She walked him to the door and gave him another small hug before he left. She'd see him again soon, she told herself. But maybe one of these days was going to be the last time. That thought hit her like a truck when she'd finally, after watching him walk his way down the driveway, closed the door. She went up to her mother's study and walked in.

"Damien go home?"

Allyssa nodded.

"Are you okay?"

Allyssa shook her head.

"Do you want a hug?"

Nodnod.

Her mom hugged her while she cried.

"Your friend is going to be okay, sweetie. Just give it time, okay? Medicine has gotten really good these days, I'm sure it'll be okay, okay?"

Sniff.

Nod.

"Now go take a shower or something, you smell like gamer."

Allyssa stuck out her tongue and went to her room. She worried about Damien for the rest of the day.

—

Damien got home and put his backpack by the door, went into the kitchen and took a candy bar from the cupboard. His mom was reading the paper at the living room table. She was still in her work clothes, the black turtleneck and jacket in stark contrast to her crimson skin.

"Hey hun, did you have fun at the Wright's?"

"Uh-huh", Damien chewed as he pulled his sweater and then his shirt over his head. His mother didn't react to his disrobing, just drinking her tea and reading.

"What time is it, Damien?"

"Five minutes to, mom."

"Alright, be with you in just a second, dear."

"Cool, thanks."

"Don't forget to draw the circle, hun."

Damien unrolled a yoga mat in the middle of the living room floor.

"Already on it, mom."

He grabbed a piece of chalk off the mantelpiece and drew a circle on the mat, then a pentagram inside it. He was just about done with the writing on the outside of it when his mother joined him, and looked at his handiwork.

"Nicely done, Damien. You're getting really good at this."

"It *has* been two years, mom."

"Fair enough. Are you ready?"

"As I'll ever be."

He knelt down in the circle and took a few deep breaths. His mother knelt down in front of him and made herself comfortable, tucking a strand of hair behind one of her horns, then looked at the clock.

"Ten seconds. Deep breath, dear", she said, as she turned around to give him some privacy. Damien wasn't ready, was never ready, but he didn't have a choice in the matter. He took a deep breath, and almost filled his lungs to capacity when it started.

He felt as though his entire body was on fire, and his skin became a deep red, with a purple hue. The pressure in his forehead was focused on two points, and he knew that the nubs there would soon break skin and begin to extrude, two horns pushing and curving elegantly backwards and upwards. One thing he was grateful for was the painlessness of the process. That was something, at least. He felt the bones in his face shift and grind as it restructured itself, the muscle and tissue changing to make him almost unrecognizable, framed as it was by rapidly growing long, black hair.

That done, the rest of the transformation began to take hold all at once. With a terrible tearing sound that he'd gotten used to over the years, two large feathered wings erupted from his back, feathers a deep red. His spine made clicking sounds as it shortened slightly, and he felt the familiar weight of the expansion on his chest, combined with the consistent loss of muscle tissue as he grew smaller, but far from weaker. His hips widened and he was glad for the sweatpants he'd been wearing. At first he'd made the mistake of wearing jeans and he'd nearly peed himself the first time. Finally, a long tail grew from his lower back, ending in a black, heart-shaped tip. And it immediately swished left to right as he flexed and stretched both it and his wings.

He panted. The process was exhausting and he was glad his mother was there, in case he felt like collapsing. When it looked like he didn't, she handed him a shirt over her shoulder, which he gratefully pulled over his head.

"Ready", he said with a voice that was distinctly different than it had been before. It wasn't high-pitched, but it had a husky, seductive quality to it he'd never been able to shake. His mom turned around, and he could tell she was trying not to fawn over his transformation too much.

When he'd become sixteen, the transformations had started. At first, without the protection of the infernal circle, he'd caught fire and nearly burned his room down. After that, his mother had made sure to be there every time. She'd feared this might happen, she'd told him. His father had died before he'd been born, and when he was born she'd been under the impression he'd be a simple human child. But on his sixteenth birthday, his infernal heritage had shown itself, and his mother had been delighted, and then intensely disappointed when she'd found the new form to be temporary.

"I don't know, "she'd said, "why you keep switching back and forth between human boy and demon girl."

"I hate it", Damien had cried, and she'd consoled him, making a mental note not to be too happy about this transformation, and do some research into this at a later date. In the meantime, until they had it figured out and he could control his transformation, he needed to stay at home whenever the transformation hit. Humans got really weird about stuff like this.

Damien got up and stretched, his wings shivering a little bit.

"Still no breakthrough on why I'm like this?" His mom got up and put her hands on her hips.

"Still nothing. Nothing you can think of?"

He shook his head. "Not really."

"All right, you can go...do whatever, alright? I'll clean this up."

"Thanks, mom", he said, and went up to his room, careful so as not to bump his wings into the doorposts.

He hated his transformation. He hated that it kept him from living a normal life. He hated how it made him feel different and other. He hated that it kept him from his best friend, who could never see him like this, would never accept him.

But most importantly, he hated that it wasn't permanent. That it didn't let him live one way or the other. He hated how it made him feel fake. Like he was wearing a girl costume that was taken away just before dawn. He flopped down on his bed face-first, and drifted off to sleep.

2

Backstroke of the West

Damien woke up to the sound of the alarm. Bleary-eyed, he picked up his phone. It was that time already, huh? He got and de-frumpled his right wing, stretching, and accidentally punched himself in the boob. "Ow", he said, eloquently.

His demonic form hadn't been as developed two years ago, but apparently it was doing a lot of growth in a short time, and he wasn't exactly used to a lot of it yet. In fact, at first the changes had been almost exclusively demonic. Skin, horns and wings. But after a few months the voice had begun to undo everything puberty and testosterone had done to it, and his hands and feet had begun to slim out, his face had become rounder and softer, his lips fuller. He'd had no idea what was going on. At least he knew when it was going to happen, thanks to his mother.

She knew an app-developer from the Old Country, who had synched up a bracelet to his phone, so that he always got a notification when a change was about to happen. It was something? At least the return transformation wasn't explosive, and didn't require any preparation. He sat on the edge of his bed, browsing on his phone, until the transformation kicked in. His wings folded in on themselves. His horns retreated. His skin regained its fleshy tone. His chest became flat again, his shoulders widened. He took off the shirt with the open back, and swapped it out with one with the Amazon from his favorite game series on the front, who was looking heroically at something undefined in the distance.

He pulled on some longer slacks. He didn't like sleeping with anything more than boxers when he was in demon form. For one thing, he liked the way his smoother legs felt against each other. In human form, the fuzziness of his legs wasn't nearly as appealing. He got up and went downstairs, made himself some breakfast. He needed calories after transforming back, and he was going to get them. As he walked into the kitchen, he passed his mother who was reading something on her tablet, cup of coffee in the other hand, and a bagel in her mouth.

"Morning mom."

"Mffrnng Bmmn."

"Mom."

She swallowed.

"Good morning, Damien", she grinned with a husky singsong voice. Hecate was in her human form, ready for work. She'd given up demonning a long time ago, it had never been her thing. But making the world a slightly worse place, that was simply in her nature, in her very existence. Which is why she worked in advertising, and she was damn good at it.

"You're up early."

"Yeah, the change happened half an hour ago. The agreement says I have to go."

Today was going to be an actual school day, and he was going to have to actually participate. And it was P.E. Fan-freaking-tastic. He *hated* swimming.

Well, that wasn't exactly true. He used to love swimming. But he hated doing it around other people. He felt at home in the water, but ever since his "condition" had started acting up he'd been uncomfortable with how exposed he felt when he was swimming. As if his bare chest was something to cover up. It didn't make any sense, but not a lot of this did yet.

"You gonna be okay, hun?" His mother did her best not to look too concerned. If it was up to her, she'd homeschool him, but she was too busy. Even as a demon, being a single mom was hard work. School, he'd argued to her, was a good way to keep him occupied, teach him useful stuff. Even if it wasn't a full education, it was good for him to get out of the house. He didn't mention that it allowed him to hang out with Allyssa.

He nodded. "Yeah. I should have a couple of hours at least." She took a bite of bagel-with-coffee, and chewed thoughtfully while looking at him.

"Not what I asked, Damien."

He scratched the back of his head. "I...Yeah. It's still not easy, mom. I just...I don't know why I can't change at will. Or why I keep getting... "He looked down at his chest with a mix of terror and confusion. Why did it bother him so much? He'd seen his demon form in the mirror so many times and it was disjointing. The body itself didn't bother him, it was quite...well...*very* attractive. But the suddenness, the fact that it wasn't a choice to be this, that was weirdly difficult. Like, he wouldn't...*mind* being able to turn into a demon at will. Or even a demon girl. But being yanked back and forth like that? He was a guy, and being forced to look like *that* made him very uncomfortable. Guys weren't supposed to look like that, for obvious reasons.

Besides.

What would Allyssa think?

He shook his head. "I'll be okay, mom. Maybe I just need more time? I think school might do me good. Even if it's P.E." Hecate downed the rest of her coffee and put the cup down on the kitchen counter, then ruffled his hair.

"If you say so, tater tot. You call if something's up, all right?"

"Promise."

"Atta boy."

"*Mom*."

"Right, right, you're not a little boy anymore." She grabbed her coat and bag, and gave him a little kiss on the forehead. "Try not to let stuff get to you, okay?"

"k"

She stood in the doorway for just a second and looked wistfully at her child, then sighed. Damien knew she wished she could do more. She already did so much, honestly. He should tell her that more.

—

Allyssa rolled out of bed with a thud and an "oof" She stretched and admired her *adorable* pajamas in the full length mirror of her closet. Today was P.E., she knew. Deep breaths. She opened the door to her bedroom at the same time as her sister Dani did in the opposing room. They made eye contact for one terrible, horrible second, then both broke into a sprint, all elbows and shoves. Finally, she dodged a tackle and slammed the bathroom door closed behind her and locked it. Danielle made a frustrated noise on the other side while Allyssa triumphantly brushed her teeth. After approximately five seconds, there was a knocking on the door.

"Hey, hurry up."

"Waid youh tuhh, Hew."

"What?" She spat out her toothpaste.

"Wait your turn, Mel."

"Uuuuugh, Lissie, pleeeaaaase, I have to use the bathroom."

"There's a bathroom downstairs." She looked in the mirror at her pajama'd visage. "I'm not wearing clothes, you can't come in."

"Fiiiiiiiine."

A moment of peace and respite as she washed up and got dressed. Finally done, she opened the bathroom door and Dani gave a little curtsy as she walked past, which Alli returned gracefully. Then Dani stuck out her tongue and went inside.

Allyssa went downstairs to see her mom and dad having breakfast. The twins, Melanie and Kat, were scarfing down their Official Off-Brand Breakfast Cereal, and her oldest sister Amy was just finishing her morning tea. The adults gave her a cheerful "good morning" or a little wave as she sat down and grabbed herself an apple.

"No breakfast today?" Her mom asked with a raised eyebrow.

"B.E.", Allyssa responded with her mouth full. She had difficulty moving much when she'd just eaten.

"Fair enough."

They sat in silence for a bit, and Danielle joined them for some buttered toast. Breakfast was a little ritual at the Wright residence. A moment of shared togetherness before the day. Since not everyone came home at the same time, this shared meal every day was important. Even if the twins didn't quite realize why yet. After what she hoped was the proper amount of time, Alli asked if she could be excused and ran up to her room. P.E. was stressful as all hell to begin with, for all the obvious reasons. But she *also* knew that her best friend was going to be there, and she was simultaneously excited to see them again and absolutely terrified for Him. The physical exercise couldn't be easy, with their illness.

She sighed, grabbed her backpack, and did a quick lap of the breakfast table, giving everyone a hug and a peck on the cheek, then ran out the door.

—

Damien surfaced and took a deep breath, just in time to hear the whistle that marked the end of class. Going under water again, he lazily swam to the edge of the pool. He was able to hold his breath for minutes — a demonic little trait he'd ever let his classmates or his teacher know about — and he liked spending time under water. He was invisible there, and it was quiet. He launched himself up on the edge of the pool and took off his goggles. His teacher waved him over.

"You did well today, Damien. Your technique needs some work, but considering the classes you missed...If you keep this up, you've got a passing grade." Damien nodded.

"Thank you, Sir", he said, smiling slightly. He slinked away backwards before the swimming instructor could attempt something like a pat on the shoulder, and made his way to the private changing stalls. It was one of the perks of his condition, and one he happily used. Let them think whatever, he could change in peace and quiet. On his way there, he looked around and just saw Allyssa go into the girl's locker room with the others. He wasn't brave enough to wave. She was, and tipped an invisible hat at him. He grinned back sheepishly, and got his stuff from his locker. His backpack was vibrating aggressively.

Oh no. He fished inside it frantically, until he managed to retrieve his phone. Five alerts. The last one seven minutes ago. "Alert", it said. "Ten minutes remaining."

Fuck. No. Fuck.

He rushed over to the private changing stalls and threw his stuff in a corner, then rooted around in his backpack, and retrieved a pack of emergency chalk, and frantically drew a circle on the ground. His hands were shaking. Fuck, he'd missed the alarms while he was in the water. The armband normally vibrated but he'd turned that feature off (he'd had a good reason at the time but he couldn't for the life of him remember what it *was*) and now he'd missed all the useful alerts. He was panicking. The circle and the pentagram were far from perfect, but they'd have to do.

He knelt down in the circle and managed to get a quarter of a breath in when the transformation hit. The protection circle was imperfect, and the transformation was not pleasant. It hurt, his skin burned. But it helped. He was *fairly* certain he wasn't going to burst into flame and set off the fire alarm. But as his skin reddened and his horns started to grow, thinking became really hard. His head felt like it was going to explode. He lost track of time, until he heard the voice of the P.E. teacher.

"Damien, are you okay?"

Oh, Fuck.

"Uh...Sir, I think my uh... "He winced, trying not to sound too pained. "I think my uh...I think my illness is...hng...is kicking in."

"Do we need to notify your mother?" The voice was filled with genuine concern.

"I uh...I'll call her myself, thank you. But I...I don't think I'll be able to join the class on the way back to school, ah, sir."

"You're sure, son?"

"Yes, sir. Thank you."

Footsteps walked away from the changing stall. He breathed a sigh of relief, and then a sigh of pain when his wings ripped themselves from his shoulder blades and unfurled, feathers and all. He'd call his mother when the transformation was complete. An emergency had happened before, though not like...like this. Hecate would come and get him with an old oversized parka, cover his face with a breathing mask to cover up his red skin, and the tail could be tucked into a pair of pants. But he couldn't leave on his own. He felt his face change, much more painful than the day before, and the headache became almost unbearable.

"Hey Damien? Are you in there?"

Oh no.

"I just...didn't see you leave with the others."

Please no.

"Mister Reeves said you had a flareup and that your mom was coming to pick you up."

Not her.

"Are you gonna be okay?"

He couldn't answer. He didn't trust his voice to sound right. His transformation was coming to its end and he sat there, a daemonette in full glory. He couldn't speak, and tears rolled down his crimson cheeks when he heard her voice, more and more scared, in pain. He wished he could talk to her. Tell her it was okay. He heard her sit down against the door, and just sat there, kneeling, looking at the spot where she'd be sitting.

"I'm just...I'm really worried about you, Damien."

He breathed a deep sigh and wiped his tears away. He could only hope she'd leave soon. Maybe she'd believe he was unable to speak.

"I don't want to lose you, okay? You're my best friend."

"You too", Damien whispered softly, and placed a hand against the stall door.

It would have been a meaningful and powerful moment for both of them, if it hadn't been for cheap engineering. The soft pressure of Damien's hand against the door clicked the latch out of the lock and the door swung open inwards. Allyssa fell backwards with a yelp and her head landed on Damien's bright red thighs. She looked up at...someone who looked like her friend. But bright red. And what looked like black eyeliner. And a slightly rounder face. And horns. And uh...Alli glanced upwards at Damien's chest. If things had been different, she'd have been aggressively aware of just how *gay* she was. But even with her head on someone's thighs with two perfect breasts metaphorically staring her right back in the face, she could only focus on one thing. This (beautiful? gorgeous?) creature was undoubtedly her childhood friend.

"Damien?!"

"Hi", he squeaked.

3

Red In The Face

Allyssa walked out of the changing rooms chatting to her girl friends, making their way to the exit. The guys joined them after, and Alli craned her neck to look for Damien. Couldn't find him, just the swim coach looking somewhat perturbed, coming from the private stalls. She scurried over to him.

"Sir, is Damien okay?"

"I...He's going to wait here for his mother to come pick him up."

"It's his..." The coach nodded quietly. Allyssa chewed her lip.

"I know his mom well. Is it okay if I stay here? I have no classes after this."

The coach looked at his watch and sighed with relief. He wasn't in the mood for a lawsuit primer, but apparently they'd just hit four o'clock. Technically, she was allowed to leave.

"I don't see why not, Allyssa." He looked over his shoulder. "Your friend is going to be okay." She looked towards the private stalls.

"So everyone keeps telling me." He sighed. This was above his pay-grade. He scratched his neck, and made his way to the rest of the group with an apologetic smile.

Allyssa sat down on a chair in the lobby. Kicked her feet. Looked at the clock and followed the second hand with her head until her neck wouldn't turn that way, and realized the woman at the desk was giving her the side-eye. Alli sighed and got up, and made her way to the private stalls. "Waiting on a friend", she reassured the woman in passing, and scuffled off, hoping that would be enough not to get her stopped. Allyssa did *not* have the patience to sit in a lobby while her friend might be in pain. After four, the pool was pretty much deserted on a monday, and she only heard sounds coming from one of the stalls. Doing a quick count, she realized that was definitely the one Damien was in. She put her hand against the stall door.

"Hey Damien? Are you in there?"

No answer, just a slight gasp. She feared he was in pain and gritted her teeth. She'd never seen him in the middle of an attack, and she could only hope she was in the right space to help him through this.

"I just...didn't see you leave with the others."

She hoped to elicit some response from him. She vaguely remembered being told to 'keep them talking' when people were in a lot of pain. Or was that people who were wounded? Or for panic attacks? Fuck, this was not the time to forget every single thing she'd ever been told. She was scared for her friend and it was getting a little difficult to think clearly. She licked her dry lips and tried again.

"Mister Reeves said you had a flareup and that your mom was coming to pick you up."

That wasn't it. Just statements weren't going to cut it, were they? She needed to connect with him, right? That was it. Give him something to hold on to. If this was his illness flaring up, he'd need to know that someone was here for him.

"Are you gonna be okay?"

Still no answer. A stabbing pain in her chest accompanied really bad intrusive thinking. She leaned against the door and felt her legs give out, and she plopped down, gently bonked her head against the barrier between them. He needed to know someone cared. That she was here and that he wasn't alone. He must be so scared, she thought.

"I'm just...I'm really worried about you, Damien."

She heard a deep sigh and some rustling. Good, at least he wasn't unconscious or something. She heard a sniff. He'd been crying. She put a hand over her eyes, as if to keep her own tears inside. Her friend was in pain and she couldn't do anything. Couldn't even see him. Couldn't hold him. She didn't even dare tell him things were going to be okay because she had no idea if they did. But maybe that didn't matter? Maybe he just needed to hear support?

"I don't want to lose you, okay? You're my best friend."

A moment of silence, and then, ever so gently, she heard a response.

"You too", a voice on the other side of the door said. It was Damien's, but much softer than she'd ever heard it. It had a silky quality to it she couldn't quite pin down. She didn't have the time to try, anyway, because just like that, the door she'd been leaning against fired open and she fell backwards. Instead of her head hitting the tile floor, it bounced off something soft. Something she realized must be thighs, because she was most definitely observing the world from a girl's lap all of a sudden.

A red girl. Like, *red*-red. A girl with horns and long, black hair. A girl with an almost perfect face, as if sculpted to be both powerful and seductive. It was accented by meticulous make-up. It was the exact kind of girl Allyssa would fawn over in secret when she'd come across its image online. You know, if it wasn't for the fact that she was quite *obviously* some kind of demon. The red eyes and red skin and horns gave that away. And...were those wings she could see over the girl's shoulders?

The girl looked absolutely mortified, had no idea what had just happened. She was also entirely topless and it was almost enough to distract Allyssa from just *how much* this daemonette looked like...

"Damien?"

"Hi", the cute demon girl said. The voice was seductive. Not so much in intonation, as it was almost...by design? In one word, she felt herself drawn to it, almost, as if the girl's lips had been invitingly covered with honey.

Allyssa didn't know what to say. Could barely speak, her head was swimming. That might have been the fall backwards. Might have been. She was almost scared to move. And not entirely in the mood to move, she didn't get many opportunities to rest her head on a cute girl's thighs. But if this was her friend then maybe they weren't a girl's thighs? Or maybe her friend wasn't...Hold up.

"*Damien?!*"

"Yeah."

"What's going on?"

Damien looked sheepish. Neither of them dared move, as if to break some kind of spell. Allyssa thought she was dreaming, unaware that Damien was mostly terrified she'd start screaming. He was both very close and very off the mark. Allyssa was feeling many things, but horror or fear were not any of them. Damien swallowed.

"This...is my condition..."

"You turn into a hot demon girl??"

"Yeah, I d— wait, hot?"

"That's not what I...listen..." Allyssa took a deep breath and closed her eyes. Then she reached up with both hands and grabbed Damien by the horns and yanked him down until they were eye to eye. "*I thought you were dying, you ass!*"

"I'msorryI'msorryI'msorry", Damien stammered. Allyssa was *really* close to his face all of a sudden, and he'd never really been held by his horns before. A lot was happening really fast and his breath was caught in his throat. Allyssa let him go and sat up, closing the stall door so as not to alert the woman at the front desk.

"What the fuck, Damien? Is Damien even your name? Is this your real form? Are you like, a real devil? Were you a girl this whole time?!" Damien stammered and tried to cover up his chest. Allyssa had made an admirable effort not to let her eyes wander but it was *really hard*. The girl in front of her was one-hundred percent her type. Despite...who was she kidding, the horns only amplified the image.

"I'm...I...Listen...I gotta...My mom's gotta pick me up...I can't go out looking like this..." Allyssa giggled, pushing down a wave of hysteria that was threatening to overtake her.

"Yeah, I can't imagine you'd make it past the front desk with your tits out."

"Alli! Please!"

She took a deep breath and tried to calm down.

"What is going on, Damien?" He took his shirt and tried to cover his chest with it. He didn't have any with him that would accommodate his wings, so this would have to do. It wasn't perfect.

"I'm...Ever since my 16th birthday, this just...happens sometimes. It's random, but I usually know in advance."

"Your mom knows?"

"Yeah, she's...like this."

"What, like she turns into a girl?"

"No, I mean, demon."

"Oh fuhhh—..." Alli panted. "You've actually gone and said it. So this isn't like, a weird disease, you're just gonna straight up go 'yo I'm a demon and so is my mom' Fuck."

"Sorry?"

Deep breaths. Deeeeep breaths.

"Call your mom first. I don't want to do this in a changing stall."

Damien nodded, and did as requested.

"Yeah. No, I didn't get the alerts in time. Yeah, across the park. Okay. Thanks, mom."

He put the phone away.

"Ten minutes."

"I have questions." He sighed and slumped down a bit."

"Hit me."

"Devils are real?"

"Yup. Angels too."

"So like, what, y'all try to steal souls?"

"Nah, apparently that whole thing is over. My mom's retired, just lives as a human now."

"What do you mean 'that whole thing' is over?"

"Yeah, like the whole clash between upstairs and downstairs. They settled their differences and now neither side really cares anymore?"

"O-kay. Big theological minefield there. I'm gonna leave that right there for now. You said your mom is like you?"

"Well, sort of. She's like, a full-on demon so she can change at will. It's not like with me. I'm half human."

"Is that why it just happens randomly?"

"Yeah."

"No idea why? Seems kind of odd."

"Yup. There's like, a stress thing? Maybe? But like, yesterday, at your place, I wasn't particularly stressed out."

"Weird."

"You're telling me."

"So like, do you have any abilities? Set stuff on fire or fly or whatever?"

"Mom says they won't manifest until I 'stabilize.' That there's too much turmoil."

Allyssa cocked her head and looked at the frazzled demon girl that had been her best friend. That was still her best friend, she corrected. Shit, that was probably important to mention.

"Listen, Damien…"

"Yeah?"

"I just…You're still my friend, right?"

"I…I mean…you're not, like…scared?"

"Oh my god. You ass. Yes, of course I'm scared. I'm scared for you. You're my best friend and I'm not going to lose you. No matter what you look like. Not even if you're like…"

"Demon? Infernal?" Not the words she would have chosen. The ones on the tip of her tongue were closer to 'blindingly attractive.' But she wasn't gonna say that *now.* She nodded.

"I'm not giving up on you. Ever." Damien cried and then did something she'd never expected. He lunged forward and hugged her. *Damien* hugged *her.* She sat shocked for a moment, then returned the gesture. The demon's skin was very warm to the touch, but not unpleasantly so. Damien also smelled slightly of fire and cinnamon. It was pleasant, but it didn't last forever.

"Thank you", Damien sniffled, and after a brief moment scrambled to cover up his chest again.

"That didn't bother you?" He shook his head.

"I'm more comfortable with…touch, like this."

"Oh?"

He shrugged. "Don't know why."

"Fair enough. I had one more question."

"Shoot."

"Are you a girl turning into a boy or a boy turning into a girl?" Damien opened his mouth several times like a goldfish suddenly fished out of its bowl, staring into the eyes of a cartoon cat. He stammered for a few seconds, but no real words were coming out. Then, there was a knock on the stall door.

"Damien, hun, are you in there?" Hecate said. Without thinking, Allyssa opened the door for her friend's mom. Hecate's eyes grew wide at the sight of Allyssa, and then looked at the crumpled form of her child. "Well then." She crossed her arms and looked at them both. "Looks like we have some talking to do."

Allyssa looked back at Damien, who was still seemingly in shock. "I think we might do, Miss H."

4

Be The Change

The way to the car was quiet. Hecate had brought Damien a fitting shirt, then covered him with the oversized parka. His horns made it look like he had a weird head, but it wasn't obvious from a distance. His tail was tucked into sweatpants. Finally, another blanket over his shoulders, to disguise the folded wings underneath, some surgical gloves, and finally a full-cover face mask. When they guided him past the front desk, his mom gave a well-practiced "I'm sorry but I also wasn't going to not do this" nod to the front desk, and went out the front door before questions could be asked. Once they were all seated in the car, Damien took off his mask, but he didn't say anything, frowning to himself.

Allyssa was worried. She kept looking at her friend, but didn't want to force anything. She buckled up and looked up, and found her gaze caught in Hecate's in the rear-view mirror. The woman was distinctly human. Her eyes were distinctly *not*. They were yellow in the same sense that the inside of a furnace was yellow, all accents of red and glowy bits that reminded Allyssa of something primal inside of her, the monkey part of her brain that told her *fire dangerous*.

"So." Hecate's words cut through the air. Allyssa could have sworn she felt a soft whiff past her ear and her split ends being cut off by half an inch. The air in the car became a little drier, and a little hotter. She swallowed and tried to make herself small. "Allyssa."

"y", she said.

"Do you have anything to say?" Allyssa felt an overwhelming urge to apologize. Like she'd been called to the principal's office, about to receive the scolding of a lifetime. She hadn't done anything wrong, had she? She hadn't really considered what it had meant that "Mrs. H" was also a demoness. Daemonette? When Damien had told her she was retired Allyssa had kind of assumed she was just...a mom...worried...about...oh dear.

"I...Not, really, ma'am."

"Don't you 'Ma'am' me, Allyssa Wright, what did you see or think you saw?"

"Your so—..." She paused. Damien had never answered the question. "My friend had an illness flare-up."

"Don't play stupid with me, Allyssa, you're not good at it." The fact that she had, perhaps unintentionally, received a compliment, caught her off-guard.

"Your child is a demon girl? I think? And you're one too? But y'all are good people, so I don't..." Hecate reacted by sighing and hitting the steering wheel gently with her forehead, honking the horn softly.

"Damieeeeeeen, you told her." Damien still didn't say anything.

"I'm sorry, Miss H."

Another dejected sigh. "You're...fine, Allyssa. I just..."

"Miss H?"

Another toot from the horn. "This was easier in the old country." Allyssa considered for a second, which turned into a horrified minute, about 'the old country' "Could have just eaten you back then." There was a slight...something in her voice.

"Are you...joking, Miss H?"

Hecate sat up straight, and finally turned towards them. "You're fine, Allyssa. Nobody's going to hurt you." It was hard to really believe her, gently glowing eyes and all. But her face radiated Big Mom Energy, and she seemed to genuinely want to put her at ease. "Just...we just want to live in peace and quiet. We're not hurting anyone, Allyssa..."

Allyssa nodded. "Ma'a— Miss H. Damien is my best friend. And you've always been very good to me. I'm not...I'm not going to just out someone like that." Hecate smiled slightly, but the relief was visible in her eyes. It was like someone had turned down the furnace in her eyes.

"You're a good kid, Allyssa. I'm glad Damien has a friend like you." She turned back to the steering wheel, and started the car. She was focused on driving and Allyssa took a deep breath. That had gone...as okay as could have been expected, surely? Her first ever talk with Demon Mom had been intense. She'd met Hecate before, of course, back when hanging out at Damien's house had been a more regular occurrence. Mrs H. had always been a gracious host, ready with a smile, and had often invited her to stay for dinner. Allyssa had always suspected it was because her son didn't have many friends.

Alli turned to Damien. "Are you okay?" She resisted the urge to reach out and touch her friend. Damien looked...small, despite the fact that he took up considerably more space with his wings behind him. She wanted to hug him, hold him and tell him it was okay, that it was all going to be okay, even if she still didn't really understand what 'it' was. She just wanted to help her friend.

He shook his head slightly, and finally spoke. "I don't know. I'm just...After what you asked..."

In the driver's seat, Hecate's ears perked up. "Asked what?" Allyssa asked obliviously.

"I just... when we get home, all right? You...you're staying for a bit, right? You're not..." Allyssa finally gave in and reached over and took Damien's hand in her own. Again she was surprised at how warm, how soft his skin was. *Just like a girl,* she thought with a smile, and then tried to push that thought out of her head.

"I'm not going anywhere." She paused for a second. "Ass."

"What did I do?" She squeezed his hand, then nudged his shoulder.

"That's for thinking I'd leave you alone."

"I..." He started tearing up again.

"No no no! I didn't mean..."

"It's a good cry, Alli. Thank you."

He was the one to reach out, now, and grab her hand in his. They sat like that in silence until the car pulled up to the driveway. They hurried Damien inside. The blinds were closed to the front lawn anyway, and their backyard had very high hedges. Once comfortably inside, Damien took off the layers of material that hid him from the world. Allyssa finally saw him in this form in his full glory. His wings stretched out, gorgeous red feathers on red wings spreading ten feet wide. The muscles in his upper back were defined, presumably, she thought while trying not to stare at what she realized was a girl's naked back, to support his wings. They rippled under his soft red skin as he flexed and stretched his wings. He turned around and caught her looking, and blushed. That was new. Damien blushed a deep purple.

She turned her head in embarrassment. "You wanted to talk? About something I asked?"

Damien folded his wings up quickly and became small again. She rushed over and gave him the hug she'd been wanting to since they'd been in the car, then took his hand and guided him to the sofa. He sat down, knees together, hugging himself. *Not a cute girl not a cute girl not a cute girl not a cute girl,* Allyssa repeated to herself. She had to keep forcing herself to remember that this was her friend Damien.

"You asked me if I was..."

"Hmm?"

"If I was a girl who turned into a boy or a boy who turned into a girl."

"Yeah. Was that...Was that not okay?"

"No! I mean, yes, it's okay. I just...I've never thought about it like that. I thought...You remember me before my sixteenth birthday. I'd always been a guy."

"I mean...I just thought that this..." she waved noncommittally at his new form. "Was who you really were."

"You.. Oh you...I mean I..."

"Are you okay, Damien?"

"I just...What if I'm not a guy who turns into a girl sometimes?"

Hecate was listening intently from the kitchen. She'd shifted into most of her non-human shape. Horns, long black talons, black sclera, and the same deep red skin her child had. Allyssa was possibly getting the breakthrough when it came to Damien that she'd never been able to achieve.

"What does that mean for you?"

"What if I'm...I think I look like this whenever...when I think I might want to... "

Damien sighed.

"I didn't want to be this because I didn't want to lose you and I thought that I had to be..."

"Hey..."

Damien looked up at Allyssa, who smiled and put a hand on his back "Be you. I'm not going anywhere. Not unless you ask me to leave."

"I would never..."

"Then I won't."

"So you're okay with me looking like..."

"...a girl?"

"...a demon?"

They looked each other in the eye. Allyssa had no idea, of course, that the same kind of explosions that were going off in her chest were happening in her friend's. "I'm okay with both."

"Can I be both?"

"Do you want to be?"

5

Taken In Vain

Hecate had been 'cooking' She'd been attempting various culinary tasks, all of which she'd failed at because she was completely and utterly incapable of focusing on the task at hand. Allyssa, bless her heart, was getting through to Damien in a way that Hecate had never figured out how to. She'd tried to give him the comfort to find himself, but it seemed that Allyssa was just asking the question Hecate had never considered.

Damien looked at Allyssa. She was...so good. She smiled at him like she always had but it felt different. He'd had feelings for her, what felt like a lifetime ago. From what social clues he'd been able to pick up on, she'd even reciprocated them, but it had never felt *right*. The way he saw it, Allyssa deserved girls. Girls were soft and good and pretty. He didn't like the thought of inserting a guy into that equation. It felt wrong. Gross, even. He tried not to think that way too often, because it felt like he wasn't being accepting of Allyssa's bisexuality.

But something in their dynamic had shifted. Well, "something" Obviously it was him. He'd changed, in a sense.

"Do you want to be?"

Fuck, what a question. He didn't know what to say. He wouldn't be opposed. And he *knew* what he'd look like. He looked like it almost half the time anyway. In fact, he looked like it almost every time he was aware of how much he didn't want to look like a lanky, angular guy. But on the other hand, most people had issues with their body. He wasn't any different from them, was he? Aside from the demon girl transformations and the demon mom thing, anyway. He couldn't imagine that most people didn't have a deep revulsion to body hair, the way it made something as simple as legs look completely repulsive, especially the muscled, no-soft-edge-in-sight version that men got. He found it hard to believe that not everyone felt a discomfort when looking in the mirror, beyond a kind of resigned acceptance. What he wanted didn't seem to come into it.

Allyssa saw the internal conflict on his face. "Okay, let me ask it differently. If you could just...pick a shape, and you would've always looked like that, and I would always have known you that way and we still would've met and I'd still be sitting here with you, which one would you pick?"

Her hand on his was so soft and cool. It was hard to think. He looked in her eyes and his limbic system did a backflip. 'More of this' it said. It was painful, in the best way. He found it hard to breathe.

"I think, if I have you here, Alli, then I think I would like to just..."

Pause. Around the corner, Hecate had given up on the onions, on all pretense of food preparation, and was just standing perfectly rigid, ears perked up, holding her breath, unwilling to miss a single word.

"I think I'd like to be a girl, Allyssa."

Allyssa took her friend's hand in her own and squeezed it gently, and smiled with so much love and caring it was already starting to make them both cry.

"Looks like you already are."

"I...I don't..."

"Hey, you're okay. Just breathe."

"O— Okay."

"I have a question. Just a small one."

Nod.

"Do you want me to keep calling you Damien?"

"I...I'm not sure? I know it means a lot to my mom. She's a traditionalist. But it doesn't...Does it fit? Me, I mean?"

Allyssa cocked her head.

"I'm not sure. I think that's mostly up to you, right?"

"Yeah but...what would you call me?"

Allyssa looked at the red skin, the searing eyes.

"You know, I'd call you Red, but that nickname is already taken, I think. How about..."

She chewed her lips thoughtfully for a second, then perked up.

"Oh! How about Scarlett?! It's a cute name, and it fits you!" She bounced in her seat a little bit. Even if they didn't find it fitting, disagreeing with someone so adorable would be nigh-on impossible. But there wasn't even the desire to do so.

"I like that. I think I like that a lot."

"Nice to meet you, Scarlett!"

"Nice to meet you too, Allyssa", Scarlett said, with a smile and a tear.

"You get to be a girl!"

"Oh my god."

"Right? I promise you, it's awesome. Do you...have any clothes that fit you? Like this?" Scarlett shook no.

"I've just been cutting the upper backs off shirts and wearing sweatpants, honestly." Allyssa got even bouncier.

"I can borrow you some clothes, and maybe we can go shopping together!"

"I...I'd like that, Alli, but can we take this, like, slow? I'm still coming to terms with some stuff over here."

"Oh, yeah. Dang, yeah, of course. Uh...Oh, do you want to like, change pronouns?"

"Uh, sure", she said.

"Cool! I just...Yeah. You're cool, Scarlett. Can I tell you something?"

Scarlett scooted her legs underneath herself. It was like a small switch had flipped in her head, that told her that femininity was allowed now. From one moment to one a little later they had flipped from 'two life long friends' to 'two girls' *I get to be a girl*, Scarlett thought. *Holy shit.* She tried not to be too aware of just how close she was sitting to Allyssa. Their knees were practically touching, and Alli still had her hand on Scarlett's.

"Of course!"

"I'm just...I'm really okay with you. Like this. I really like looking at you."

Scarlett tried to say words. She'd done so many times in her life and she was surprised to find that it wasn't happening right now. All that came out of her mouth were an assortment of shocked and surprised noises. Allyssa giggled.

"I just mean...You're a lot cuter like this. Like kinda hot."

Allyssa thought she was helping. She really wasn't. Scarlett was short-circuiting like a toaster in a microwave in a bathtub, and it was Allyssa's fault, who had no idea of what she was doing to her friend.

"It's just...the horns? The red skin? It looks really good on you. Like *really* good. wink. "She had said the word wink out loud without actually winking.

"Alli!" Scarlett squeaked.

"What?"

"Aaa!"

"What?!"

"You can't say that kind of stuff! I'm still trying to figure this stuff out and...I mean, I still like girls..."

"Haha, me too", Allyssa said like an idiot. Then the words dawned on her.

"Haha", Scarlett said. Allyssa sat frozen. She looked at their hands. Then at Scarlett. Looked her in the eyes. Scarlett looked a little panicked, panting with her mouth open. Allyssa stared intently at the parted dark red lips, couldn't tear her eyes away.

"Oh", she mumbled quietly.

"Yeah", Scarlett mumbled in response. The person sitting opposite wasn't Damien. Not anymore, not really. Scarlett was Scarlett now, and Scarlett was gay as Hell. Scarlett did not have any trouble imagining Allyssa dating, say, a girl. Hypothetically. Hypothetically a girl with red skin.

"Alli?"

"Yeah?"

"Do you really like the way I look like this?"

"I really do."

"Even the horns?"

"Especially the horns. Wait, I'm...I'm sorry. I didn't mean to yank them that hard earlier...Does it hurt?"

"No, they're just...sensitive."

"Oh fuck I'm so sorry!"

"No! No, they're eh...good sensitive. I didn't...mind. That you grabbed them."

"Oh...I...Oh!"

"Yeah..."

Hecate had slinked out of the kitchen. The conversation had turned from 'my baby is discovering herself'to 'my baby is *discovering* herself' and despite her heritage, this wasn't actually something Hecate had even the least bit of interest in hearing anything about.

"Is this...why you never...did anything, Scarlett?"

"I just...didn't want to say anything. Not as a boy. Or a guy. Whatever. It didn't feel right."

"Well yeah, that's because you were a girl."

"I...You're right."

"Do you want to..."

" "

"Just...see what...it would be like?"

"Like what would be like?"

Allyssa was staring intensely at Scarlett. Her eyes darted all over her friend's face, her friend she didn't have to think of as a guy anymore, her friend who liked her back, her friend who was suddenly a really cute girl, her *really hot demon girlfriend.*

"Like... "She squeezed Scarlett's hand. "Being a girl..."

"But I'm already..."

"...with another girl."

"I...I'm...oh..."

"Would you..."

"I mean if you..."

Allyssa squeezed her eyes shut. She seemed frustrated for a second, and for a scared moment Scarlett was afraid she'd done something wrong, that she'd upset Alli somehow.

Then, Scarlett stopped being afraid, as Allyssa reached forward, grabbed Scarlett by both horns, and pulled her friend's blood red lips against her own.

179

6

Over Dinner

"So…you can feel this?"

Allyssa ran a finger over the ridged black-and-red horn in her lap, Scarlett purring gently. As an answer, Scarlett's eyes rolled up into her head and she bit her lip. Her left leg twitched a little bit, and she folded her other one over it.

"Oh."

"Y—…Yeah."

"That good?"

"M-hm."

"Do you want me to stop?"

Scarlett made a soft sound in protest. Her wings were splayed across the couch and Allyssa was gently admiring, well, all of her. After they'd kissed, they'd both scooted backwards from each other, as if unbelieving of what had just happened. They'd looked at each other and smiled, both seemingly terrified that the other might scream, or possibly dissolve in a puff of smoke. Scarlett had bit her lip, nodding. Alli had sighed and launched herself at Scarlett again. Their first kiss had been a soft, transcendental affair, blowing their minds into galaxies and burning stars. This was different. Scarlett got to kiss a girl *as a girl* and it was everything she could ever remember wanting. Both careful, unsure, it had been awkward and amazing, Scarlett's hands uncertainly on Allyssa's hips. Alli's arms around Scarlett's neck.

They'd stayed like that for a few minutes, until Allyssa'd had to come up for air, slumping back into the sofa breathlessly. Scarlett had just sat there and stared. Allyssa panting wasn't something she'd been opposed to seeing, but the situation had been kind of absurd. And they'd laughed. Giggled, at how long it had taken them to get, well, here, at how long they'd been running circles around each other.

But most of all, they'd laughed out of sheer delight that they had found each other.

Scarlett had slumped over and gently put her head on Allyssa's lap, so as not to stab her with the horns.

"Do you want me to stop?"

"Nnnooo. But it eh…"

"Are you uncomfortable?"

"I'm um…too comfortable."

"I…Uh. Oh…I mean…is that…a bad…"

"It's a good thing, Alli. But I want to take things slow. If…If that's okay?"

"Of course! Yes, of course, yes, sorry!"

"You don't have to say sorry, Alli. You didn't do anything wrong."

"All right. Thank you."

They sat in content silence for a bit.

"Are you okay?"

"Hell yeah. It's just a bit much to take in, you know?"

"You're one to talk. My childhood friend is a demon girl."

"Hey! *I'm a girl.* That trumps your thing."

"I've got one better!"

"Oh?"

"My childhood crush likes me back."

"Asfgj", Scarlett said, and covered her blushing face with her hands.

"Struck a nerve?"

"Aaa."

"Hey, assface."

"What?"

"I like you."

"Aaa!"

Allyssa nudged Scarlett.

"I like you too", Scarlett squeaked between her fingers.

"I know", Allyssa said, and kissed Scarlett on the forehead, who made a delighted high-pitched noise, muffled shortly after by Allyssa kissing her on the mouth again. More quiet sitting, this time slightly more involved as they lost themselves in each other again.

"How long did you know?" Scarlett looked up at Allyssa.

"Know what?"

"That you, you know, liked me."

"Gosh. Sixth grade? Maybe?"

"Shit."

"What?"

"Me too."

"Oh my god."

"Yeah."

Allyssa absent-mindedly ran a finger along one of Scarlett's horns. Scarlett squirmed, moaned, and Allyssa jerked her hand back. Her head was beet red. Scarlett was a deep purple. They avoided looking at each other, blushing and hiding smiles.

Hecate walked past the living room and saw her child smiling in a way they only ever really did when they were around Allyssa. She'd been rooting for those two since forever, and she was glad they'd finally found each other. Hesitant as she was to disturb them, she nevertheless walked into the room. Both of them turned their blushing heads lazily towards her.

"Food's going to be ready in a bit. You're free to join us, Allyssa, just call your parents."

Allyssa and Scarlett looked at each other with big, happy smiles, then Allyssa nodded. They slowly untangled themselves from each other, and Scarlett stretched her wings and Allyssa tried not to sigh wistfully as she saw Scarlett's well-defined shoulders flex powerfully, then scuttled off to call her mom. Scarlett joined her mom, once again attempting to cut an onion, in the kitchen.

"So...mom..."

"Yes, dear?" A long career of being infernal hellspawn was the only thing keeping Hecate's voice level. She was putting in a lot of effort not to sound too eager, like she hadn't heard most of their conversation earlier.

"I...I think I know why the changes have been happening." Hecate turned around, happily curious. This was news. "I think that.... Hm..."

"Take your time, hun."

"I think, every time I maybe like...thought about...wanting to be...." Hecate's eyes grew a little wider. It was taking every bit of self control not to whoop unceremoniously. "I think every time I like, consciously, wanted to be a girl...I was."

"So you're saying..."

"I think I want to stay like this, mom."

Hecate smiled proudly. "Then you can stay like this, hun." She opened her arms invitingly, and Scarlett stepped into them happily. "I heard your friend call you Scarlett..."

"Yeah. I like that better."

"I like it too, sweetie. I'm proud of you."

"Thanks mom."

They melted, for just a moment, into their very first mother-daughter hug. Hecate was proud, of course, that her daughter had found a way to be comfortable with her infernal heritage. But what really struck a chord in her chest was the fact that she'd found who she was as a person, that she'd realized she was a woman, and, maybe most of all, that she'd been comfortable enough to tell her mother about it. Hecate took a step back, smiled, and ruffled Scarlett's hair. It was a lot harder now that it was longer.

"I'm gonna get back to cooking sweetie. You see if your friend needs anything."

Just then, Allyssa walked into the kitchen. Hecate grabbed the kitchen knife as she turned around, was momentarily distracted by Allyssa walking in, bumped into the fridge, and found the blade shoved down to the hilt into her chest. They stood frozen there for a second.

"M—... mom?" Hecate stared at her hand on the knife with disbelief. Allyssa was frozen with shock.

Then, Hecate rolled her eyes. "Ugh, and I *just* got this shirt." She removed the knife with an annoyed glare, as if it had personally slighted her, and then rinsed it in the sink, talking to Scarlett and Allyssa over her shoulder. "I'm going to go upstairs and get changed and cleaned up. I'm so sorry about this. Why don't you guys order a pizza? I'm not going to get anything *done* today I can already *feel* it, anyway, I love you sweetie order me something with mushrooms..." Her voice trailed off as she made her way upstairs.

"Aaa?" Allyssa asked.

"Oh. Oh! Right!" Scarlett was quick to take Allyssa's hand in her own for reassurance. "My mom's fine. She's...a lot sturdier than normal people, Alli. Just a bit clumsy. Don't worry about it." She looked up in her mom's general direction. "She's fine."

"She stabbed herself in the chest, Scarlett!"

"Look, I can do it too if it helps? Do you want to—"

"I'm not going to stab you, you ass! I just...I had no idea your mom was so..."

"... weird?"

"Cool!"

"My mom isn't cool."

"She's a demon! Who shrugged off a knife to the chest like it was a blueberry jam stain!"

"I promise you she's a mom first."

"Fair. Valid. I guess." There was a bit of a pause as they just stood in the kitchen, holding hands. Alli pulled Scarlett in for a kiss. Neither could really get over just how *soft* the other was. Allyssa was the first to pull away, and bit her lip. "So...Pizza?"

"Yeah. Something with meat, please."

"Okay!" Allyssa practically skipped back into the living room, and Scarlett just stood there with eyes happily glazed over. Her mom was still upstairs, so she went up to make sure everything was okay. Quietly walking up, she heard her mom talking.

"...nally figured out what was happening."

Not one to pry but also not one to avoid a trope, Scarlett stood behind the corner and listened. Her mom was clearly talking to someone on the phone.

"Yeah. No. No, that's not...Nope. Yeah. It's Scarlett now. Yeah. Exactly. Yeah I hadn't considered that either. Yeah. I think that...Yeah. No, I think it's because we were too close, you know? Yeah. No, *she's* fine."

Something about the way her mom had said 'She' made Scarlett really happy. It was as if she'd just gently but sternly corrected someone.

"No. No I didn't. Remember her friend from school? Yeah, her. The Wright girl. She's the one who helped her...yeah. She was really good about it. And...Oh yeah, no, they're finally...Yup. Called it. You too, huh? Anyway, gotta get downstairs. Yeah. Bye. Okay. Bye. I love you too."

Scarlett realized the conversation was ending and she quickly and quietly shuffled down the stairs. She walked up behind Allyssa, wrapping her arms around her from behind, giving her little kisses on the back of the neck, until she turned around and they enjoyed some more gay.

Finally, her mom came back downstairs, at around the same time as the doorbell rang. Pizza was put on the table, and they enjoyed their meal in comfortable silence.

"So, Scarlett?" Her mom asked after washing down her last bite.

"Yeah, mom?"

"What are you going to do now if you change back?"

Scarlett froze mid-bite. She hadn't considered that. She thought that, now that she knew, she could just stay that way. Hadn't considered the possibility that, when the alarm went off again, she'd be turned back into that weird masculine shape. She didn't want to, *really* didn't want to go back. She was Scarlett, she couldn't go back to looking like...*him.* Tears began to well up in her eyes.

"Oh. Fuck."

7

Improvise. Adapt. Overcome.

Immediately, Allyssa scooted closer to Scarlett and put a hand on her back. "Hey, I'm here." She looked panicked at Hecate, who was just as frazzled as she was. Hecate was clearly somewhat mortified that she'd just upset her daughter with what she'd thought to be an innocuous question.

"We don't know what's going to happen, Scarlett. Don't...don't panic, okay?" Scarlett nodded, but the fact that tears were dripping onto her plate told them that it wasn't quite that easy. Allyssa pulled her close and kissed her softly on the side of the head.

"It's going to be okay, no matter what, okay? I'm going to be here for you. I have no idea how any of this stuff works, but we'll figure it out together." Hecate got up and joined them, kneeling down next to her daughter.

"Hey, it's entirely possible the changes won't happen anymore. You told me they happened when you wanted to be like this, right? So now that you're, you know, all girl, maybe you won't switch back." Scarlett sniffed and nodded again, and for a moment tried to be brave. It took her two seconds to fail and burst out crying again. This time, both Allyssa and Hecate hugged her.

"It's going to be okay", Allyssa whispered against her shoulder, over and over again. Hecate softly rubbed her back. "We're here. You're going to be okay." They were interrupted by the worst, most horrifying sound in the world.

Scarlett's phone gleefully beeped its alarm. "Five Minutes" the display said. Scarlett panicked, like a caged animal confronted with a predator. She pushed herself away from the table, tried to get away from the phone as best she could, trying not to scream.

"No no no no no!" She struggled against herself, against the arms of Allyssa and her mom, who both scrambled to get a hold of the situation. Allyssa frantically tried to turn off the alarm while Hecate tried to keep Scarlett from hurting herself, her wings thrashing against the furniture. Hecate took a step back and in an instant, her own wings had torn through the back of her shirt and she wrapped them protectively around Scarlett and Allyssa. Scarlett collapsed into a sobbing, whimpering mess, leaning against her mother, Allyssa wrapping both arms around her and holding her close.

The alarm began beeping again. "One minute." Hecate's left wing shot out and shattered the phone.

"I'll buy you a new one", she whispered. Scarlett curled up into a ball, inadvertently cocooning into her wings, with the two most important people in her life wrapped around her. They weren't going anywhere. She cried in deep, heaving breaths, until it was the only sound in the room.

Slowly, the horns protruding from the top of the ball of feathers began to withdraw. The feathers lost their deep red color as the wings began to retreat. The tail shrank away into nothing. Scarlett sobbed. Allyssa held her close, crying in sympathy and pain.

"I'll be here for you, no matter what, Scarlett. You're my...you."

The red tint of Scarlett's skin became the mundane human one. Her fingernails became soft pink instead of jet black. The transformation stopped in silence. The whole room held its breath. Then, carefully, Hecate retracted her wings and gently stroked Scarlett's hair. Scarlett's long, black hair. She looked at Allyssa, eyes wide in recognition.

"Hey, Scarlett, honey?"

Sad sounds.

"Hey, hun, open your eyes for a second? Try to take a deep breath for me."

Scarlett did as her mother told her. Took a deep, shuddering breath. Then another, a little more evenly. Then finally, a third, deep breath, that carried with it a feeling of...resolution.

Scarlett opened her eyes. Her hands had been clutched to her chest. She unclenched them, saw the marks her nails had dug into the palms of her hands. She also saw the thin, slender fingers. She unfurled herself, relaxed a bit as her long hair fell in front of her face, and she touched it like it was the first time she'd ever seen it. Touched her face. Looked at her hands, her arms, which were soft with only a barely noticeable hint of light fuzz. Paused for a moment, and grabbed her breasts. She looked up at Allyssa and Hecate.

The face that was looking at them, was familiar, even without the horns or the red skin. It was the face of Scarlett, a beautiful, eighteen year old girl, cheeks wet with tears, framed by beautiful black hair. She touched her own face again.

"Am...am I..."

"Hold on", Allyssa said, and fished her phone out of her pocket, and handed it to

Scarlett with the front-facing camera on. "Look." Scarlett looked at the girl on the phone, and tears ran down her face as she smiled.

"I get to..." Hecate and Allyssa held her again.

"You do."

"I get to be a girl, mom." She cried, happy tears this time.

Hecate gently nudged Allyssa away. "You'll get to dote over her in a second." She lifted Scarlett like she was nothing and carried her to the sofa. "The transformation can be exhausting. Especially when it comes to a new form. You sit with her, I'll go make some tea."

Allyssa sat down next to Scarlett, who scooted up against her and they nuzzled up against each other.

"I'm sorry."

"What are you sorry for?"

"Panicking over nothing..."

Allyssa gently bopped Scarlett's head, and then kissed her in the same spot. "Your panic was entirely valid and justified. I'd panic too."

"Okay." Sniff. "Thank you."

"Can I do anything to help?"

"Just...I get why you would. This is weird and scary. But...please don't leave?"

"Hey Scarlett?"

"Yeah?"

Allyssa kissed her. "I'm not going anywhere. In fact..."

"Thank you. What is it?"

"Do you want to be my girlfriend?"

Scarlett made affirmative girlfriend noises. She kissed Allyssa all over her face as they both giggled, then settled down again. Allyssa looked pensive after a moment. Raised eyebrows from Scarlett asked the question for her, and Allyssa responded.

"Why do you think this happened?"

"I don't know. All I could think about before it happened was that I just...I knew I wanted to be a girl. Even as a human."

"Do you think it's possible you just thought 'Want to be human girl' and that's what happened?"

Hecate set down two cups of tea in front of them, sat down on the coffee table, and took a sip of her tea. Scarlett did the same. Allyssa did too, and burned her tongue. She realized only after this that the other two probably weren't as bothered by the heat as she was, and she sheepishly blew on it. Hecate looked at her with amusement, then turned to Scarlett.

"That seems entirely possible. I switch between two forms all the time without really thinking, but it's all about intent."

"You think I can just…Switch back and forth?" Her mom looked thoughtful, cradling her teacup.

"Should be, I think. Do you want to give it a try? Something small. How about…Just one feature? Something from the other shape. Try *really* wanting it."

Scarlett took a sip from her tea, then closed her eyes. After a few seconds, a long, slender tail tipped with a little upside-down heart snaked its way from behind her and swayed back and forth in the air in front of her. Allyssa smiled and pawed at it. Scarlett booped her in the nose with the pointy tip.

"I think that proves the hypothesis." Hecate said with satisfaction until she spilled tea on her blouse. "Oh shhhh-ucks."

"Mom, I think that shirt is plenty ruined already, honestly."

"What do you…oh." She looked behind her, at the ragged parts of her shirt where the wings had torn through. "Oh, fair enough. Still. Waste of good tea."

"So now what?"

"What do you mean, Allyssa?"

"I mean…Scarlett can switch back and forth, now, probably. Maybe. But like…I think people are gonna notice that", and she made really overt quotation marks in the air, " 'Damien'looks a bit different now than before."

"Shoot, yeah, I hadn't thought of that", Hecate said. "We could shift you to a new school?" Scarlett responded by immediately intertwining her fingers with Allyssa's.

"Hard no."

"You only go to this one half the time anyway."

"And the other half of the time my best friend is there with me."

"Hum." Hecate crossed her arms and legs and chewed on her thoughts for a moment.

"Could you turn back into a boy?"

"Mom! No!"

She held up her hands. "All right, fair enough. Just considering options."

"I mean…" Allyssa looked at Scarlett.

"With a hoodie and maybe like, a face mask, that might work? We can blame some of the changes on the illness, maybe?"

"Would you be willing to do that, hun?"

Scarlett thought about it for a minute. "I'd have to try, I guess? I don't want to stop going to school, but this seems…risky."

"Worth a shot?"

"I'd say so, yeah."

"Then let's have a crack at it."

"Can we do that later though?"

"Of course, sweetie. It's been a long day."

Scarlett nodded. "I also kinda want to…"

She stood upright. Aside from the tail, her wings now also unfurled themselves again. Her skin darkened and her horns grew back in. It was only when she smiled down at Allyssa that the latter noticed that the transformation was...different, from before. It was the row of sharp teeth that really gave it away. The forked tongue was just the icing on the lesbian.

"Oh", Allyssa said. She didn't even notice the hooves until Scarlett grew another five inches. "Oh", she repeated for emphasis.

"I'm impressed, hun!" Hecate said. "I didn't think you'd find your full form just yet."

"My full..." Scarlett looked down and back up, felt her new teeth with her new tongue. "Oh, cool!"

"Do you have full control now, do you think?"

"I'm not sure. Why?"

"Well, you didn't draw the protective circle."

"Oh shit", Scarlett said, and the couch caught on fire.

8

Friendly Fire

Immediately, Hecate jumped up and dunked her tea on the flaming parts of the couch. It helped only a bit, and the carpet was starting to turn black as well. She didn't pause and hurried her way to the kitchen, shouting instructions over her shoulder.

"Stand on the tiles, sweetie. Try to focus!"

Scarlett stepped over to exposed tile of the floor, which singed with every step. She kicked a carpet aside and tried taking deep breaths. Flames were licking her hair, flickering in and out of existence around her head, hands and feet.

"Focus on what, mom?!" she shouted at the kitchen.

"Just...not being on fire!? Try to be calm!" came the muffled answer.

Allyssa stepped over to Scarlett. The air around her was hot. It was like being close to an open oven. She stood in front of Scarlett.

"You need to focus, right? Calm down?"

Scarlett nodded anxiously. Allyssa reached out and touched Scarlett's face, cradling it in her hands. Scarlett's skin was hot. Painfully so. Alli bit her tongue to keep from wincing. "Look at me, Scarlett."

Scarlett's eyes, glowing red like burning coals, looked into Allyssa's soothing, cool, blue ones. She took a breath, and the temperature in the room began to drop. The fires on the couch and carpet went out. Allyssa held Scarlett like that, smiling through the pain, until she was entirely focused on not setting her girlfriend on fire. Hecate ran in with a fire extinguisher and saw the pre-extinguished situation.

"Oh."

The tension dissolved. Allyssa withdrew her hands, which were a deep red from the heat, and tried to hide them. Hecate was much too quick for that, and she put the fire extinguisher down in a corner, then strode over.

"Thank you", she said. Then, without saying much of anything else, so as not to give Allyssa chance to protest, she snatched the girl by the wrists and inspected her hands.

"I can work with this. Sit."

When Hecate got like this, her voice sharp, what she said didn't sound like a command. It sounded like she made a statement as to how the world was going to be in a second and then the world obliged. Allyssa was sitting on the edge of the sofa before she'd realized anything had been said. Hecate cracked her knuckles, and then her neck.

"It's been a while." Then she transformed. This was the first time Allyssa had seen Scarlett's mom in her true form. Hecate grew a foot taller, then two. Two giant ram's horns curled from her head, two giant black wings extended from her head. Her eyes burned, flames licking her eyebrows, a glow in her eyes so intense it was like looking into the sun. Two hooves clacked on the floor. Fingernails extended into black talons. A long, elegant tale swooped through the air, ending in an inverted black heart. Teeth became sharper and longer, a forked tongue flitting between them as if tasting the air.

"Try to...relax." Hecate said, and knelt in front of Allyssa, who had no idea what was going on but she was too awestruck to do anything, say anything, try anything or think anything of value. Hecate took the dumbstruck girl's hands in her own, and blew on them. Allyssa's entire body was instantly filled with a supernatural heat, like she was being baked. Her hair blew as if she was standing in front of an inferno, and it was hard to keep her eyes open, hard to breathe. And...just like that, it was over.

She looked down, and Hecate looked like her normal self again, though she hadn't seemed to bother getting rid of her horns. Just as impressive was the fact that her hands no longer hurt.

"Burns aren't too hard", Hecate said, trying not to sound smug.

"Thank you, Ms. H." She looked up in awe at this...she realized she had no idea what Hecate *actually* was.

"Don't mention it."

"Okay."

"I *mean* it." Hecate's eyes bored into hers.

"I'm not saying anything, Ms. H. Promise."

"Atta girl." Hecate ruffled Allyssa's hair, and then realized that that wasn't something she could do with every child.

"Listen, Allyssa. It's getting late. I think you should go home. Why don't you...Why don't you come by after school tomorrow, and we can see about getting Scarlett some clothes?"

Scarlett looked between the two of them and nodded. If she stayed much longer, her parents would get worried.

"You're right. Yeah. Let me just eh...say goodbye to Scarlett."

"Go right ahead", Hecate smiled, hands on her hips and not moving.

"Alone?"

"Oh. Oh! Yes. Of course!" Hecate shuffled out of the room as quickly as she could while keeping her composure. Scarlett and Allyssa looked at each other, and slowly closed the distance between them. Tentatively reached out.

"Hey."

"Hey you."

"Today was fucking weird, Scarlett."

"It really was. I'm glad you were here." Scarlett smiled.

"Me too."

"Really?"

"Really", Allyssa nodded.

"I'm just glad I get to keep you." Her voice cracked halfway through that sentence. "Just a few hours ago I thought I was going to lose you, Scarlett. I was so scared."

Scarlett pulled her in for a hug, their cheeks gently touching.

"I'm sorry, Alli. I just didn't want to push you away with...with what I am."

"You knew I liked girls, dumdum."

"I meant the whole demon thing?"

"Right. Uh. I'm okay with that too."

"You're a weirdo."

"Ass."

"Thanks for having been my friend forever, Alli."

"You too."

"I lov—..."

"Shhh."

Scarlett clamped her mouth shut. She thought for a second she'd gone too far, and froze. Allyssa gently scratched the back of her girlfriend's neck.

"Me too, silly. I just...I want to say it when the time is right. Not standing in a singed living room."

She took a step back and held Scarlett's hands.

"Whatever you feel for me, I promise I'm feeling it too. But I want..." She looked away shyly.

"I want it to be special, with you. You're my favorite person. I wanna do it right."

Scarlett pulled her back in for another hug, and then kissed her. "You're amazing", she said.

"You too. Dumbass." Allyssa said. They kissed a few more times, then Scarlett helped Allyssa gather her stuff, and walked her to the front door. One more kiss. The specific kind of kiss that only lesbians know when they say goodbye to someone they'll see tomorrow. It was a kiss that said "I know I'll see you tomorrow, but I'm going to treat the time between then and now as if it was infinite." It was a *good* kiss.

Allyssa stepped out the door, was just about to leave when she spun around and grabbed Scarlett by the collar of her shirt and pulled her in for much more down to earth "I need to taste you one more time" kind of kiss which, while much less poetic, was nonetheless very effective for both of them. She looked self satisfied and was about to turn again when she perked up.

"Oh! Can I eh...tell my mom about you?"

"Tell her...what, exactly?" Scarlett stared at her.

"I want to...tell her about us, you know? But I don't want her to use the wrong name."

"Oh, that! I thought you meant about what my mom and I are."

Allyssa had literally not considered that.

"Ah, no. I just want her to think of you the right way."

"Oh. Th—thank you." Scarlett reached out and squeezed Allyssa's hand. "Of course you can."

"Thank you", Allyssa bounced, and gave her another quick kiss. Then she tried to walk down the driveway, constantly looking over her shoulder and tripping over everything, waving as she went. She managed to make it home without slamming her face into the pavement, which was a win, considering how much her head was spinning.

When she got home, most of the family had gone to their respective rooms to do homework or, in case of the twins, get ready for bed. She found her mom in her study again.

"Hey pumpkin."

"Hey mom!"

"How's your friend? Damien? His mom called to say you helped him out when his illness was getting bad and that you got him home safe. I'm glad she offered you dinner. Is something wrong?"

She'd seen, of course, how Allyssa's face had scrunched up. Allyssa sat down on the other desk chair in the room and spun the chair, pulling her legs up.

"Okay, mom, don't freak out."

"What's up, Lissie?"

"It's not really...Damien anymore?"

"Oh? What do you mean?"

"*She* uses Scarlett now."

"Oh! Okay, I'll try to get it right from here on. Do you mind if I tell your father?"

Allyssa shook her head no.

"I'm going to be honest, sweetie, I thought you were going to tell me you two had finally...you know..."

Allyssa stopped spinning. Her mom grinned triumphantly.

"Really?"

Nodnod.

"I knew it. Your father owes me five dollars." She got up and went over to the chair Allyssa was making herself small in.

"I'm very glad for you two. Da—… Scarlett has always been a good kid, if a bit quiet. I'm happy for you." She gave Allyssa a kiss on her forehead and then pulled her in for a hug.

"Alright, go downstairs, grab yourself some ice cream, and don't tell your father."

Excited nod.

"And hey."

Allyssa turned around.

"I'm proud of you."

Question mark.

"For being there for your friend. Accepting them. Makes me proud to have raised a good kid."

"I'm proud you're my mom."

Allyssa ran downstairs, which her mom was grateful for, so she could hide the fact that she was crying.

Meanwhile, half a block over, Scarlett was curled up against her mom on the sofa with a spaghetti western playing on the television.

"How are you doing, tater tot?"

"I'm good, mom. Thank you."

"You two are really cute together."

"Mo-om."

"I mean it. I think she's good for you."

"You…you do?"

"Hun. Tot. Sweetie. 'Dum dum' Please." Hecate counted on her fingers. "In one day she, and I'm keeping score, helped you out when you transformed, accepted you as a demon, helped you realize you're a girl, accepted you as a girl, and not once, but *twice* she went to you to help you calm down, once actually burning herself to help you. Yeah. I approve."

"Thanks mom." Scarlett sighed happily, her mom's arm around her as Charles Bronson played the harmonica in black and white.

"Besides, it was about time."

"What do you mean by that?"

"Sweetie, you two have been 'stealing glances' at each other for like, what? Five years?"

"Wow, okay. Attacked by my own mom."

"You'll live. You've got good genes."

"Thanks mom. For everything today."

"Of course, sweetie. I'll always be your mom. And I have a daughter and that's honestly awesome."

"Thank you."

"If you so much as touch my bras I will *fight* you."

"Deal. I love you mom."

"I love you too, tater tot."

That night, both Allyssa and Scarlett's mothers went to bed with satisfied smiles on their faces. Sometimes, being a mom was really, really rewarding work. Their daughters, respectively, went to bed thinking of their new girlfriends, and how different their lives were about to be.

They dreamt of fire and first kisses.

9

Out Of Left Field

Scarlett woke up the next day and rolled out of bed. She could scarcely believe yesterday had *actually* happened. She made to reach for her phone, and remembered its explosive demise the day before, smiling at her mom's protectiveness. After her morning rituals, freshly showered, she went downstairs, where her mom was taking her time eating breakfast.

"Morning hun", she waved with a full mouth.

"Hey mom. Not going to work today?"

"Nuh. Taking a day off. We need groceries, and you can't do school anyway."

"True", Scarlett said, and butter herself a piece of toast.

"Besides. You need a new phone."

"You remembered", Scarlett smiled as she stuffed the bagel into her face-hole.

"Of course I remembered, I had to pick shards out of the ceiling."

"Ooph."

"I just did it because I love you, sweetie."

"I know, mom."

They finished breakfast on what felt like a lazy Sunday morning. Scarlett got dressed while Hecate finished the rest of cleaning up the damage from the night before. The couch was going to have to go. The carpet was a mess of black hoofprints. By the time it was rolled up, Scarlett was dressed and ready to go.

The day passed quickly. By the time it was almost four, they'd had a mother-daughter day, Scarlett had a new phone, and they got ice cream. On the way back to the house, Hecate got a phone call.

"Hey. I wasn't expecting to he—... You're what? How did...Really? To— Okay. I'll have to...Yeah, no...It's no problem. The girl from the other night...yeah. Okay."

She put the phone down and looked at Scarlett with a blank expression.

"Allyssa can still come over after school, but I'm afraid you're not going shopping. We're having someone...come over for dinner tonight."

"Oh? Someone I know?" Hecate shook her head and looked at the road again.

"No. It's an old friend of mine. From work."

Scarlett could tell her mom wasn't in a great mood, all of a sudden and thought better than to ask further. Still, she was worried. Her mom didn't often get like this. She usually bounced between her regular self and the occasional overprotective hellion. Sullen Hecate was a rare and unpleasant sight.

As they went up the driveway, they saw Allyssa park her bike by the garage. Scarlett jumped out of the car while it was almost stationary, and they ran into each other's arms, only slightly bumping their foreheads into each other.

"Ow."

"Hey you."

"Hey Alli. How was school?"

"Fine. Boring." Allyssa paused, and gently kissed Scarlett on the nose.

"Empty, without you."

"Eee", Scarlett said.

"Do you still want to go shopping?"

"I do, but mom said we're having someone over tonight, so...tomorrow?"

"Oh", Allyssa said. The disappointment was clear on her face. Scarlett immediately felt a pang of guilt. Alli tried to look chipper, but failed. "I'll see you tomorrow, then?" Hecate walked past with her arms full of groceries.

"Nonsense, you're staying over for dinner."

"I...yes, ma'am."

Normally, Hecate enjoyed that kind of response, but she seemed laser-focused on getting everything inside.

"Is your mom okay?"

"Yeah, I think she's just stressed about the guest coming over. Apparently it's an old friend of hers?"

Allyssa raised her eyebrows as they made their way inside, but didn't say anything. As they walked, the backs of their hands touched, and it seemed to be almost automatic that their fingers entwined. To Scarlett, Alli's cool hands were like a cold drink on a hot day. To Allyssa, her girlfriend's touch was like hot chocolate on a cold winter morning. They looked each other in the eye and, like they would many times after, fell for each other all over again.

Deciding that going up to Scarlett's room was perhaps, for now, not the right time, with how stressed Hecate was, they settled in the living room, on the part of the couch that wasn't crunchy. Once inside and comfortable, Scarlett became *more* Scarlett, horns and tail and deep red skin and was again nestled on Allyssa's lap, and they put the TV on so as to raise the veneer of doing something other than looking into each other's eyes and finding out just how long Allyssa could hold her breath while kissing.

Allyssa, in between breathless bouts of affection, gently stroked Scarlett's hair.

"How was your day?"

"It was goo—... hhhhh" Just as Scarlett had begun to answer the question, Alli, with an innocent expression on her face, ran a finger down the length of one of Scarlett's horns.

"Hmm? You were saying something?"

"Alli! Not fai— aah"

Scarlett couldn't keep a straight face as Allyssa grabbed her horn. Alli kept glancing over in the direction of the kitchen, but Hecate was too focused on cooking. Alli could tell by the muttered curses that could be heard even over the sound of the television. She turned her attention back to Scarlett

"Do you want me to stop, Scarlett?"

She massaged the horn gently as she spoke. Scarlett just whimpered. Her legs seemed to lead a life of their own as she squirmed.

"Nnn—..."

"Good girl", Allyssa said with a wolfish grin, but she let up a bit anyway. Scarlett slumped on the sofa and panted.

"Where...where did that come from, Alli?"

"I just...wanted to see how that fit. Did you...like it?"

"Ye." Allyssa kissed her on the forehead.

"Want to do that again some time?"

"Maybe not in the living room? What if my mom sees?"

Allyssa ran her nail along the horn again and Scarlett made a noise that was only barely muffled by the sound of the tv. "But that's part of the fun."

"Baaaaabe", Scarlett whimpered.

"I'll stop. Promise." Another kiss. They actually ended up watching a part of the movie that was playing, for as much as they managed to stay focused on what they were watching. There was a lot of gentle touching as Allyssa gently caressed Scarlett's neck, and occasionally they exchanged a kiss. Scarlett had almost dozed off when the doorbell rang. Hecate poked her head out from the kitchen.

"Will you get that, hun? I've got my hands full."

"On it!" Scarlett said and jumped up, ready to run to the front door.

"Scarlett!" Allyssa hissed.

"What?"

Allyssa just pointed at her head. Right. The horns.

"And the tail."

"Oops."

Looking more human, she barely managed to remember making her skin less crimson before opening the front door.

In front of her stood an imposing woman. Her features were androgynous, her jaw sharp enough to cut glass. She had laugh lines around her mouth, though she didn't look like she smiled much. Her eyes were a deep, icy blue, the most striking part of a face framed by long, golden-blonde hair. She was wearing a tan coat over a white business suit.

"Hello", Scarlett said, slightly intimidated.

"Hello. You must be Scarlett. Can I come in?"

"I...Of course. Come in. Can eh...Can I take your coat?"

The woman smiled softly, but it made a world of difference. It made her features look a lot softer. "If you insist." She handed her the coat. "Now, let's see if I remember..." The woman paused for a second, then made her way directly to the kitchen. As Scarlett hung up the woman's coat, she could hear voices from the kitchen.

"Hey, Cate." That's a name she'd never heard anyone call her mother before.

"I thought it was you. What name do you go by these days?"

"Don't..." There was a weariness in the woman's voice.

"I'm...I'm sorry...I didn't mean..."

Scarlett was a little taken aback at how quiet her mother sounded. Sullen Hecate. She took another second to 'hang up the coat'some more, but couldn't keep stalling and joined them. Hecate stood with her back to the room at the sink, and the woman had her arms defensively crossed in front of her. The awkward silence was deafening.

"Do...can I..." Scarlett tried.

"Why don't you get our guest comfortable at the dinner table, sweetie? I'll be right there. Food's almost done. Why don't you introduce her to Alli?"

Scarlett nodded, and then realized Hecate couldn't see her. "Okay mom."

She walked past the woman and urged her to follow. She quickly pattered over the living room, where she grabbed a confused Alli by the hand and dragged her along. The woman was already sitting down. She looked like she was about to take an interview.

"I...hi..." Scarlett said again.

"Hello again, Scarlett. And your friend?"

Scarlett and Allyssa looked at each other, holding hands under the table.

"My girlfriend." She grinned proudly. "This is Allyssa." Allyssa smiled happily and waved.

"Hi!"

"Allyssa this is..." Scarlett left the question hanging in the air.

"Hello Allyssa. I'm...I'm an old colleague of your mother's. Right around the time she moved to this neighborhood. Please, sit down", she offered as if this wasn't Scarlett's own house. They obliged.

"I'm in asset management." She paused, and saw their looks. They were about as enthusiastic as you got from two teens who had just been told the words 'asset management'

"In short, when two companies merge, it's my job to make sure everything goes over smoothly. My company", she motioned first at herself, then at the kitchen. "Acquired your mother's. We've been working on getting everything fixed."

Just then, Hecate came in with a large oven dish. It looked and smelled amazing. She'd clearly been working on getting this perfect for *hours*.

"No work talk at the dinner table, please", she said briskly, and handed everyone a plate.

"How come you were in the neighborhood?" She cut right to the chase as she poured herself a glass of water. Scarlett and Allyssa felt very much like wheels three and four on the world's most awkward bicycle.

"I wasn't, Hecate. That's why I'm here. This isn't a courtesy call."

"Oh?" Hecate's eyebrows raised but her eyes stayed dull. That constant hint of...something, it wasn't going away.

"The merger is almost done."

"That's not... I thought..." Hecate seemed taken aback, shocked.

"Six months. At most. And I'm not really needed anymore."

"But I thought...You said..."

"I just repeated what they told me then. I just worked harder than they thought I could."

"But that's...I just..." Tears were welling up in Hecate's eyes.

Scarlett finally had enough.

"I don't want to be rude, ma'am, but what's going on? Why is this merger so important it's making my mom upset? Who *are* you?"

Hecate looked at the woman, and then at Scarlett, and then back at the woman.

"You're sure? This isn't...some cruel..."

"We...*I* don't do that, Cate. You know that."

"Yeah. I...I just can't believe...Go ahead."

The woman clasped her hands together and looked at Hecate and Scarlett.

"Scarlett, my name is Gabrielle. I worked with your mother *before* she came here. From the old country."

"O... Oh."

The woman took a deep breath, and looked Scarlett right in the eyes. "Scarlett, I'm your mother."

10

Union And Reunion

"You're my *what?!*"

"Jesus Christ, Gabe, you could have been a bit more tactful." Hecate leaned her face in her hands.

"I wanted to get it out of the way first, Cate."

"You haven't changed a bit."

Gabrielle looked dejected. "You have."

"I've been a mother for eighteen years, Gabe. Parenting does that to a person."

"Hold up", Scarlett interjected. "Can we rewind, please? Mom, what's going on?"

Hecate shot Gabrielle a withering glance.

"I'm your mother, sweetie. Always have been. Gabrielle here just...is too."

Scarlett frowned.

"How does that..."

"I'm not human, Scarlett", Gabrielle said. "I'm from..." she paused. "Upstairs."

"Are you an angel?" Allyssa asked. If the situation had been less serious or intense, Scarlett would have made a pod-racing joke. Instead, Gabrielle simply nodded.

"Our physiology is a bit different. We can...I'm trying not to make things too weird for you here...we can induce immaculate conception." Hecate shot Gabrielle another glance. Softer, with eyes filled with memories. "It's an involved process but...your mother and I really wanted a child."

"Then..."

Scarlett had a lot going on. She'd only come to herself yesterday. Where was this coming from? Why now?

"Where were you? If you're...my other mom...mom never talked about you..."

Gabrielle sighed. Despite her imposing presence, she looked small. Her hand on the table inched slightly towards Hecate who, through a feat of titanic willpower, reached out and squeezed it.

"Around the time you were born I was...summoned. To do work, upstairs. I was told it might take...centuries, even. And you'd been born all pink and human, with no traits of me or your mother, we feared you might be human. We decided not to tell you. We didn't want to give you a parent and then take them away."

"But then...why now?" Scarlett was confused, but Allyssa's grip on her hand gave her something to hold on to.

"I...was more capable than they estimated. The work that was going to take centuries I managed to whittle down. Considerably. Two years ago, when you first started transforming we...we hoped you'd be in one camp or the other. But what if you stabilized as a human? I couldn't take that chance. I didn't tell your mother but I moved and shook where I could. The past two years I've forced decades of work to be done. When she called me yesterday, and you'd found yourself... "

She sighed.

"A lot's happened. But your mother and I have never...lost touch."

"So...now what?" Scarlett looked confused. She'd never really had negative feelings towards her unnamed other parent. Her mother had ensured her she hadn't been run out on. She felt a pang of resentment but, well, Hecate had been an amazing mom.

"I would like to be a part of your life, Scarlett, if that's okay. Now that I know I won't lose you to time, that I know I'll get to spend time down here... "Scarlett slumped in her chair.

"This is a lot to take in."

"I understand. Of course. I just...I've missed the past eighteen years. And your mother tells me you have...some of my traits." Scarlett looked confused. Gabrielle scratched the back of her neck.

"It took me a long time to realize I was a...let's just say I'm grateful you found out who you were as early as you did."

"Oh! I...Oh!"

Hecate smiled again. "There's also the more obvious genetic thing."

"What's that, mom?"

"Demon's wings don't ordinarily have feathers, hun." Hecate smiled softly. "You get yours from her."

Scarlett blinked. She just thought that they were like...like hair color. Something slightly different for each person. She'd never considered it was hereditary.

"So I'm...part angel?"

Gabrielle made a non-committal hand gesture.

"Ehhh, yes and no. Think of it like...mostly Demon, some human, and a little bit of Angel. You take after your mom, for the most part, and immaculate children are usually mostly human. That you're more comfortable in your infernal form is proof that you're more your mother than human, though."

Scarlett nodded slowly. "I think I understand. So...you're moving in here? I just...met you. I'm not...I'm not sure I'm..."

Gabrielle held up a hand. "Nothing that fast or drastic, Scarlett. Your mother and I have a lot of catching up to do. I've rented an apartment in the area, and I'd like to visit, often, to get to know you and your girlfriend, and...reconnect with your mother. Turns out there was no rush to begin with." Hecate and Gabrielle, for the first time, smiled at each other.

Scarlett was happy for them. She was also still confused at all of the revelations. "We..."

She paused. Allyssa took over. "We should probably eat before dinner gets cold?"

"Excellent idea...Allyssa, was it?"

"Yeah! Alli is fine too. Only my mom calls me Lissie."

"Nice to meet you, Alli."

"You too, miss Gabrielle."

"Just Gabrielle is fine, dear."

"I have a question", Scarlett said, chewing thoughtfully.

"Are you *that* Gabriel?" Gabrielle steepled her fingers together.

"Not anymore, Scarlett. I'm not the person I was. Besides, being a girl fits me much better, don't you think?"

"I'll say." Allyssa said. "*Woof.*" Allyssa had tried to mumble under her breath, but she was just loud enough for Hecate to hear while she was drinking. Water came out her nose as she snorted. Gabrielle laughed and Scarlett simply looked flustered between the two of them.

"Impressive, Hecate. Not many people can make you do that", Gabrielle grinned.

"She's very...quick-witted for her age, Gabe. I was just taken by surprise."

"I'm very sorry, Ms. H!" Allyssa said quickly.

"You're fine, Allyssa", Hecate said as she cleaned her face with a napkin. "I'm glad you're here too. I figured it would help Scarlett if you were here."

Scarlett smiled gratefully. "Thanks mom." Gabrielle turned to Allyssa again.

"So you...know? All of it?"

Allyssa shrugged. "I doubt it. But I know Scarlett is Scarlett, I know she's got horns and hooves and wings."

"And that doesn't bother you?"

"It's like finding out one of your friends has like...a birthmark? It's not a personality trait, doesn't change who she is, right?"

"I mean, there's...theological implications."

Alli took a bit of food and happily spoke with her mouth full. "I was raised agnostic." She swallowed her food and took a sip of water.

"You're literally the only human being at the table, Alli", Scarlett said. "How can you be agnostic now?"

"Well..." she paused to collect her thoughts. "Clearly nobody who ever wrote anything down about this stuff had any idea what they were talking about, and I still don't really *know* anything. But I know Hecate is a good mom and a good person, Scarlett is an amazing girl, and you seem cool. It looks like my soul is still mine, I haven't really been corrupted, and there's no smiting going on. So yeah, still agnostic. I have no idea what to believe, so I'm definitely not going to start worshiping shit." Oops. "No offense."

"None taken, Allyssa", Gabrielle said. "It's a healthy attitude, honestly. It's been a while now but...nobody really cares anymore, up there. There's too many of you and too many moral and ethical questions that can't be answered. Nobody wants to do the math anymore."

"What do you mean?"

Gabrielle looked over to Hecate, who shrugged. "Go for it."

"Hell's been, uh, canceled."

"Excuse me?" Allyssa and Scarlett said with various added expletives.

"Yeah. Look, the world as it's been going on...there's no way to make things, eh...ethically justified."

"What do you mean?" Allyssa asked.

"Up until about, uh, twenty years ago, everyone was going...down."

"What?!"

"Yeah, look, like I said, it's an ethical quagmire. Your entire civilization is built upon the backs of other people, on unethically sourced food and resources. If you consume any of it, media, food, you name it, you're a willing participant. And you lose your spot up there. So people downstairs started getting overworked..."

"Ugh, you can say that again", Hecate interjected.

"... and people upstairs were getting upset. Humanity was supposed to deserve *rest* after the toil of life."

"So..."

"Hell's been canceled."

"Where do people go, then?"

"Mostly where they believe they're going to go, really."

"So like, what? Nazis? Serial killers? Everyone gets to go to heaven?"

"Sort of? Everyone gets their own slice. It's not like we're going to run out of space. But there's a lot of management, and we try to make things ethically sound *up there* at least. Think of it like...for most people it's a very happy retirement home, and for the, uh..."

"Dickheads", Hecate offered.

"*Less savory characters*", Gabrielle disagreed, "it's more of a rehabilitation center. Sort of."

"So the whole merger thing you mentioned..." Scarlett thought out loud.

"Yeah. I've been putting people to work in getting the whole thing set up. Did you know there are over a hundred billion people up there?"

"Oof."

"Yeah. Oof. But happy people don't need as much work as they do downstairs. So a lot of Hecate's people moved upstairs for a cushier job. Not everyone was happy with the merger, and a lot of people on both sides retired and moved here."

"Like, this neighborhood?" Scarlett suddenly wondered how many people she knew were angels or demons.

"No, like, the earthly plane. The mortal realm, whatever you want to call it."

"So Hell is over, everyone goes to heaven?"

"Pretty much."

"Neat." Allyssa said.

"It's pretty neat. But it's been a lot of work. But we just about did it."

"So...God is real too, then, right?" Scarlett interjected.

"I mean...yeah. But they're not really, eh... "

"They've been busy with other projects", Hecate helped Gabrielle out. "Still full of infinite love for all creatures, great and small and all that jazz, just not very *actively* these days. The last time they even looked this way was to approve the merger."

"O-kay. That's...Um..."

"Yeah. We know", Gabrielle said. "We're doing the best we can. And uh...don't tell anyone?"

"I'd like to see how that conversation would go", Allyssa said with a grin. "Do I start with 'my girlfriend is a demon' and work my way up to 'hell is canceled' or work backwards?"

"Fair point", Gabrielle smiled back. "By the way, Cate, the food is delicious."

"Thank you!" Hecate said. "Nobody said anything, I was beginning to worry."

"Mom, you *know* you're a good cook. When you're not stabbing yourself."

"When you're not *what?!*" Gabrielle's head snapped to face Hecate.

"Hoo boy", Hecate laughed with exasperation. As she told the story, the table laughed. Slowly, the metaphorical temperature in the room went up. The lights seemed to get a little bit brighter, a little warmer. The four people at the table started to relax around each other, and found common ground where it wasn't expected, and found love where it was feared lost.

Gabrielle found herself welcome in their home. After living nearby for six months, she eventually moved in. After another six months, Scarlett called her mom. She and Hecate renewed their vows, promising to never grow old, together. They both cried but Hecate was better at pretending she hadn't. When Scarlett eventually moved out, Hecate and Gabrielle moved to the countryside. They had a little cottage that was slightly larger on the inside, and grew their own vegetables. Over time, they had acquired a reputation as lesbian witches, and adopted two cats. The orange one was *really stupid*. It was perfect.

Scarlett and Allyssa had gone upstairs that night, to give Scarlett's two moms the time and space to reconnect, not considering the consequences. The two teenagers had found themselves sitting on Scarlett's bed, looking awkwardly at the wall, until they'd turned towards each other and Allyssa had tackled Scarlett backwards. She'd requested, sweetly, with a sing-song voice that could convince varnish to strip, that Scarlett grew her horns back. Scarlett had happily obliged, and with more than just her hands, Allyssa had made Scarlett squirm all sorts of ways that night.

When they'd woken up together the next morning, they'd looked into each other's eyes and told each other how they truly felt, for the first of many more times to come. After a few years, Scarlett had moved out, and moved in with Allyssa. They had bought a small penthouse apartment in town, and found themselves with more happiness than they knew what to do with.

There had only been one snag.

"Scarlett?" The call came from the bathroom.

"Yeah, babe?"

"I've got another gray hair."

"I love your gray hairs, baby, they give you character."

"That's...not what I meant."

Scarlett joined Allyssa in the bathroom and wrapped her arms around her, kissed her neck, as she looked at her girlfriend in the mirror.

"You look beautiful."

"I look older."

"I...I mean..."

"I look older than you. By a few years."

"I'm...I'm sorry."

Allyssa had been aging more rapidly than Scarlett who, in a few years, would simply *stop getting* older. It was something they'd spent days talking over, a horrifying possibility that they didn't want to think about, but had to. After a particularly long conversation with her mother, Scarlett had sat down Alli opposite her on the couch.

"So...My mom and I...I think we have a solution."

"I...oh? I don't see..."

"There's a way to these things but apparently some of the...old rules, they still go."

"What do you mean?"

Scarlett reached under the couch and put a musical case in front of her. From it, she retrieved a golden violin.

"Play you for it", she said with a devilish grin. "But if you lose, I get your soul." Recognition dawned on Allyssa's face.

"Forever?"

"For all eternity, Alli."

"Gosh, if only I knew how to play the fiddle."

"I've always wanted a demon servant."

Allyssa reached over and stroked Scarlett's face.

"Sweetie, we both know you're a bottom."

"I'm going to hit you with this fiddle."

"No, you're not", Allyssa grinned, and kissed her. Twenty minutes later, after a lot of noise from two terrible fiddle-players, they unanimously agreed that Allyssa had lost her soul, which now belonged to Scarlett, to do with as she pleased.

Allyssa had still grown old. Allyssa had still died. And when she did, Hecate had helped Scarlett file a request for a body, to very detailed specifications, for one (1) soul that had gone overlooked during the great merger.

Allyssa, now plus one order of short, cute, stubby horns, and Scarlett, horny as ever, now had all the time in the world.

And you can bet they made it worth their while.

About the Author

Ela Bambust is, ostensibly, an author. What this actually means is that she spends a lot of time drinking coffee and stressing about the relationship status of fictional characters, and bothering her cat, before severely abusing an old and battered keyboard for several hours. Somehow, words come out the other end, and the result appears to be something approaching literature.

You can connect with me on:

 Elamimaxima

 elamimax